"It's your wish..."

"No, we're going to do this together," Brian insisted. "Think, Rachel. Put together the wish of a lifetime."

Contrary to her saner instincts, Rachel closed her eyes and began to build a wish. She heard the surf, felt the cold January afternoon against her face. The steady, enveloping warmth of Brian's body pervaded her senses, and suddenly all the dreams and desires she had put aside for all those years rose up inside her like a spring. Powerless to push them away, she went completely still, concentrating.

Brian stood as quietly as she, and Rachel could feel his churning energy waiting to be released with the wish and the balloon.

"Ready?" he whispered, his breath ruffling the curls at her forehead.

"Ready."

"Okay, three, two...one." Simultaneously their hands opened to release the tugging balloon, the back of her hand against his warm palm. He wrapped his arms around her as they stood in silence to watch the clear bubble bob away from them. At first it appeared to fall, then it sailed up until they had to lean back to watch it. When the balloon crossed the sun for a moment, it was invisible, but then it danced aside, a brilliant ball of fire. With one last, graceful pirouette, the balloon floated away on its mission of chance....

ABOUT THE AUTHOR

Muriel Jensen started writing in the sixth grade and has never stopped. She writes from the heart about firsthand experiences and wants that emotion to come alive in her stories. Muriel makes her home on the Oregon coast with her husband, her three children and her collection of cats, both live and porcelain.

Books by Muriel Jensen

HARLEQUIN AMERICAN ROMANCE

The Duck Shack Agreement
Muriel Jensen

Harlequin Books

TORONTO • NEW YORK • LONDON
AMSTERDAM • PARIS • SYDNEY • HAMBURG
STOCKHOLM • ATHENS • TOKYO • MILAN

To Dave and Katey,
Sam and Dorothy,
and Wanda and Andy,
for all the wonderful times.

Published April 1988

First printing February 1988

ISBN 0-373-16244-8

Chapter One

"Are you coming back to the shop after the delivery?"

"Yep." Rachel Bennett pulled a white sweatshirt over her head and settled the ribbed hem on her hips. "I've still got to make the bank deposit and catch up on posting. Statements have to go out tomorrow." She adjusted the collar of her blue blouse over the neckline of the sweatshirt and smoothed the colorful lettering across her chest. "Ballooney-Tunes" was spelled out in primary colors, and a bouquet of balloons in red, blue and yellow was appliquéd just above the lettering.

"Okay. Where am I going?" Rachel reached for the straw hat on a hook on the storage-room door and settled it at a jaunty angle on her shiny fall of shoulder-length brown hair. Bending her knees to check the result in the small framed mirror behind the counter, she frowned and patted the curling ends of her hair.

"How come your hair never frizzes in the winter?" she asked her employee.

Penny Mitchell snickered, looking up from the order sheet. Penny was short and plump and what she lacked in glamour she made up for with a sharp wit and unfailing loyalty. "It's too limp to frizz." She ran a disparaging hand through her short blond mop then grabbed the bouquet of helium-filled balloons suspended beside her. Bells attached to the bottom of their colorful ribbons prevented them from floating to the ceiling. "Do you know what some women pay for permanents to make their hair look like yours does naturally?"

Rachel turned to Penny and took the balloons. "Shocking, isn't it," she asked seriously, "when eight hours a day spent working with you could achieve the same result?"

Penny swatted Rachel's arm with the card that accompanied the balloons. "Don't get smart with me or I'll go on a diet, lose forty pounds, lure some rich man into marrying me and taking me away from all this. Then where would you be?"

Rachel feigned an expression of horror. "You wouldn't leave me?"

"No," Penny decided on second thought. "You deliver balloons with great style; you write cute ditties; and you look like a cross between Sally Field and Jessica Lange; other than that—you are totally incompetent."

As Rachel puzzled over what such a cross would look like, Penny helped her into her parka, holding the balloons. "You did get the song written?" Penny asked. "You aren't going to congratulate this gentleman on his bar mitzvah when it's really his fortieth birthday?"

Rachel grimaced at Penny. "Yes, I got the song written. His mother gave me some great stuff to use. I hope he has the sense of humor she thinks he has."

Ballooney-Tunes differed from other agents in the relatively new field of balloon deliveries because Rachel's background in music allowed her to offer a unique service—balloons delivered to the accompaniment of a song. If the giver of the gift so wished, Rachel would write a song using information on the person provided by the benefactor. Brian Tate's mother had been full of whimsical information about her son, anxious, as she said, "to needle the old boy."

"Why you gave up an exciting life on the road to do this..." Penny began.

Rachel's expression became dry. "You'd have to live amid all that glamour to understand." Then she smiled at her friend and took the balloons. "And what would you be doing if I hadn't fallen in love with the Oregon coast and made Cannon Beach my home? Huh? You'd have some sedate job in a bank or an insurance office or a department store."

"Yeah," Penny replied wistfully.

Rachel frowned and reached for the doorknob. "Ingrate. Now, where am I supposed to find this Tate? Did his mother check his schedule like she promised?"

"Right. He's at a Coast College board meeting at the Shelton."

"Good. See you later, Pen."

Rachel pushed her way out into the cold and blustery January afternoon. Twelve helium-filled balloons held at arm's length gave the block-long race to her van an added dimension of adventure. The balloons finally stuffed inside the van, Rachel drove the six-block length of Cannon Beach's main street to the highway, then the half mile to the Shelton Inn. Situated on a bluff overlooking the ocean where picturesque boulders had been flung out in some prehistoric eruption, the inn was a gathering place for most Cannon Beach organizations, which had no such luxury as meeting rooms in the small art colony. Parked near the rear entrance, Rachel shed her coat and carefully removed the balloons and the card that was to accompany them.

She ran for the inn's back door and stopped in the dark corridor to catch her breath. A bellman, an older man who had directed her on previous deliveries, walked toward Rachel with a tray of drinks.

"Ah." He smiled, the tray balanced expertly on the flat of his hand. "And who are we ballooning today?"

"A Mr. Tate in the Coast College board meeting."

He nodded. "Right. Follow me."

At the end of the corridor the bellman pushed open a door on which hung an elegant brass sign that marked the Beachview Suite. From the doorway Rachel saw that the room was paneled in a dark wood and contained a long table strewn with notepads, a computer printout, pencils and Styrofoam coffee cups. A small bar against the wall held several coffee carafes, more cups and a pitcher of water.

As she made her entrance, twelve pairs of eyes, the majority of them male, looked up to investigate the cause of the intrusion. She felt a moment's trepidation. A year and a half in her unique business had taught her that women were fun to balloon because they loved the fuss and attention that accompanied the gift. Men, on the other hand, tended to become embarrassed and, on a rare occasion, even rude. This group, a cross section of men ranging in age from early twenties to near retirement, looked a little stuffy. The two women in conservative suits, one young and one with graying hair, looked downright forbidding.

Fortunately, the six years she'd spent on the nightclub circuit, singing to audiences that either didn't listen to her or paid more attention to her than she cared for, had made her impervious to everything but the job she had to do. She settled her hat more firmly in place and advanced into the room.

Her eyes settled on three fortyish-looking men grouped together on one side of the table. "Mr. Brian Tate?" she asked brightly.

A stricken murmur of "Oh, God!" came from a dark-haired man at the far end of the table. Laughter and a spatter of applause rose from the men as they turned to look at him. Good, Rachel thought, they're not as stuffy as they look.

Brian Tate rose to his feet with reluctant courtesy, studying the intruder and quickly deducing her mission. He gave her a look that dared her to go through with it, suggesting a slow and ugly retribution if she did.

He wasn't a particularly quiet or private person, quite the opposite really, but he hated being part of a scene. And she was coming toward him with a confident smile that told him he could glare at her all he wanted but she wouldn't be intimidated. Her job was to embarrass some poor victim with the dubious honor of a dozen balloons.

As the woman drew closer to him, Brian was momentarily distracted from his silent vow of revenge by the sparkle of her darkly lashed brown eyes, the disciplined carriage of her body, and the sweatshirt that displayed her business logo.

"Happy birthday from your mother, Mr. Tate," she said as she handed him the balloons.

His mother. He should have guessed.

Rachel reached into her pocket and affixed an adhesive label to his sweater that read, "I've been ballooned by..." A sweeping, flamboyant hand had filled in "Mother." As she patted the label in place on the resistant knit of his gray turtleneck, Rachel felt strong bone and a warm, tough musculature. Intelligence and annoyance lit eyes that were a very unusual teal blue. Interested, she studied him more closely.

His hair was dark brown and a little long, and as she noticed the curling ends around his ears she thought idly that he probably had the same trouble controlling his hair that she did. Dark eyebrows made a formidable line over his eyes, and a strong, straight nose led her eyes to a full but neatly trimmed mustache.

A very attractive man, she thought, momentarily distracted from her purpose.

Brian Tate folded his arms and looked down at the label then into Rachel's thoughtfully perusing gaze.

"Is there more?" he asked as she continued to stand there, studying him.

She shifted her attention quickly to the matter at hand. "Yes, there is. A song written especially for you."

He cast a glance over his shoulder at his companions that was part amusement and part dread. They cheered again, obviously enjoying this joke at his expense. A wicked gleam flashed in his eyes, and he turned to secure the balloons to the table by placing his notepad on the jingling tails of the ribbons.

"Well, then, Miss Ballooney-Tunes. Let's put you where everyone can hear you." And with a swift, sure movement he lifted Rachel onto the chair he had occupied, then took her hand, steadying her as he urged her to step up onto the table. Paper cups and notepads were hastily pushed aside, the printout folded.

She looked down at him, caught between irritation and surprise. His attempt to embarrass her was annoying, but she wouldn't let him get the best of her. She pulled her hand away.

"You're on," Brian said quietly. Then he resumed his seat, relaxing in a corner of it, prepared to enjoy her discomfort.

Rachel turned away from him with a haughty lift of one eyebrow and walked the length of the table, the performer in her taking over. She had hated working in front of an audience, but she had done it very well, and all those performances had taught her poise and control, which remained part of her. She turned back to face the group and noted that they were eager for her to begin.

"This song was written by Ballooney-Tunes," she announced with a bright smile, "especially to commemorate Mr. Tate's fortieth birthday."

The younger of the two women, a petite blonde in a navy jacket and white silk blouse, gasped then giggled. "Brian! You're *not* forty?"

He gave the woman a thin smile then challenged Rachel with a glance. "And getting older by the minute. Do go on, Miss Ballooney-Tunes."

Borrowing the melody from an old German Christmas carol, "O Tannenbaum," Rachel began in the high sweet voice of a balladeer:

"Our Brian Tate, he has no mate, though he's approaching forty. He has more luck with mallard duck than women . . . Lordy! Lordy!"

Laughter rose immediately. Encouraged by the playful participation of Tate's acquaintances, who were obviously aware of his passion for duck watching, Rachel went on.

Through several verses, Rachel poked fun at his recent success as a best-selling author, his poker playing until all hours, his love for his Porsche Carrera and his weakness for Bruce's Candy Kitchen's starfish confections. But the theme carrying through the ditty was what had concerned his mother most when Rachel had spoken to her—his continued bachelorhood.

Before she was finished, a chorus of hoots and guffaws was aimed at Rachel's victim, who took it all with a dry grin. Rachel finally closed the distance between them and sat on the edge of the table to sing the final verse while looking into his eyes.

He closed them for a moment, as though bracing himself for whatever was coming next, then opened them to watch her evenly, apparently determined to be a good sport. Rachel smiled at him, pleased and surprised by his continued good humor.

"Oh, what a fate, poor Brian Tate, alone and single still. A man should stand with wife at hand when going o'er the hill."

While loud applause cheered Rachel's performance, Brian stood, taking her hands and helping her to her feet. His hands were strong and warm, and Rachel found herself sharply aware of how they felt against hers—large, a little rough, full of energy. His unusual blue-gray eyes studied her face, feature by feature, going slowly over her hair, then finding the mild confusion in her eyes and pausing there.

"Happy birthday again, Mr. Tate," she said quickly, casually trying to pull her hands away. "From your mother and from all of us at Ballooney-Tunes."

He retained his grip for a moment; his eyes had found her mouth and studied it with paralyzing thoroughness. Feeling awkward, she removed her hands from his.

With a small bow, Rachel spun around, walked to the door and closed it behind her as laughter and hoots of good-natured derision began again.

"HOW'D IT GO?" Penny wanted to know, studying her employer's expression for a clue. Rachel looked thoughtful and slightly distracted—unusual for a woman who prided herself on being controlled and logical. "Don't tell me. He didn't have the sense of humor his mother thought he had?"

Rachel placed her straw hat on the hook and pulled off her parka, moving into the tiny back room that served as both office and storeroom. She draped her jacket over a stack of boxes and sat at her desk, leaning back in her office chair as she thought about Brian Tate.

"He was pretty good about it," she said finally.

"Then why do you look like that?" Penny persisted.

Rachel turned in the chair to look at her friend. "How?" she asked curiously.

"I don't know. Dreamy, sort of. A little out of it."

Rachel tossed her head back, her ripply stream of hair falling free. That about described how she felt. Out of it. She was usually very content with life, loving her daughter, enjoying her business and the many friends she'd made in Cannon Beach. But there were times when five years of widowhood seemed like an eternity and she longed for a man's big appetite to cook for, a companion in the day-to-day struggles of life, a shoulder to lean against in the quiet hours of evening, arms to lie in at night.

She expelled a deep breath, reminding herself that while she did not have the pluses found in a relationship, she did not have the negatives, either. She could make decisions without consulting anyone, purchases she didn't have to explain and mistakes that were no one else's business but her own.

"Just how good-looking is Brian Tate?" Penny asked, perching on the edge of one of the boxes. It was becoming obvious that Rachel's last delivery had made an impression on her.

Rachel stared blindly at her calendar, thinking of the very different color of his eyes. "Blue," she replied softly, her mind wandering, not registering Penny's question. "A very unusual shade of blue."

Trying to decode that reply, Penny was silent for a moment. "You mean you've fallen for a Smurf?"

Rachel frowned at Penny, who sobered quickly. "Sorry. Go on."

"His eyes are blue," she explained with a side glance that was both smiling and censorious. "Teal blue. And full of light." Shaking her head over her own reaction, Rachel sighed again. "Nothing happened. I mean I went in, I sang my song..."

"Did he think it was funny?"

"Not at first." She related how he had put her on the table, hoping to embarrass her.

Penny nodded knowingly. "And all that did was get your adrenaline flowing, right?"

Rachel grinned. "I was really pretty good. And once I got into it he seemed more amused than annoyed."

"Then what happened?"

Rachel shrugged. "I wished him a happy birthday from his mother and all of us at Ballooney-Tunes and...he took my hands..."

Noting the sudden blur in Rachel's eyes, Penny suggested, "And you fell in love?"

"Of course not." Rachel focused on her friend's face and shook her head. "It's just that...every once in a while you meet a man who isn't like all the other men you come across. I could sense his intelligence, feel his energy and yet...there was something very calm about him, very steady."

Penny got to her feet as though ready for action. "Well, what are you waiting for? Let's kidnap him and share him."

"Pen, I'm trying to be serious."

"So am I."

"What I'm trying to say," Rachel went on determinedly, "is that meeting him got me thinking about my single status."

"You hated being married," Penny reminded her, a little concerned now by this glimpse of her friend's vulnerability.

It required just a moment's thought to make Rachel nod in agreement. "I know. I don't think I'd want to be married again, but a ..." She sighed thoughtfully. "A relationship would be nice."

Penny frowned. "You mean an affair?"

"No," Rachel said with mild impatience. "I mean a relationship. Loving somebody, somebody loving me, without all the tyrannies of marriage." She sighed again, knowing she was pining for the impossible. "But then there's Jessica, and that wouldn't be very healthy for her."

Rachel turned briskly back to her desk and pulled the file box that held her accounts receivable toward her. "I don't know what's the matter with me."

"Dormant puberty," Penny diagnosed. "You got married so young, you never really experienced a giggling, hormonal adolescence. Apparently, Blue Eyes brought it out in you. And as for the relationship without the tyrannies, that's probably something we all dream about. I just doubt that it exists."

Rachel held the dream one more moment. "Pity, isn't it?" she asked Penny.

Penny replied with a heartfelt nod as she moved toward the outer office and the ring of the telephone. "You can say that again."

Finally diverting her mind from its disturbing thoughts, Rachel turned her attention to writing monthly statements. She was making good progress when she heard a commotion in the outer office. Penny appeared, closing the office door behind her and leaning against it, her eyes bright, her cheeks pink.

"He's here!" she whispered loudly.

Rachel turned away from the desk, her brow furrowed. "Who?"

"Brian Tate!"

Rachel's heart pounded. "You're kidding."

"I'm not!" Penny's eyes widened farther. "And he's brought his mother. They want to see you."

Impatient with herself for being nervous, Rachel got to her feet. "Well, send them in."

Penny opened the door and Brian Tate walked in, filling the small back room with his tall, broad presence. Forcing herself to appear composed, Rachel knew she hadn't imagined the energy and sexy magnetism earlier this afternoon. The air around her seemed to crackle with them.

He aimed a deadly smile at Penny, who stood by the door. She blushed visibly. He extended his hand.

"You are...?"

"Penny Mitchell, Rachel's assistant." She put her hand in his.

"I'm pleased to meet you, Penny," he said.

Penny nodded and drew her hand away, still staring.

As she sidled out of the room, Brian Tate looked behind him as though expecting someone to be there. When he found no one, he disappeared into the storefront then returned, towing his mother by the arm. The woman resisted but he was firm.

"I know you two have conducted business over the phone," Brian said, giving his mother a judicious glance, "but I think you should be formally introduced. Mrs. Bennett..." He surprised Rachel with the use of her name. "Penny told me," he said in answer to her raised eyebrow. "I'd like to present my mother, Alicia Tate. Mother, Rachel Bennett."

Alicia Tate, in high-heeled black boots visible under a long magenta cloak, was almost as tall as her son. Rachel concluded that she had to be close to sixty if her son was celebrating his fortieth birthday, but she still had beautiful skin, short but full, artistically windblown gray hair and an air about her that was decidedly youthful. At the moment she looked annoyed and embarrassed. She extended a hand to Rachel.

"Forgive this intrusion, my dear, but this stick-in-the-mud son of mine insists on getting his revenge for my little joke this afternoon. I hope you understand."

Rachel patted the hand holding hers. It was adorned with beaten silver bangle bracelets. "That depends," she said cautiously, "on which one of us he's getting back at."

"First me." Alicia indicated herself with a long magenta fingernail. "And then you. Although your penance is far more palatable than mine." At that she looked at her son pleadingly. "Brian, I can't do this."

"Sure you can," he replied with a heartless smile. "Just remember the alternative."

Alicia sighed, rolled her eyes, then pushed up the sleeves of her cloak. "I'm sorry to put you through this, dear." She took Rachel by both arms and urged her into her chair. "You'd better sit down."

Beginning to wonder if it was time to call the police, Rachel sat tensely on the edge of her chair.

Alicia drew a deep breath then began to sing in a high, off-key soprano. Though difficult to distinguish at first, the melody seemed to be "Camptown Races."

"I've been asked to sing this song..." Alicia's voice cracked and she stopped abruptly, closed her eyes, then turned around, prepared to abandon her task and leave. But Brian caught the billowy sleeve of her cloak and pulled her back.

"Uh-uh," he scolded and turned her to face Rachel. "You've got a few more bars to go. And don't forget the doo-dahs."

Alicia gave her son a long, murderous look, then began again, up-tempo this time. "I've been asked to sing this song, doo-dah, doo-dah, and to promise that it won't take long, oh, the doo-dah day. Brian would like to know..." She stood on tiptoe, straining over the high note. "If you would like to go with him to dinner and to a show. He'll pick you up at seven or so." The last three words were slurred together to fit them into the crowded bar of music.

There was a moment's silence while Alicia drew a sigh of relief that her task was accomplished and Rachel stoutly held back laughter.

"Before you give me an answer—" Brian smiled at Rachel while putting an arm around his mother's shoulder "—you should know that, should you refuse, I'm sending Mother to Lapland for the rest of the winter."

In the tiny room, Alicia had but to reach out to capture Rachel's hand. "Dear, please consider my future. I'm still a young woman. I'm in the middle of an affair. I have my own teeth, my own hair and a headful of the most outrageous fantasies..."

Laughter burst from Rachel. After composing herself, she shook her head regretfully. "I am sorry about your affair, but I can't."

"Oh, but—" Alicia began to argue.

"I'll handle it, Mother," Brian interrupted. "And because you tried so hard, we'll give you another chance. But, Mom..." He looked gravely into his mother's face. "Don't ever leave your watercolors to try your hand at the musical stage."

Alicia reached up to pat his cheek. "If you promise not to abandon writing books to become a lyricist."

He raised a hand to swear. "I promise."

Alicia kissed his cheek. "Good luck, darling." She turned to smile at Rachel. "He's really a very nice man. A little..." She waggled a hand to indicate a condition for which there apparently was no suitable word. "...of course, I don't know how he got like that."

With a swish of magenta, Alicia waved and left the room. And Rachel found herself alone with Brian Tate. She was no longer nervous, but warmly amused and a little disappointed that she had to decline his invitation. He was wearing a leather bomber jacket and jeans. A deep blue sweater visible at the open collar of his jacket darkened the shade of his eyes.

"About dinner—" he began.

"Mr. Tate, I have a child—" But before Rachel could finish her explanation, the door burst open, forcing Brian to catch it before it rammed his shoulder. A curly blond head appeared around it at about the level of his waist. Soft brown eyes shone up at him, and a friendly smile apologized for the abrupt entry.

"Hi," the child said, walking past him to fling herself, books and all, into Rachel's chair. She looked up at her mother grimly. "Mom, math is going to kill me. Can't you pull me out of school for health reasons?"

Rachel rolled her eyes and put a hand to her daughter's earlobes, which were bright red with the cold. "Jess, I sent you to school this morning in a hat for health reasons."

"It's in my lunch pail."

"It's supposed to be on your head." Rachel shook her head at her visitor. "Mr. Tate, I'd like you to meet my daughter, Jessica. I'll be having dinner with her tonight."

Jessica frowned at her mother. "No, you won't. I'm spending the weekend with Leslie, remember? It's her birthday and we're all going for pizza, then she's having a slumber party." To Brian, Jessica added, "And I'm her best friend so I get to stay until Sunday. Are you a supplier?"

"No," Brian replied with a smile. "I'm sort of a... customer."

"Good!" she said feelingly. "January and February are slow months, except for Valentine's Day. We need all the business we can get."

Concluding that her daughter was spending far too much time listening to shop talk, Rachel made a mental note to enroll Jess in that tumbling class she wanted to take, whether or not the tight budget would allow it.

"Leslie's mom is waiting for me." Jessica stood and reached up to wrap her free arm around Rachel's neck. "We're gonna stop at home to pick up my stuff and the present." Jessica suddenly frowned in concern. "Are you going to be okay all by yourself?"

Rachel hugged her daughter. "Of course I will. I'm the mom and you're the kid, remember? I'll be just fine."

"Would you feel better if I took your mom out to dinner?" Brian asked Jessica, his tone and his gaze blandly innocent as he ignored Rachel's stare.

"You mean a date?" Jessica asked.

"Yes."

Jessica looked up at Rachel, giving the question a moment's thought. "Mom never has dates. I mean, she goes out to chamber of commerce meetings and stuff like that. And once Penny took her to see this male strip—"

A swift hand over her daughter's mouth halted the flow of words and Rachel glared at her guest as he coughed.

"That was not my idea."

"Of course."

Rachel reached down to give Jessica another hug. "Have a wonderful time, sweetie, and please be good and helpful."

"I will." Jessica reached for the doorknob then gave the stranger another look. "You aren't married are you, Mr. Tate?"

"No," he replied. "And you can call me Brian."

"Mom's not married, either," she confided. "She's a widow. But Penny says she needs a man."

As Rachel fell into her chair and covered her face with her hands, Brian opened the door for Jessica. "I see," he said. "Then you think dinner's a good idea?"

Jessica nodded. "Yup. I do. Bye."

"Bye, Jessica." Brian Tate closed the door then turned to Rachel with a satisfied smile. "So you're free after all."

"It's been a long day, Mr. Tate—" Rachel began.

"Okay." In two steps he had closed the distance between them. She noted that his smile was nice but determined. "Just dinner. We'll skip the show. Morris's Fireside is a relaxing setting."

He did have beautiful eyes, Rachel thought. And it had been a long time since she'd had dinner with a man she really wanted to be with. Interest finally overpowered caution. "All right," she agreed. "Dinner."

Chapter Two

Brian studied the woman sitting across the table from him as she stared pensively into her tulip glass of white Zinfandel. She was very pretty. Not beautiful like many of the executives and society women who had crossed his path in his checkered career in the business of sports news, but...soft in a way no longer considered fashionable, except by closet chauvinists like himself.

She looked up at him as he formed that thought, and as though she read his mind, her gaze focused on his and her lips firmed. She didn't want to appear soft. He saw strength and tenacity in her eyes and wondered if those qualities were inherent in her or if she had earned them.

He had a fleeting image of her strutting and singing on the boardroom table that afternoon and remembered how she had made the most of the opportunity when he had hoped to embarrass her. Yet her performance had poked fun at him without being offensive.

That delicate balance of softness and strength was the essence of woman, yet many of those he'd met had lived too hard and had lost the softness, or had never been challenged and showed no strength. Rachel Bennett had an intriguing combination of both qualities.

"You're staring at me," she said, her tone not as much disapproving as curious. He liked her lack of pretense.

"You're very pretty." He leaned back in his chair as the waitress brought their salads and offered pepper from a silver grinder. "I find it hard not to stare."

Rachel took a roll from the basket and offered it to him. "My mother was an English war bride with that flawless British Isles complexion. My father's a big, strapping Kansas farm boy. I'm not pretty, just healthy."

Brian passed her the small silver dish of butter. "Did you grow up here?"

"Kansas." She speared a pat with that tiny fork he could never get to work for him and nodded, her sudden smile wide and uncomplicated. "On a wheat farm with six brothers and sisters."

An only child, Brian tried not to blanche. "Seven kids?"

Rachel passed the butter back, frowning. "You don't like kids?"

"I like other people's kids," he admitted candidly. At her continued frown, he changed the subject. "I hunted pheasant and quail in Kansas when I was in the army. Visually, it's a pretty uninteresting state."

"That seems to be every visitor's concept of Kansas, but I think it's a beautiful place." Her eyes softened as she smiled at him, opening her napkin with an absent flick of her wrist then spreading it on her lap. "It isn't as spectacular and bold as the northwest, of course, but it has its own particular beauty. We had a couple of hundred acres, and just before the harvest, that field of wheat dances in the sun and it sings to you in the night breeze. Then, after the harvest, the land is so flat for endless miles that you can see the curvature of the earth." She sighed and said emphatically, "I loved it."

"Then I guess the obvious question is, why did you leave?"

Her expression changed instantly. Sudden pain and sadness clouded her eyes then they were gone. "I got married," she said tersely.

Brian reached briskly over to top off her wineglass, sensitive to her sudden discomfort. "Scratch the question," he said. "Tell me about Jessica. At her age... Eight? Nine? She's already got a finger on the pulse of your business and a careful eye on your social life."

Rachel laughed softly, unabashed pride lighting her smile. "She'll be ten in June. She's in many advanced classes at school."

"That's easy to believe." Brian was trying to be unobtrusive about chasing a pat of butter with the silly little fork. As the butter somersaulted to the rim of the dish he groaned, deciding to eat his roll dry. But Rachel reached over to perform the task for him. Her hand brushed his and he felt a very adolescent quiver of excitement. He cleared his throat. "Thank you. How long have you been in the balloon business?"

"Almost two years."

"Does your musical talent come from your mother, too?"

"No, my dad. He used to sit on the porch and strum his guitar and sing all the old country ballads. We all joined in. Most of my family have some musical ability, but I'm the only one who went into music as a career."

The waitress removed their salad plates and served the main course of butterfly shrimp and steaming baked potatoes with long, tender stalks of asparagus. They both took a moment to sniff appreciatively.

"You've sung professionally, then?" Brian asked, taking knife and fork in hand.

"Yes," she answered quietly. "While I was married. I hated it."

Brian nodded and promptly withdrew from the subject, scanning his mind for a safer topic of conversation. "Would you pass the..." He pointed. "That thing with sour cream and bacon bits and onions."

Smiling, Rachel obliged. "That's called a potato wheel." When he looked surprised that she could put a name to it, she explained. "My first job as a singer was in our high-school hangout in Danvers. I had to waitress as well." She was silent for a moment then looked up at him briefly as she cut a bite of succulent shrimp. "I met my husband there."

About to despair of finding a subject for conversation that didn't lead back to her husband, Brian's head came up in surprise when she asked warily, "Do you want to hear about him so we can get it out of the way? There's probably a limit to how long we can dodge around the subject and, frankly, it's making me nervous. Everything about me—my daughter, my career—leads back to Jarrod. It'll be hard to find anything in my life that doesn't relate to him somehow."

Brian was silent for a moment, startled by her candor.

"I'm sorry," she said quickly, brushing the soft hair from her cheek with one finger in a gesture of embarrassment. "Penny keeps telling me that my middle-America honesty makes people uncomfortable."

"I'm not uncomfortable," he insisted quickly. "Just...surprised. If you don't mind talking about it, please do. We seem to keep bumping up against it anyway."

Apparently unconvinced that she hadn't embarrassed him, she shook her head, concentrating on her plate. "I don't mind talking about it, but someone else's mistakes can be pretty boring dinnertime conversation."

He sipped his wine then fixed her with a steady look. "I doubt that you could bore me. Tell me."

She looked up at him then, a trace of doubt lingering in her eyes. "You're sure?"

"Absolutely."

Rachel ate the bit of shrimp and watched Brian's hands move as he worked easily over his dinner.

"I promise not to go into painful detail."

Brian nodded. "Whatever you're comfortable with."

Rachel opened her mouth to begin, then closed it and put her fork down. "I wonder what made me think talking about Jarrod would be a good idea? I mean, it's never made me nervous before. It was over between us long before he died and my grief was more for him than for myself, because even if he had lived, nothing would have changed. I hardly ever think of him anymore." She frowned at Brian, realizing that she was babbling. "Why am I finding it hard to tell you about him?"

He smiled gently, pushing her wineglass toward her. "I think you just started, Rachel. Just keep going. Or maybe start at the beginning."

Wondering why she had ever suggested talking about Jarrod, sure Brian Tate was now considering sending her to Lapland along with his mother, Rachel tried to form a coherent story in her mind. "I was singing in our high-school hangout..." She looked at him, wondering if he recalled what she had told him.

He nodded. "Right. The potato wheel. Go on."

"Jarrod was passing through with a friend. He had a small rock band. His friend was the drummer." She played with the base of her wineglass while Brian, totally attentive, continued to eat. "He was only a few years older than I, but he seemed to know so much, and I had stars in my eyes." She shook her head sadly and gave Brian a thin smile. "I tend to learn things the hard way."

He nodded again. "You've got a lot of company there."

"He offered me a spot in the band and big dreams. In a couple of weeks I was on the road as Mrs. Jarrod Bennett, part of the Country Crowd Road Band. My family was devastated." She sighed and Brian understood suddenly where a lot of the pain she felt rested. "But I was in love with Jarrod and he loved me... at least as much as he was able. I'll admit I didn't make it very easy for him. I hated the life almost right away—always on the move, seedy nightclubs, rude crowds, hot, dusty fairs and rodeos." She sighed again, shaking her head as though seeing it all in front of her eyes. She looked up a little guiltily. "Do you want to hear any more?"

"If you want to tell me."

She frowned, wondering at herself. "I do."

He poured them both more wine. "Then go on. I'm listening."

She had to think for a moment. Something about just looking at Brian Tate pulled her right out of her grim thoughts and she had to immerse herself in the past to bring them back.

"Jessica came before our first anniversary," she said finally, "and I pleaded with Jarrod to stop. We had friends, contacts—I begged him to try to cut a record—find another kind of work—anything that would keep us in one place. But he loved the applause of an audience and life on the road, even though he needed alcohol to deal with the pressures." She stopped, taking a quick sip of wine and leveling challenging brown eyes on Brian. "You're wondering why I stayed."

He shook his head, returning her steady gaze. "No. I'm not. You were young, with a baby and probably no business skills to get a job. I'm sure a good voice is a great asset but in the time it would take to succeed in the music world, you and the baby could have starved." He smiled gently. "And at eighteen, going back home and admitting you were wrong ranks just above death in order of preferred solutions."

Warmed by his perception, Rachel uttered a small laugh. "Don't tell me you were once a road singer with a baby to support."

He lowered his head and the soft restaurant lighting glinted in his dark hair. "No. But I've been young with the world falling down around my ears. I know that sometimes all you can do is coast until a solution presents itself."

Rachel's eyes were shot with pain again, and Brian suddenly realized that the solution that presented itself for her must have been Jarrod's death. Ready to let her back out of the rest of the story if she wanted to, he waited quietly while she toyed with her potato then put her fork down. When she finally raised her eyes to him, the pain was diluted by a world-weary wisdom. She sat a little straighter in her chair and went on sadly.

"We were traveling from Portland where we'd had an engagement." She smiled grimly at him. "I always refused to call it a 'gig.' Dumb word. To the Red Lion in Astoria for another performance. Jarrod and Dandy, the drummer, were killed when they missed a turn on the Sunset Highway. They were sharing a bottle."

Brian closed his eyes for a moment, feeling her pain. "You weren't hurt?"

"After Jessica was born, I refused to ride with them. We were with our bass and lead guitar in a second car. I had lost Jarrod long before he went off the road and I felt sorriest for all the dreams we'd had, and all the plans that couldn't be. Or maybe I only imagined that we had shared them because I'd given up so much, hurt so many people to follow him. I buried Jarrod here because he had no other family. My parents came out for the funeral but I . . . I sensed a difference in them. I think I killed something there that I can never recapture.''

She sat back in her chair and sighed, throwing her head back for an instant as she drew in air. The soft blue wool of her sweater rose and fell and Brian was distracted by the motion. ''Well!'' she said, purposefully picking up her fork. ''I haven't dragged all that out for anybody, even myself, in a long, long time.''

For the next few moments Rachel ate as though she'd just noticed the food. She looked up at Brian, savoring a bite of shrimp. ''This is wonderful. Anyway, there was a little insurance money and I decided to go back to school, then try my hand at business. I liked the Oregon coast and decided to stay. Jessica doesn't remember much of the past and has adjusted happily here.'' She lifted a shoulder and gave him a sassy little smile. ''Now do you want me to talk about you?''

His pulse reacting to that smile, Brian decided that the safest course of action was to let her follow her own peculiar conversation pattern. He waved a hand to indicate that she should proceed and sat back in his chair, waiting to see just what she knew about him.

Rachel closed her eyes for a moment, calling up all the details Alicia had given her about her son. ''You're an only child who had a propensity for climbing things and exploring the woods outside your home in Green Lake, Wisconsin. You went to Madill School of Journalism at Northwestern University, got a job on the sports staff of the Chicago *Daily News* where you eventually became a widely syndicated columnist. You are now the west coast's accepted expert on fly-fishing and have written a book of practical but comical advice for outdoorsmen that has become a bestseller." She paused for breath and continued. "You love to play poker, you have a sweet tooth, a formidable temper, a curiously archaic preference for boxer shorts and a weakness for blondes. Does that cover it?"

By the time she had finished Brian was laughing. Their conversation was suspended while the waitress cleared away their dishes and promised to return with the dessert tray. Alone with Rachel once more, Brian leaned across the cleared table and confided quietly, "I appreciate your not working the boxer shorts into the song this afternoon."

Rachel accepted the thanks with an inclination of her head. "Ballooney-Tunes is ever discreet."

"I do appreciate that." Brian nodded gratefully. "But one of your facts was incorrect."

"Oh?"

His eyes ran lazily over her thick dark hair, straining against the confinement of a tortoiseshell comb just above each temple. Then they lowered to hers. "There's been a switch in loyalties from blondes to brunettes."

Rachel looked into his inviting gaze and felt for a moment as though she had slipped inside it, lost to all that existed around them. The dark warmth of it seemed to enclose her, entrance her. She turned her head away, fighting to regain her self-possession just as the waitress leaned toward her with a tray burdened with sinfully rich pastries.

Rachel shook her head, putting a hand up in denial. "I couldn't possibly." Then on the next breath pointed to a pyramid of cream in the middle of the tray. "That one."

Laughing, Brian selected a wedge of carrot cake. The waitress returned with coffee and Brian watched Rachel at work on the cream-covered square of chocolate and strawberries. She ate with such enjoyment, he wondered at the trim but enticingly rounded, blue-wool-draped torso that had been tantalizing him all evening. Either she had a lively metabolism or she ate only once a week.

She caught his eyes on her and nodded penitently. "I know. It's probably disgusting to watch a grown woman who should know better put away a dessert like this, but Jessica never lets me have this stuff." Then she studied him questioningly. "Wouldn't the little blonde in the blue suit be upset?"

He gave the question a moment's thought, and unable to relate it to whom she was talking about, Brian leaned toward her on an elbow and asked, "Give me a hint."

"The blonde on the college board."

"Oh, Priscilla Cummings." He asked in bewilderment, "Would she be upset if you had dessert?"

"No." She rolled her eyes. "If you switched your allegiance from blondes to brunettes."

"Ah!" Relieved to finally have a handle on the conversation again, Brian shook his head. "No. We've been out a few times but neither one of us really enjoyed it."

"Why not?"

"She has a tendency to whine and cling. I have a tendency to hate that."

Rachel nodded, able to understand his aversion to that kind of behavior. "What brought you here from Chicago?"

His dark eyes widened in disbelief. "You mean my mother didn't tell you?" At her smiling shrug he went on to explain more seriously. "She and my father retired here about eight years ago. Mom's a fine watercolorist and she's done some beautiful work here. Anyway, my father died two years ago. I wanted her to come back and live with me but, despite her apparent youth, she complains of feeling arthritic and didn't think she could put up with Chicago winters again. I'd been wanting to quit the column and concentrate on a longer project. So I came out to be near her. That's the nice thing about writing books— it doesn't matter where you do it."

"You're working on another one?"

"Right. I've got an April deadline."

"Same subject?"

"It worked the last time."

"An April deadline and you've got time to go out to dinner?" Rachel pushed her empty dessert plate aside and took a long sip of coffee. It was hot and strong and after all that wine and her companion's heady presence, she felt she needed it.

"And breakfast and maybe lunch." He smiled at her across the table. "Busy tomorrow morning?"

Rachel wasn't sure if she was relieved or disappointed that Saturday was Penny's day off. "I have to work."

"Tomorrow night?"

"Ah . . ." Rachel hesitated, hating herself for sounding like a nervous adolescent, groping for an excuse. But for a woman who only this afternoon had been pining for a relationship, she was now panicky at the thought that one might develop between her and this man. He was studying her with a determination she found unnerving. "I've got to make the most of my weekend with Jessica away," she said with forced brightness. "This is my chance to get her room cleaned up, and her laundry done and..."

He looked right into her eyes and though he was smiling she got the distinct impression that he saw right through her.

"I'll bet her room is in perfect order," he said, "and that she does the laundry for both of you while you're at work."

That was close enough to the truth to silence Rachel completely. He arched an eyebrow when she didn't refute his remark.

"You're right," she admitted finally, leaning back in her chair and crossing her arms. "That was a fib. I'd like to see you tomorrow but I'm not sure it's a good idea."

"Why not?"

She waved both hands out in a helpless gesture. "Because I never act like this. You make me chatter."

She looked a little nervous, Brian thought. After the controlled performer he'd met this afternoon, and the almost painfully honest woman he'd just shared dinner with, he found a case of nerves somehow endearing.

"Maybe it's the wine," he suggested.

Rachel looked into her empty glass, realized she had emptied it several times during the course of the evening, and put it down with a frown. "Maybe."

"Or maybe you work too hard, at the shop and at being a mother, and there's been no one with whom to share all that sadness. We all tend to talk when there's a sympathetic ear."

She looked at him doubtfully. "I've only known you..." She glanced at her watch. "Seven hours."

"You referred to telling me about Jarrod as getting it out of the way." He shrugged. "Now we can concentrate on getting to know each other. And I won't have to keep shifting the subject every time he comes up.''

Still uncomfortable about the way she had behaved tonight and reluctant to think about seeing him the following day, she tried to shift some blame on him by accusing, ''You don't even like kids.''

He laughed softly. ''So far I have only proposed breakfast, Rachel, not marriage.''

''I know,'' she said, lifting her small clutch bag off the floor at her feet. ''But when you have a child, you're always thinking ahead. Would you take me home now before I make a total fool of myself?''

He walked around the table to pull her chair out. ''Honesty never makes a fool of anyone. And I like other people's children, remember? Jessica seems like a doll.''

In the foyer of the restaurant Brian paid the check then helped Rachel on with her coat. After slipping it over her shoulders, he reached his warm hand in between her hair and the nape of her neck, pulling the dark mass of it from inside the collar of her coat. He caught a whiff of flowers and herbs while she went ahead of him to the door, battling an urge to take her in his arms.

They were silent most of the way home. When Brian walked Rachel to the door of her duplex, he stopped, leaning a shoulder against the siding to look down at her. She put her key in the lock and opened the front door, flooding the porch with light from the living room.

She looked up at him and smiled. ''The dinner was wonderful. Thank you. And I enjoyed...'' She was forced to stop because his head was coming down. And her mouth was too busy trying to decide whether to reach up to his or pull away to finish the sentence.

The decision was taken from her when he put warm hands on either side of her face and tilted it up. His lips, warm and firm, covered hers for one long, delicious moment, then he pulled away.

"If you change your mind about tomorrow," he said, "or if you need me for anything, call. I'm in the book. If I'm not at home, leave a message."

"Okay."

His eyes went to her lips and rested there. And just when she was convinced he would kiss her again, he turned away and ran lightly down the steps to his car, tapping the horn as he pulled away.

Rachel waved, watching with mixed feelings of relief and disappointment as the Porsche disappeared into the darkness. She touched a finger to her lips and remembered his kiss. It had been sweet, but she told herself sensibly that it offered nothing more than a salute to the age-old game of man in pursuit of woman. Then she remembered how much she had laughed with Brian, and how much better she'd felt after talking to him. With a little thrill of well-being, she turned to go into the house.

Chapter Three

Through the shop window Rachel watched the winter wind whip at the blue-and-white restaurant awning across the street. A lone shopper struggled to retain her grip on an armload of packages while holding her coat closed at the collar.

It was a quiet Saturday in downtown Cannon Beach, and even those shoppers who had braved the weather were heading home to warm fires and smells of dinner cooking on the stove.

Rachel felt a pang of homesickness. Not a yearning for Kansas, but a longing for a home with a man in it. Someone who would lift Jessica into the air and make her feel special. Someone who would come toward her, Rachel, with desire in his eyes and hands that were strong and magical. Images of her evening with Brian had distracted her from paperwork for most of the afternoon.

The telephone rang and she wandered slowly back to the worktable to answer it. "Ballooney-Tunes," she said. "Inflation is our business."

"Hi, Rachel. It's Brian." The voice was deep, yet quiet and unmistakable.

She wanted to be brilliant and witty, but the only response that came to mind was: "Hi."

"I was just checking your ad in the phone book." She heard the rustle of pages being turned, then Brian read: "Hours: Monday through Friday, 9:00 a.m. to 6:00 p.m. Saturday, 9:00 a.m. to 1:00 p.m."

Wondering about the point of his call, she said cautiously, "That's right."

"Then you're off in fifteen minutes."

Rachel glanced at the clock. It was 12:45. "Yes."

"Well..." The simple word seemed to hold a vast potential of promise. "It's a great day for a late lunch of chili and corn bread. Want to join me?"

She smiled into the receiver. "I thought I turned you down last night."

He laughed softly. "You turned down breakfast and dinner. We never discussed lunch."

"You're sneaky," she accused.

"Astute," he corrected. "You'd have let me think you had to work all day. Fortunately I'm not so easily discouraged. Want me to pick you up?"

"No." There was a moment's silence while she once again considered then dismissed caution. "Where do you live?"

He gave her an address.

"I'll find it," she said. "Want me to bring anything?"

"Just you."

"1:15?"

"Perfect."

A half hour later, Rachel paused a moment to admire the size and architecture of a beachfront house that was blatantly modern, all angles, glass and weathered cedar. A wide deck surrounded it, and there were two window boxes filled with ornamental cabbage.

Beyond the house a tidal pool was visible, trapped between the shore and an exposed sandbar. Sandpipers darted back and forth and gulls bobbed and bathed contentedly, ignoring the inclement weather. Where the coastline bulged out into the ocean, a grass-covered dune supported a condominium that sprawled unobtrusively into its environment. A colorful wind sock and an American flag were whipped by the strong wind.

Brian's car was not in the driveway and Rachel began to wonder if she had the correct address. Then the front door, cut into the house at an angle, was pulled open and Brian stood there in jeans and a black cashmere sweater. The darkness of the color and the softness of the sweater's texture intensified the unusual blue of his eyes. He smiled and pushed the door wide.

She held out a bunch of daisies, purchased at the last moment. She had considered a bottle of wine, but had no idea if anyone had ever established what went with chili. Then she had spotted the jaunty bouquet near the checkout stand, guessing that it was the product of some sunny, southern California field. Unsure how he would react to a gift of flowers, she had decided to take the chance.

"Ah." He made a soft sound of approval as he took them from her then ran one large palm under the petals. He looked genuinely pleased. "I know an abandoned meadow in Jewell," he said, "that's covered with these in early June, just when the hay starts. Thank you, Rachel."

A little embarrassed, she shrugged a slender shoulder. "Seemed only fair. I don't think a man has ever cooked for me before."

He pulled her inside and closed the door behind her. Taking her jacket, he hooked it onto a tall, brass coat tree, then nudged her toward the living room. "Make yourself at home. I'm going to put these in water and check the chili."

Rachel wandered around a spacious living room decorated in the colors of the beach: sand, pale blue and the soft orange of a winter sunset. Bright watercolor landscapes adorned the walls, and in the center of the room, a sand-colored fireplace kept the sharpness of January at bay.

The large room opened onto a dining area where she saw a round table set for two, a tall, cylindrical basket filled with exotic grasses and another watercolor, this one of a lonely figure on a windswept beach.

When Brian returned to the living room, he found Rachel standing in front of a bookshelf, laughing over a volume she held in her hands. She looked up at him, her eyes bright with humor.

"No wonder this became a bestseller. It's hilarious." She giggled and looked back at the page she'd been reading. "You don't even have to be a sportsman to appreciate what it must be like to carry your elk out of the woods on a moped."

He grinned and looked over her shoulder. "Everyone should experience the fun of having your truck die seven miles from civilization when you have a twelve-hundred-pound elk to get home. Come and sit down."

Still holding the book open, she followed him to the sofa. "And this part, where you tell about buying your first truck for two hundred dollars and having the bed fall off when you went up a steep hill."

"It was hardest on my friends who were sitting in the bed."

Rachel laughed again, her mind's eye conjuring up the amusing picture his words painted. When she stopped, she saw Brian, a soft smile on his face, staring at her.

"You're doing it again." She relinquished the book as he took it from her and closed it, setting it aside. "I wasn't finished . . ."

"You can borrow it. Doing what?"

"I should buy it," she said as he put an arm on the sofa back and pulled her closer. "Staring at me."

He nodded, whether agreeing that she should buy his book, or acknowledging that he had been staring, she was never sure. Then he leaned down, and she felt his soft mustache against her upper lip and the dry warmth of his mobile mouth as it touched hers and then teased it. It had all the sweetness of last night's kiss, but with a new, complex quality that was both explorative and assertive.

Brian felt her immediate though somewhat tentative response. She seemed not to mind the gentle invasion of his tongue, or the hand that began to explore down her spine. He felt her hands at his neck, her fingernails moving into the short hair behind his ears. He felt an unsettling tremor.

She pulled away, and reluctantly he loosened his hold. But she wanted only to look at him, not to draw out of his arms. Her soft, dark eyes looked into his, their expression probing and grave.

"What do you see?" he asked, trying to read the message in their shiny depths but unable to.

"Sweetness," she said in mild surprise. "A small flare of passion. Patience."

His laugh was soft and wicked. "I can vouch for the passion, though the 'small flare' is in great danger of becoming 'conflagration.' As for sweetness, you're probably seeing yourself reflected. The patience you must be misreading. I don't think either one of us is big on it."

"I don't feel patient right now," she admitted in a whisper.

His, "Neither do I," was barely a sigh as his mouth covered hers again. It ran riot over her face, dipping into the V of her sweater then running back up her throat to her ear.

She hunched her shoulder, laughing breathlessly, as her nerve endings pulsed madly.

"Ah," he said on a note of delighted discovery. "Ticklish there?" As he dipped his head to ravish that sensitive spot once more a loud crash came from the direction of the kitchen. It was followed instantly by a heartfelt but youthful-sounding, "Damn!"

Brian muttered his own quiet oath and, putting Rachel gently aside, rose and ran to the kitchen. Rachel followed him, wondering idly if he had a pet.

On a blue-and-ivory-tiled floor were the remnants of a terra-cotta pot and a philodendron. The plant was apparently still whole, but damp earth and shards of pottery were spread all over the kitchen.

At Brian's loud "Davey!" Rachel looked up to find a picture that required a double take for even minimal comprehension. Perched on the sill over the sink, one leg in and one leg out of the window, was a boy about Jessica's age, his respectably sized sneaker-clad foot in the sink. The boy's eyes were dark and large, his expression uncertain.

"Hi," he said to Brian, trying a smile and then deciding to withdraw it when it wasn't returned. "When did you put the plant on the counter?"

"This morning," Brian said, confronting the intruder with arms folded across his chest, "when I watered it."

Davey swallowed. "I'm sorry. I didn't see your car. I thought you weren't home."

"It's being waxed." Brian's tone was stern. "Look, I know I told you you're welcome to come over any time, even when I'm not home, but I'd rather you didn't break and enter." He frowned at the floor. "Or enter and break. What happened to the key I gave you?"

"Lost it."

Man and boy studied each other in a manner Rachel suspected wasn't new. Brian looked exasperated but tolerant, the boy, contrite but expecting to be forgiven. With a sigh Brian finally reached over the sink to the boy's waist and swung him easily to the floor.

"Rachel, this is David Callahan," Brian said. "Davey, this is my friend, Rachel Bennett."

Davey was just about Jessica's height. He had a thick thatch of dark hair and a pair of jeans and a flannel shirt that looked like they hadn't been off his back in several weeks. But his smile was open and warm.

"Hi," he said to Rachel. Then with a quick glance at Brian he added, "I'll get the broom."

When the boy disappeared into the garage, Brian reached down and snatched up the philodendron. "Well, I guess this is a loss," he said, trailing earth as he crossed to the sliding doors beyond which Rachel could see a trash can.

"No!" Rachel followed him and grabbed hold of his forearm. She felt warmth, wiry hair, muscle. "Don't you dare put that in the trash. Just get another pot."

"I don't have another pot."

"A large butter tub, a plastic bowl, a bucket," she enumerated. "Anything will do in the meantime. Really," she scolded, following him as he went to the sink, reaching under it to retrieve a plastic bucket. "To think an outdoor writer would have so little respect for a living thing."

He handed her the bucket. "It's not lack of respect, but lack of knowledge. I don't know anything about houseplants. My mother thinks I need them."

Rachel beckoned the boy. "Over here with the broom, Davey."

Brian watched while Davey wielded the broom according to Rachel's directions, sweeping the rich dark earth into a mound. Then, on her hands and knees on the tile, Rachel scooped the dirt up in handfuls and put it in the bucket, then hollowed out a nest for the roots, packing the earth neatly around them. Then she got to her feet, put the bucket in the sink, and put a small amount of water in it. She moved to place it on the counter then looked at Davey consideringly.

"Do you always leave the same way you came in?"

He laughed. "When Brian's home I use the door. You can put it there. Well..." He smiled in embarrassment at Brian. "I didn't know you had company. I'll put the broom back and see ya tomorrow."

Davey leaned out the still-open door to the garage, replaced the broom against the wall and pulled the door closed. He directed a small wave toward Brian and Rachel, then pulled the sliding doors open.

Rachel heard a small sound of exasperation from Brian's throat. He looked heavenward in supplication.

"Davey!" he called, just as the boy started to push the doors closed.

Davey stuck his head inside, his expression casually questioning. But Rachel had been a mother too long not to see beyond what was apparent. Davey wanted very much to be invited to stay.

"Had lunch?" Brian asked.

The look was still carefully nonchalant. "No." Then the boy hesitated and admitted, "I had soup with Grandma a little while ago, but I'm still hungry."

"Is she all right?"

Davey nodded. "Yeah. She's asleep."

"Chili," Brian informed him. "Want to stay?"

The boy grinned broadly. "Sure."

During lunch Rachel learned that Brian made chili that could fuel a jet. She also learned that Davey lived across the road with his grandmother, who was in her late seventies and not in very good health. Brian did her shopping and kept up her yard, and on one occasion, when the woman had spent three days in the hospital, Davey had stayed with Brian.

"We went duck hunting," Davey told Rachel.

"Oh?" she said politely. But the look she cast at Brian was disapproving. Davey, however, missed nothing.

"Oh, we don't shoot 'em," he put in quickly, "we just hunt 'em to look at 'em. By this time of the year they've chosen mates anyway so we don't think it's right to kill 'em." Davey looked at his hero for corroboration. "Right?"

Brian nodded. "Right."

Rachel smiled tauntingly at him. "So only the married are safe, huh?"

"And those steadily seeing someone." Brian nodded, his expression deadly serious. "You should come with us sometime."

"It gets really cold on the river," Davey discouraged, looking Rachel over and obviously deciding that she looked too delicate for the job. "You wouldn't like it."

"Sure she would," Brian said, standing to retrieve the coffeepot from the stove. He refilled Rachel's cup then his own and replaced the pot. "More milk, Davey?"

"Yeah," the boy replied.

"Yeah, what?"

"Yes, please." Davey corrected his reply, and dutifully stacked up the empty bowls and carried them to the sink. While Brian poured his milk the boy filled the dishwasher. He obviously spent a lot of time with Brian, Rachel noted, and was familiar with his routine. She remembered being concerned about Brian's attitude toward children because of his remark about liking only other people's children, and wondered how many men would make the kind of time Brian did for a little ruffian like Davey.

"So what do you say?" Brian prompted. "Want to come duck watching with us tomorrow morning?"

When she just looked at him, thinking it was one of the most curious invitations she'd ever considered, he cajoled her with, "I've got a duck shack with all the amenities."

She frowned. "I thought the ducks lived on the river."

Davey giggled, promptly covering his mouth with both hands when Brian sent him a quelling glance.

"The ducks don't live in the shack," he explained patiently, though he did sound in danger of choking, "the hunter does. Or at least he uses it as his base camp. It has a refrigerator, stove, beds. We'll pick you up at 6:00 a.m."

"Six?" she asked in horror.

He frowned. "I thought you were a farm girl."

"That was a long time ago." Rachel looked at him consideringly. "Jessica will be home in the middle of the afternoon."

"We'll be back by lunch."

She'd never been *on* the Columbia River, she thought, only watched its beauty from one of the many towns along its banks that she and Jarrod and their band had played.

It would be a new experience, and there had been so little in her life lately besides work and caring for Jessica.

"What do I wear?" she asked.

Brian laughed. "Everything you've got and your warmest socks. Davey's right; it's very cold business."

As Rachel got to her feet she caught Davey's watchful expression. She saw disappointment register in his eyes before he quickly turned away to start the dishwasher. She felt a stab of pain for him. Obviously he prized Brian's friendship and saw her as an intruder.

"Lunch was delicious," she said quickly, starting to move toward the living room, "but I've got to go. I'm supposed to meet Penny this afternoon for—"

"A male revue?" he guessed with a teasing grin, recalling Jessica's short litany of her mother's activities.

"A movie," she corrected with dignity. On her way to the door, she detoured to a wall of the room that held three watercolors, two seascapes and a mountain scene with a stream and a small cabin. "Are these your mother's work?"

"Right."

These were not soft, muted watercolors, but paintings with bright splashes of strong color. Rachel smiled, remembering Alicia's high-fashion look and her rampant sense of humor.

"What a neat lady," she said. Then entertaining the thought for the first time, she looked up at Brian and asked, "What was your father like?"

When he would have replied, she put both hands to his chest in a halting gesture. It worked as he lost the very breath he had drawn to speak.

"No, don't tell me!" she said, narrowing her eyes on him. "Let me guess." Sorting out what she knew of him and separating those qualities she could attribute to his mother from the rest, she said slowly, "The patience comes from him."

"I tell you I have no patience," he said, repeating his earlier claim.

Rachel shook her head, denying that. "You haven't seen *you* with Davey."

He inclined his head thoughtfully. "That's right. I must be due for canonization."

"Your father had a temper," she guessed.

"Most definitely."

"But he could be sensitive and kind."

Brian hesitated for just an instant. "True."

"Protective."

He frowned. "Yes. But where'd you pick that up?"

"You look out for Davey and his grandmother."

He shifted his weight, folding his arms. "I thought we were discussing my father."

"We are. By what I know of you." She punched lightly at his tough shoulder. "He must have been big, too. You could have gotten your height from your mother, but with her slender wrists she could have never given you those shoulders. Was he a writer, too?"

Fascinated by her analysis and her unorthodox method of assembling it, Brian nodded in surprise. Maybe one day he'd explain about his father. "Yes—of textbooks. Medical stuff."

"Aha!" Proud of her conclusions, Rachel dusted her hands. "Did he develop weapons for the government?"

Perplexed, Brian raised an eyebrow. "No. Why?"

"The napalm in your chili."

Groaning at her joke, Brian caught her neck gently in the crook of his elbow and walked her out to the van. He pulled the door open for her, then turned her to face him.

Before she could move or protest, he had planted a chaste kiss on her lips.

"Don't forget the warm socks," Brian reminded her, helping her step up into the van. "I'll take care of breakfast at the shack." And before she could close the door, he leaned in for one more kiss. It was quick but emphatic, and Rachel finally drove away with a heartbeat working as hard as her van's engine.

Chapter Four

Had they been serious about duck hunting, Brian judged that they would have had a perfect morning for it. It was drizzly and cold. The sky, slow about shaking off its midwinter darkness, was still deep blue and quilted with clouds. It would be nasty on the river; the cold would be bone-chilling, the rain continuous. He loved this kind of morning. He smiled as he turned onto the road where Rachel lived. It would be interesting to see what she thought of it.

He pulled up in front of her duplex and he saw a hand brush a curtain aside. Driving his truck instead of the Porsche in which he'd taken her to dinner, he jumped out, waving to identify himself. She came out instantly, running lightly down the steps.

"Good morning," she whispered as he reached a hand out to help her into the truck. Then noting that there was no one in the cab of his pickup but the two of them, she asked as softly, "Where's Davey?"

"Seems he caused a little problem at school on Friday," Brian replied. "The teacher called his grandmother and she's grounded him for a while. When he told her about our trip, she felt she had to stand firm."

Rachel felt sympathy for Davey. "Poor kid. He doesn't lead a very easy life, does he?"

"No." Brian shook his head. "But he's got to learn that flouting school authority, or any authority, isn't going to make it any better."

"What did he do?"

"Frogs in the girls' rest room," he replied, his struggle with a smile calling one up from Rachel. "Not very inventive, but effective. I guess it took more than an hour to calm all the young ladies down. Longer than that to catch the frogs."

Rachel giggled. "The little devil." Then she sobered and asked, "Well, do you still want to go? I mean, you had planned the trip for him originally."

Brian looked at Rachel before answering. Most of the guys he hunted and fished with used a woman's figure in a bikini or in lacy underwear as a standard for judging her longevity in camp. He liked a woman dressed to her ears, every enticing curve and distracting indentation covered with down and fur. If there was still a spark in her eyes and a smile on her lips, it was bound to be a warm, companionable trip.

Rachel's eyes sparkled in the dark cab of the truck.

"You still game?" he challenged.

"Sure. If you are." She paused and added firmly, "And you promise not to shoot anything."

"I am. And I promise."

She smiled and settled in her seat, pulling on her seat belt. "Then let's go."

He turned on the motor and pulled out onto the quiet street.

The sky was changing from dark blue to murky pewter an hour later when Brian turned off the highway that had led them through Seaside and Gearhart then turned inland along the river. Rachel judged that they were about twenty miles beyond Astoria as they meandered down a narrow road. In summer, the road would be overgrown by trees on both sides, probably forming a canopy over their heads. But now only naked branches reached for the truck.

Brian stopped at a railroad track, pulled off the road and, nudging the nose of the truck into the bushes, braked to a stop. Rachel looked around. There was no duck shack that she could see.

"We walk," Brian said, reaching between their seats for a pack.

"Okay." Rachel leaped out of the truck and fastened the collar of her down jacket as rain fell steadily on her head and shoulders. She wondered how far they would have to walk but didn't ask. Something about this morning had turned the usually verbal Brian into a man of few words. It wasn't that he was unpleasant, or even that the silence bothered her, it was just unusual behavior for the man she was coming to know. Maybe this was the strong-silent-hunter persona that he took on when he worked. She smiled at that thought.

They were standing at the rear of the truck and he had opened the camper shell to reach in and take out two camouflage ponchos. He pulled one over her head, guiding her arms through the hole formed by the snap that kept the sides closed.

When Rachel's head surfaced with her knit cap down over her nose, she faced his general direction with a hand on her hip.

"Is this so the ducks don't recognize us?" she asked.

He yanked the hat off and teasingly swatted her cheek with it. Cold air filtered through her hair, nipping at her ears and neck.

Removing his gloves, he gave them to her to hold. "Never a dull moment with you, is there?" he chuckled. He resettled the hat over her hair, narrowing the cuff so that it covered more of her ears and just skimmed her eyebrows. "Better?"

"Yes." Her voice splintered, her heart uncertain of its work as his hands continued to fiddle with her clothes. "Thank you."

He raised the camouflage hood up and looked her over. Then he noticed her feet. "Tennis shoes?"

She looked down at them, then up at him, having to pull the hood back in place. "You said warm socks, you didn't say anything about shoes. Don't people wear deck shoes on a boat?"

He shook his head, more to himself than at her. "Yachts, yes. Duck boats, no. You're going to freeze your feet."

Rachel looked at his stout hiking boots and shrugged, no easy accomplishment under all she wore. "I don't own anything like those, anyway. Just dressy shoes and these." She smiled winningly. "If my feet freeze I won't complain, I promise."

He shrugged into his own rain poncho, a larger version of hers, and emerged from the neck hole asking, "Let's see the soles of your shoes."

She lifted one, frowning. "We're getting a little intimate for a second date, aren't we?"

He looked with disapproval at the scores of tiny circles that made up the bottoms of her aerobic shoes. "In jogging sneakers with good tread you might have had a chance. With those you're going to find this icy railroad track very slick. Watch your step. And it's our third."

"Third?"

"Date."

She smiled and handed back his gloves. "Why, Brian Tate. You're counting. Can I carry something?"

He had just slung the pack over one shoulder and a smaller bag on the other.

"Just keep yourself upright," he said, returning her smile. It was different from what she now thought of as his "city" smile. Just as he was more quiet, his smile was more introspective, as though it were a little harder to pull up and almost too precious to share. "We'll go about half a mile along the tracks, then turn off the road. Go on."

She frowned. "Isn't it wilderness etiquette for the big, strong one to get out in front?"

"If you don't know where you're going. If you do, the smallest one sets the pace so she doesn't get left behind. Or fall down unnoticed."

She turned away with a grin. "I'll bet you just want to watch me walk."

"Right," he called to her as she started off, moving out ahead of him. "You're so seductive in that outfit."

She gave her stride an exaggerated swing and he laughed. Until she hit an icy patch on the track and slipped, frantically flailing the air. She caught herself and stuck her tongue out at him over her shoulder.

"Quit clowning around and watch where you're going," he shouted, but in a good-natured tone. She made him feel good. As he watched her walk, her arms held out for balance, her slender legs in jeans carefully picking their way, he realized without surprise that he wanted her. This was not quite what he had in mind. He had wanted to see her because the winter was quiet in Cannon Beach and he needed a distraction from his deadline. The day they met, he hadn't suspected that she had a child, or that there was such a warm and witty woman underneath the performer.

He didn't want anything like that—nothing that smacked of something long-term. Kids were a constant distraction and he had work to do. Warm, witty women wanted warm, witty men, and they wanted them to stay around. He liked to pick up and go when he wanted to—when he needed to.

Silly to worry about it, he decided finally as the sun rose a little higher and decided to show its face. Then Rachel turned to him with a big grin and pointed a mittened finger at the sky. "Sun!" she said, as though it were her own personal discovery.

He nodded, his heart tripping over itself. "Turn left on that road just ahead of you," he shouted.

The air was noisy now, filled with the quacks and honks of ducks and geese. Rachel followed the road, which ended abruptly and deposited her on a boardwalk of sorts built over water.

"The river?" she asked as Brian caught up with her. She had stopped to inspect her surroundings.

"A slough," he corrected. "A sort of bay in the shore of the river. Follow the planks to that building."

Rachel complied, wondering if she was about to enter the much-touted duck shack. If so, she decided as she stepped inside, Brian's idea of amenities was poles apart from hers.

Crooked doors hung on loose hinges and small squares of watery sunlight filtered through holes in the roof to dapple the creaking wooden floor of the structure that was built around a dock. A small boat bobbed inside the room in the square of slough in the middle. Duck decoys hung all around on the rough wooden walls.

"Boat shed." Brian pulled her back out and along the planks that led to another small structure, adjoining the front of the boat shed. "Duck shack."

She was relieved to find that their preferences in amenities weren't quite that far apart after all. Rachel stepped into a small square room to find a refrigerator, a sink with running water, a wood stove, cupboards and a table with two chairs. Immediately on her right and filling a quarter of the room were bunk beds. A pair of waders hung on a hook and a small shelf against the wall held a few tools and a small radio.

"You can stay here a couple of days at a time and be quite comfortable," he said, moving into the room to shed the pack and the other bag. He removed some things from the pack and put them in the refrigerator. "We'll be out for a couple of hours. There's a bathroom right outside."

"Right." Smiling to herself, Rachel thought there was more of a parent in that man than he realized.

"Feeling warm enough?" Brian asked. "Your feet?"

"I'm fine," she assured him. Her feet were cold but she doubted that they would make her seriously uncomfortable. "Are we ready?"

Her eyes were bright, and she was wearing a big smile. Brian began to seriously regret the fact that this was not an overnight expedition.

Leaping lightly into the duck boat, Brian turned to offer Rachel a hand down. She placed a foot where he pointed, then uttered a little scream when the boat drifted away from the dock, threatening to separate one half of her body from the other. Brian reached for her waist and hauled her off the dock, depositing her on her feet beside him.

"Baryshnikov would have been proud of that one." He laughed, pushing her onto a padded bench. "You okay?"

She was still smiling. "Embarrassed, but okay."

He reached out to cup the back of her woolen-capped head in a large gloved hand. "Don't be silly," he scolded gently.

The sun had retreated again and the run through the slough as Brian pushed the throttle and headed the boat for the open river filled Rachel with wonder. A whole world she had never known about existed so close to hand.

Tall pines, beaten by the north coast's harsh winds and rains, bordered both sides of the slough, their exotic, mossy undergrowth trailing into the water and disappearing. A whole colony of duck shacks nestled under them, lining the route to the river. Some of the shacks looked about to collapse, while others had the elegance of serious houseboats, with curtains visible and window boxes filled with ornamental winter plants. But most of them looked like Brian's, reasonably well cared for, no-nonsense shelters—an escape from the tidy demands of the everyday world.

An irregular column of ducks swam toward them and Brian slowed the boat, reaching into a paper bag at his feet and tossing out a handful of bread torn into pieces. After devouring his offering, the ducks moved on to the shack with the window boxes. A plump, older woman stepped out and tossed something their way. She waved at Brian and he waved back.

"They have an established begging route," Rachel asked, "just like dogs and cats?"

Brian nodded. "Those do. Mrs. Froman's husband found that female two seasons ago. She was just a duckling and her mother had been killed. Mrs. Froman nursed her back to health and she brings her babies back regularly to show them off." Brian pushed the throttle and Rachel tore her eyes away from the pretty picture the ducks made as he guided the boat toward the river.

They seemed to break out of the slough all of a sudden. One moment they were sheltered by the pines and the shacks and suddenly they were on a broad expanse of river dotted with small islands, mere clumps of earth that supported tall stalks of reeds and cattails waving in the cold wind.

For two hours Brian wove in and out of the small islands, sometimes stopping behind a thicket of grass and killing the motor to lure the ducks closer for Rachel's admiration.

He would yank on a string near the controls and a "blind" he had made by weaving grass through a length of netting snapped upright into place to conceal the occupants of the boat. Brian explained that mostly mallards inhabited this part of the Columbia River and that they were a garden-variety duck. But common or not, Rachel found its vibrant green head, white neck band, and rusty breast spectacular. Even the females, simply brown with a spattering of white freckles, were beautiful in their simplicity.

"They wear the sweetest, schoolteacher expressions," Rachel whispered. She and Brian were seated together on the padded bench, hunched down to watch a family of ducks inspecting their blind. "They bustle around so importantly..." She folded her arms and raised both elbows like wings, rocking back and forth in imitation of their busybody movements. The boat rocked alarmingly, and she put both hands out to steady it, one connecting with Brian's knee. "Sorry." She gave him a swift smile then turned back to the ducks.

Brian sat calmly, trying not to react to the touch he could still feel though she'd withdrawn her hand. He wondered if she was sorry she had rocked the boat, or sorry she had touched him? Prophetic in either case, he decided.

"Seen enough?" he asked quietly.

"No," she whispered back.

Having picked up the sound of her voice, the ducks rose with an explosive splash, wings and water aflutter in the air as they shot almost straight up like some sophisticated aircraft. Rachel stared up at the picture they made against the leaden sky and felt a wrench in the pit of her stomach at the thought that anyone could aim a gun and shoot one.

She turned to Brian, her dark eyes hot and indignant. "How could anybody kill one for sport?" she demanded.

A woman of swift and sudden changes, Brian thought. He decided quickly that in this particular case, cowardice was the better part of valor. "I'm not going to fight that one out with you," he said, starting the boat. "How about some lunch and some hot coffee?"

She looked up at the sky mournfully. "I want a duck to take home."

RACHEL'S FEET WERE FROZEN. While Brian cooked bacon and eggs in a pan on top of the wood stove, she got as close to it as she could without getting in the way. Unobtrusively, she stretched out her legs, aiming her toes at the warmth of the fire.

"Feet cold?" Brian asked casually as he stepped over her feet to put plates on the table. She looked up into his eyes and found them bland—until she looked a little closer and saw the amused "I told you so" in their depths.

"Frozen," she admitted with a sigh.

As he passed her he pulled back on the hem of her jeans, revealing a long white sock with its blue athletic stripe. He gave her that small shaking of his head that made her feel as though she were a lost cause. Going to his pack, he removed something and tossed it at her. A large lump of gray wool with a splash of red landed in her lap.

"Put those on," he said. He pointed to what she wore with disgust. "You wear those in the summer to play tennis."

Unwinding the socks, Rachel found that they were thick and woolen with red reinforced toes and heels. She removed her unsuitable aerobic sneakers and her summer tennis socks and put on the Brian-approved proper footwear. She stretched her feet out to the fire and couldn't hold back the "aah" of finally warm toes.

"Here." Brian put a plate of still sizzling bacon and eggs on her lap and handed her a knife and fork. "You can eat off your lap instead of the table and keep your feet stretched out to the fire." He pulled a foil-wrapped package off the back of the stove, tossing it in his hands as he carried it to the table. He opened it to reveal fat blueberry muffins. Rachel took one with a groan of approval.

"Does this taste so good because it just is?" she asked, nibbling on a strip of bacon. "Or because it's so cold out there that warmth and food are so welcome?"

Brian sat at the table, poured coffee for both of them, then tucked into his breakfast. "A little of both, I suppose. We forget how little we need to be comfortable, even satisfied. Shelter and good food is all it takes."

Rachel wiggled her toes at the fire. "Weren't you going to mention the good company?"

He was silent a moment, and when she turned her head to look at him, he was studying her, his expression watchful, entertained. "Would you?"

"That goes without saying." Her breath seemed to catch in her throat, and she turned back to the expertly done over-easy egg on her plate. "Had I come here alone, in the wrong shoes, the wrong socks, and without a slicker, I'd probably be just a casualty of the wilderness by now, like those pioneers on that snowy pass. Donder?"

"That's one of Santa's reindeer," he corrected. "Donner. This isn't the wilderness and not too many people die duck hunting in Samson Slough." He smiled lazily at her. "But I appreciate being considered necessary."

"You also make a great breakfast. Did you bake the muffins?"

He shook his head. "Those are a contribution from my mother. But I'm not a bad cook with the basics. Most bachelors learn as a matter of self-preservation."

Rachel considered all his skills, both on a practical level and socially, and turned her head to frown across the table at him. "Why have you never married?"

He shrugged, snapping off a bite of bacon. "No one ever asked me."

Rachel rolled her eyes. "You're supposed to do the asking."

Feigning surprise, he selected a muffin from the foil packet and tore it in half. "Really? I thought with all the changes taking place in the mating game that I could just sit back and wait for some buxom, capable career woman to corner me on the sofa and say, 'Tate, let me take you away from all this. Marry me and we'll eat and play all day and make love all night.' Then she'd nibble on my ears until I agreed."

Rachel chuckled. "Your fantasies are richer than Tolkien's." Then she sobered and studied him over a triangle of toast. "Seriously, Brian."

Brian dropped the muffin on his plate and leaned back in his chair, reaching a long arm out for his coffee. His thick hair was slightly ruffled, the sturdy contours of his face ruddied by the morning spent outdoors and the warmth of their cozy fire. The eyes he raised to her were quiet and resigned.

"I have some habits that would be hard to fit into a marriage."

Somehow, she couldn't imagine that. "Like what?"

"The nature of my work, for one thing," he said, holding the stout mug between his hands and rolling it to the ends of his fingers then back to his strong palm. "Writing is a pretty solitary occupation. You need a lot of time alone to get it done. When I'm not writing, I'm doing what I do, so that I have something to write about— hunting, fishing, camping." He looked up at her. "And sometimes I just have to go, work or not. I have to get away from everything and everyone. When I was a columnist there were too many times when I couldn't do that. Now that I have the freedom to indulge myself, I can't imagine giving it up for anybody." He sighed. "And then there's kids."

"Right." Remembering how he was with Davey, she suppressed a smile. "I keep forgetting you don't like them."

"I like them," he said, an arched eyebrow acknowledging her teasing, "but I don't think it would be fair to stick a kid with a father who locks himself in a room for long stretches of time, then takes off without warning for days."

Rachel pushed her empty plate aside and took a long sip of coffee. "You know," she said, looking at him through the steam rising from her cup. "Kids have an amazing capacity for accepting what you can give them, as long as what you do give them is genuine.'' She put her cup down and lifted a shoulder philosophically. ''And maybe somewhere there's a woman who could put up with your taking off like that.''

''Would you?'' he challenged.

''No,'' she replied without pause. ''I would hate it.''

He nodded, as though her answer proved his point. ''That's why I'm still single. Probably only a woman who didn't care would put up with it. And who wants to be married to a woman who doesn't care?''

Rachel dropped her cup to the table with a laugh. ''You've painted yourself into a corner, Brian.''

He went to the stove for the blue graniteware coffeepot and topped up their cups. ''Could be. But then, you're right there with me. There must be a good reason you haven't remarried in five years. I can't believe you haven't been asked.''

''Not by anyone I would have seriously considered.''

He looked skeptical. ''You're looking for magic?''

She nodded truthfully. ''Yes. For me and for Jessica. He would have to be someone she could love, too, and who would love her.''

''But she's such a cute, smart kid. Would it be that hard?''

Rachel leaned her chin on her hand and sighed. ''You wouldn't think so. But many men share your attitude. Kids are nice, but they wouldn't want to raise one.''

He was silent for a moment then slowly drew a deep breath. ''Well, if that was calculated to make me feel small, it worked.''

''It wasn't,'' she denied instantly. ''It was calculated to show you that I have as valid a reason for remaining single as you do. Our reasons are the same—just the reverse sides of the same coin. There aren't many men who'd like to live the structured life that makes me comfortable. Anyway, I've gotten used to my independence and have even grown to like it. I don't have to consult anyone but myself before I make a decision.''

''Not even Jessica?''

''Sometimes Jessica.'' She grinned. ''But I can overrule her. With a husband it isn't that easy. Shall we share the last muffin?''

Brian looked at her for a long moment, then handed her a knife. She cut the muffin in half, buttered both pieces and handed him one. She sat back to eat hers, her free hand cupped to catch crumbs.

''But I have felt like I'm missing out on a lot,'' she admitted.

The half muffin dispensed with in one bite, Brian brushed a paper napkin over his mouth and looked at her questioningly, waiting for her to go on.

''Well, don't you ever feel like that? Like, even though you know there's no one out there you could promise to love and live with on a permanent basis, there should be someone you could go to dinner with, laugh with, tell your troubles to?''

He quirked an eyebrow. ''An affair?''

''Oh, God! You and Penny,'' she said in irritation.

He looked perplexed. ''Penny and I should have an affair?''

''No!'' she shouted, then caught his smile. His laugh was quiet but rich as he reached across the table and patted her hand.

''I know it's hard for you, Rachel, but try to make sense.''

She drew a deep breath and went on patiently. ''I was trying to explain the same thought to Penny and she had the same reaction you just did. She thought I meant an affair. But I mean just a . . . a relationship. . ." As he began to nod knowingly, she shook her head. "And not a relationship as defined by today's jargon. I mean a friendship. Two people willing to share. If intimacy develops, fine. If it doesn't, fine. There is so much a woman can't share with another woman and I don't mean the obvious. I mean . . . every little tender thing that is so much sweeter because there's a man's arm around you, or his height and his solidity beside you. A woman friend can make you laugh and cry. But she can't make you *feel* like a woman. It takes a man to do that. And if there's anything I've missed in five years of widowhood, it's that."

Looking into her thoughtful, impassioned expression, Brian was sure he had never met a more honest woman in his life. Even as her honesty made him nervous, he admired her for it. He had held back a little in telling her why he'd prefer not to have children, but she held back nothing. He knew what it cost to reveal a fear, analyze it, then share it with someone, taking the chance of being laughed at or ignored.

And he understood precisely what she meant. It was hard to share a sensitive thought with another man, to wake your buddies up because the sunrise was spectacular. Contrary to Rachel's observation about women, being with other men intensified one's masculinity, but did nothing for what made a man a man—that protectiveness, that caring, that I-can-be-bigger-than-I-am feeling that rose inside when a woman reached out to you in need.

"And . . ." Brian pushed the now cool coffeepot from between them and looked into her eyes. "Do you see us in this kind of a . . . relationship?"

Would she continue to be honest, he wondered. Then he laughed a moment later for having even given the question a moment's thought.

"Why not?" she replied, looking from her feet in the red-toed socks to his eyes. "We'd be perfect for each other—neither one of us a threat to the other."

"Good point." He leaned back in his chair, appearing to consider it. Her slim legs in jeans stretched out to the fire, Rachel looked like the incarnation of every woodsman's dream. Though inexperienced in outdoor activities, she had taken all the small inconveniences with good humor and seemed to have enjoyed her morning on the river with open-hearted love for nature and everything else it had to offer besides sunshine, blue sky and green grass. She was honest and fun and there were not two qualities more precious in a wilderness companion. And then there was the way she looked. Seeing her in jeans and an old red sweater, her hair long and full around a pink-cheeked face, it was all he could do to remain on his side of the table.

What man, he wondered, wouldn't leap at the prospect of having this kind of an opportunity dropped in his lap. A very honest, let's-be-friends-and-see-what-develops attitude in a woman was so rare. "If intimacy develops, fine," she had said. "If not, fine." He suppressed a smile as he considered his thoughts on that subject.

She tossed her hair back to look at him, and he studied her in turn. The only thing about all this that made him uncomfortable was a curious sense of foreboding that he felt every time he looked, really looked, into her eyes. Like now. Despite her lively wit and her occasional passionate turns of mood, she seemed to be a calm woman with her emotions on an even keel. But every once in a while he would glimpse something hot and hungry in her when she looked at him. And something in him would react to that and fill him with a need that hurt. That scared him. Real need had a tendency to make you forget your promises to yourself, to make you disregard the little obstacles as un-important—until you had to fit your life around them.

Noting his grave expression, Rachel asked quietly, "Bad idea?"

"No." He shook his head, looking into her eyes. "It's an excellent idea."

The longing in her eyes subsided and he smiled as the brightness and the humor returned. He glanced at his watch. "It's also noon."

"Noon!" She was out of her chair like a shot, hunting for her shoes.

"Under the table." He angled her doubled-over body in the right direction as he slipped past her to douse the fire in the stove. "Relax. We've got lots of time before Jessica is due."

She straightened up, a shoe in each hand, her cheeks flushed and her hair in wild disarray. He felt that picture of her commit itself to his memory.

"There was so much I was going to do this weekend." She was muttering to herself as she sat on the chair and pulled her shoes on over the stout socks. "I haven't ac-complished a thing." She looked up to see him turn away from the sink. He was smiling and she smiled back. "But I had a wonderful time. I'd like to come back and see the ducks again. And build a checkpoint at the entrance to the river from the slough and not let anybody through with a gun."

He laughed and tossed her a dish towel. "Get over here and earn your keep."

On the drive back to Cannon Beach, Rachel sat beside him in the middle of the truck's bench seat. The feel of his tough body right beside hers, even through their winter clothes, elicited a sigh from deep inside her.

"Tired?" Brian asked as they pulled up at a red light.

She shook her head and leaned it against his shoulder. "Safe."

"Safe." He repeated the word with a small laugh, trying to interpret what she meant.

"I feel safe," she said. "For the first time in years..." Then her head came up as she realized how long it had been since she'd felt this way. "For the first time since I left Kansas, I feel safe." She looked into his eyes, unaware of the desire that was there. "You make me feel safe."

Brian felt that answering need in him push at his heart, trying to get to her. It made him feel more threatened than safe. Still, he put his arm around her and held her close as the light turned green and he drove on.

When he pulled up in front of her duplex, Rachel drew away from him with reluctance. The last thing she wanted to do at this moment was leave him, but she remembered what he'd said about Priscilla. "She has a tendency to whine and cling, and I have a tendency to hate that."

"I had a wonderful morning," she said, trying hard to sound bright and casual, but her voice had a husky, wistful quality instead.

"I'll call you tomorrow," he promised. "Do you want to plan on lunch?"

She smiled and his heart shot up like a mallard sensing danger. "Yes."

Brian caught Rachel's face between his hands and held her still while his mouth traced a kiss over her lips. He kissed her long and thoroughly, and with a possessiveness he recognized and could find no reason to dispute. He felt the need he had seen in her eyes rise up and fill her as she touched him, a hand to the side of his face. Her fingers were gentle, but trembling.

He pulled her closer, tracing kisses from her mouth to her ear. "You are safe," he said, holding her against him, needing to reassure her. "I'll keep you safe."

It never occurred to him that he was the one in danger.

Chapter Five

Jessica arrived home with two days' worth of news to report and a million questions about her mother's dinner with "that hunk in the storeroom."

"Hunk?" Rachel looked up from stuffing Jessica's clothes in the washer and frowned. "Where did you get such a word? How would you like it if some man called you cutie?"

Jessica thought about that. "I think I would."

"It shows no respect," Rachel pointed out. "And respect is very important between people, particularly men and women. Brian Tate is a very nice man who happens to be good-looking, not a hunk."

Handing Rachel the box of soap, Jessica asked with interest, "Did he think you were a cutie?" At her mother's censorious look she amended quickly, "A very nice woman who happens to be good-looking?"

Rachel poured soap and said casually, "He's going to call me tomorrow."

"Aw-right!" Jessica leaped up in the air, clapping her hands. Rachel caught the box of soap just in time to divert disaster. "We could be just like everybody else."

Sensing the path Jessica's thoughts were taking, Rachel warned gently, "Now, wait a minute, Jess..."

"You could have a husband and I could have a dad like most of the other kids." Jessica was off on her flight of fancy, and Rachel acknowledged with a wry smile that there would be no stopping her daughter until she had spun out the dream. "We could all sit around the table having dinner, only you'd have to cook fattening stuff 'cause men don't eat salads and stuff like we do. Then we could all sit on the living room floor and eat popcorn and watch *Who's the Boss* and *Kate and Allie*. Then you guys could tuck me in and go to bed together."

At Rachel's arched eyebrow Jessica said knowledgeably, "I know all about that stuff." Then her expression turned to one of anticipation. "And then you'll have babies. Lots of them."

"Jess!" Rachel said firmly, dropping the lid on the washer with a bang. Jessica came to in wide-eyed surprise.

"Yeah?"

"We've agreed to just be friends."

Her beautiful future shot down, Jessica's thin shoulders sagged. "Mom," she said plaintively, "you're throwing away the chance of a lifetime. And you probably won't have that many more."

Rachel rolled her eyes, put an arm around Jessica and led her through the kitchen and into the living room. "As old as I am, sweetie, I'll have to risk it." Swearing that she could feel joints creak that hadn't hurt a moment ago, Rachel changed the subject.

"A young boy about your age lives right next door to Mr. Tate. We all had chili together Saturday afternoon."

"Oh, yeah? What's his name?" They walked up the narrow staircase to the bedrooms.

"Davey Callahan," Rachel replied, leaning against the doorway to Jessica's room as the child dropped her overnight bag on the bed, then fell beside it onto the mattress, an expression of disdain on her face.

"Oh, him."

"You know him?"

"He's in my class. He's kind of a jerk." Jessica opened her bag and pulled out the tapes and games she had taken to Leslie's.

Rachel took a few steps into the room.

"Why do you say that?"

"Well, he's late a lot. He forgets his permission slips all the time and he usually looks pretty messy."

Rachel sat on the edge of Jessica's bed, her heart going out to Davey. "I hope you're not mean to him because of those things. He lives with a grandmother, who isn't very well. He has to fend for himself a lot."

"I'm not mean to him," Jessica denied. "But some of the other kids are. And sometimes he asks for it. The other day he put frogs in the girls' john."

"Rest room," Rachel corrected.

"Rest room." Jessica giggled. "I thought it was pretty funny, but Mrs. Leahy, you know, she's in charge of the library?" Suppressing a smile, Rachel nodded, and Jessica went on. "She had to spend an hour in the teachers' lounge. I guess one landed right in her lap." Jessica put both hands over her mouth, laughing uproariously, and it was all Rachel could do not to join her.

"Jokes at other people's expense are never funny," she said in her best mother tone. "Maybe if other kids were friendlier to him, he wouldn't act up so much."

Jessica shrugged. "Actually, he's been a little better lately. I mean, he still does stuff like the rest room stunt but he looks a little better and he's on time sometimes. I think a relative moved in with him, or something."

Helping her daughter get ready for bed, Rachel wondered if the small change was the result of a caring neighbor's interest. The neighbor who liked other people's children because he was so sure he would never have any of his own.

"DID JESSICA HAVE a good time?" It was a simple question, but at 10:15 on a busy Monday morning, Brian's deep voice brought back to Rachel the long, relaxing hour in the duck shack with her feet stretched out to the fire in the wood stove. She saw his face in her mind's eye, the sexily tousled hair, the teal-blue eyes, the neat mustache over a ready smile.

The breath left her in a rush as she replied, "Yes. Everything she brought with her was filthy. That's a good indication."

He laughed softly. "Interesting theory. Can I pick you up at noon?"

"Noon is fine."

"Good. See you then."

As Rachel hung up the phone and turned away, Penny advanced on her, a pink balloon bouquet dancing at the end of the silver ribbons she held in her hand.

"The hunk got to you, didn't he?" she asked.

Rachel frowned. "So that's where Jessica gets her questionable vocabulary. And just what do you mean by got to me?"

"Nothing unsavory," Penny denied quickly, her expression still perplexed. "But he must have rattled your cage. This order for the new mother at Cannon Beach Memorial..."

Rachel looked up at the pink balloons. "What about it?"

"She had a boy."

Rachel sighed and snatched the cluster of balloons from Penny. "Well, with the names they give them today, it's hard to tell."

"Jonathan?" Penny asked. "Who ever heard of a girl named Jonathan?"

Rachel sighed again, a smile escaping despite her irritation at herself. "Give me a break, Pen," she said, disappearing into the storeroom. "And pray," she shouted, out of sight, "that another baby is born today and that it's a girl with a relative who sends balloons!"

Filling a dozen blue balloons with helium, Rachel wondered if she had imagined her magic weekend. Had it really been that special, or had she just been too long without a man in her life? Then she remembered the ride back to Cannon Beach, her body comfortably close to Brian's, her head on his shoulder. She put a hand to her lips, remembering, too, the kiss they'd shared before she got out of the truck.

But even if it had been that special to her, could it have meant as much to him? Or had it just seemed that way because she had been cozy and warm and flattered by a man's attentions?

"We'll need an hour and a half for lunch, Penny," Brian said when he picked Rachel up.

Penny snickered. "She can have the afternoon off; she's doing more harm than good around here today, anyway."

"Oh?"

Disregarding Rachel's warning frown, Penny went on, dusting a shelf of small gift items. "Got her mind on other things, I think."

"I'll be back at 1:30," Rachel said firmly.

"Fine." Penny didn't turn around. "I'll try to have all your mistakes corrected by then."

"Having a bad morning?" Brian wanted to know as he helped Rachel into the car. He was wearing a short, black down-filled jacket and black jeans. His gray-blue eyes seemed full of life against the somber color.

She explained about the mistake over the balloons for the new mother. She tried to dismiss it as just a typical Monday. But Brian got in behind the wheel and turned to her in the confines of the front seat. That close, his eyes seemed suddenly electric as they went over her face.

"Must be contagious. I haven't written a word this morning, and it's not that I haven't tried." He smiled, the sweetness of the gesture carrying all the reassurance Rachel needed that she had imagined nothing about the weekend. She had made friends with a very special man. "I keep thinking of you in my duck shack."

"In gray woolen socks with red toes." She laughed. "I cut such a romantic figure."

"It's all in what you're looking for," he said. "You're calm and quiet, yet full of hell." He studied her eyes and laughed softly. "Sort of an angelic little devil."

Rachel considered that analysis of herself as he pulled out into the traffic. "I'm not sure I like that."

"Doesn't matter. I do."

After lunch Brian stopped Rachel in the restaurant's small vestibule, holding her coat out. She slipped into it, feeling that prickling sensation along her spine as he pulled her long hair out of her collar.

"I need your help with something," he said.

"What?"

"The wish balloon." Out of his pocket he pulled a small business-card-sized piece of yellow paper on which Rachel had carefully typed the tag that was fastened to a clear latex wish balloon that accompanied every bouquet. He read the verse. " 'I'm your fondest wish balloon; let me float up to the sky. Make a wish for love on me; I'll take it with me as I fly.' We'll go up to Ecola Park and let it go."

"Are you serious?" she asked as he pushed her gently out into the brisk January afternoon.

"Of course."

"Where's the balloon?"

"In the trunk of the car." Brian closed the car door on her mild protest and got in behind the wheel. "Think of it as servicing your product. You brought me the balloons, it's your responsibility to see that my balloon flies and delivers my wish."

Deep evergreen forests bordered both sides of the narrow, winding road that lead to Ecola Park. Cliff sides had eroded, and gnarled roots and the undersides of a thick ground cover hung as though suspended from nothing. Large ferns swung gracefully, and Rachel thought it looked like some fantasy world that should be populated with gremlins or leprechauns.

The road continued for several miles, finally depositing them in a large open parking area. Beyond the cars, a plush green lawn spread out before them then sloped steeply toward the sea. The water reflected the bright blue winter sky and stretched like glass to the horizon. Off to the right, on Tillamook Rock, a decommissioned lighthouse stood like a fortress, surf crashing around its base.

Brian parked and came around to help Rachel out of the car. He turned to close her door, then paused, a hand going around her shoulder as he leaned against the car and stared down to their left.

"No matter how often I come up here," he said, his voice reflecting wonder, "I never get used to that view of Indian Beach." He pointed to where the coast unfolded in a crescent shape, spilling toward the horizon in purple folds. Fog nestled in wisps like twisted gauze. The back of Haystack Rock was visible to them and many other rocks stood in the shallows, tossed there during some prehistoric shower of lava. It looked like something that might have existed in Jules Verne's imagination.

"Spectacular, isn't it?" Rachel stepped away from the door so that he could close it. "Jessica loves to picnic there in the summer."

"Then we'll have to do that," he said, unlocking the trunk. The clear balloon drifted up and he caught the gold foil ribbon attached to it and handed it to Rachel while he slammed the trunk closed.

"We'll have to do that." As though he knew they would still be keeping company in the summer. Keeping company, she thought. What a quaint phrase. What a quaint relationship. How many couples went duck watching on a date and agreed to embark on an association with the understanding that it could or could not become intimate, depending on how it developed? Somehow, the lack of confinement was the very thing that made her feel just a little uneasy.

Taking note of her confused expression as he turned around, Brian took her elbow and began to pull her toward the grassy edge of the cliff. "What?" he asked.

"I was just thinking how different you are," she admitted candidly.

"Different." He repeated the word thoughtfully. "Should I be flattered or upset?"

A gust of wind attacked them from behind and Rachel reached up to prevent her hair blowing across her face. "Oh, flattered. Definitely." Wanting to divert him from asking any more questions about her strange thoughts, she said with a teasing brusqueness, "There are no guarantees on wishes, you know. You just bare your heart and take a chance.''

''Bare your heart, huh?'' They had reached the edge of the cliff, and the earth fell away to the roar of the ocean many feet below them. Brian looked up to the blue sky, a few puffy clouds arranged in aesthetic perfection overhead. He looked down at Rachel, his eyes full of sunlight. ''I guess I can do that.''

She lifted a shoulder, her eyes ensnared by his. ''As long as you understand the risks.''

''One should acknowledge risks, but not be intimidated by them.''

Brian pulled Rachel in front of him, facing the drop-off to the ocean, and reached around her for the string of the balloon. Her lungs seemed to collapse, expelling air in a loud rush. She could feel the faint roughness of his chin against the corner of her eye and the delicious crush of his upper arms around her shoulders. His hands, cold and strong, closed around her own.

''It's *your* wish,'' she protested, trying to wriggle out of his arms.

''No, we're going to do this together,'' he insisted, holding her firmly in place. ''Have you got hold of the string?''

''Yes, but it won't work. It's supposed to be *your* wish.''

''I'll let you attach a rider,'' he said, one arm holding her fast against his chest. ''Congress does it with bills all the time.'' He paused to ask quietly, ''Unless you're afraid of the risk.''

She *was* suddenly afraid—why? Of what? But admitting her fear and letting it stop her were two different things entirely.

"One should acknowledge risks," she said dryly, "but not be intimidated by them."

"Very profound. Now." Brian held her closer still. "Think, Rachel. Put together the wish of a lifetime."

Contrary to her saner instincts, Rachel closed her eyes and began to build a wish. She heard the surf, felt the cold January afternoon against her face and smelled its perfume. The steady, enveloping warmth of Brian Tate's body pervaded her senses, and suddenly all the dreams and desires she had wearily put aside all those years ago rose up inside her like a spring. Powerless to push them aside, she went completely still, concentrating.

Brian stood as quietly as she, and Rachel could feel his churning energy waiting to be released with the wish and the balloon.

"Ready?" he whispered, his breath ruffling the curls at her forehead.

"Ready."

"Okay. Three, two...one." Simultaneously their hands opened to release the tugging balloon, the back of her hand against the now warm palm of his. Then he wrapped his arms around her as they stood in silence to watch the clear bubble dance away from them, catching the sparkle of the sun. At first it appeared to fall, then bobbed up and up until they had to lean back to watch it. The balloon's luster made it invisible when it floated in the path of the sun, but they watched until it danced aside and seemed to stand still for a moment, a brilliant ball of fire. Then with one last, graceful pirouette, the balloon floated away on its mission of chance.

Rachel stared at the balloon, a mere speck on the horizon, and wondered if Brian had experienced the same sensation that she had.

Brian stared at the sky as a shiver went through his body. Bringing Rachel here had been a whimsical, romantic notion—a desire to provide for her one of those "tender little things" that made a woman feel like a woman. He hadn't been prepared for the experience to make him feel quite so much like a man.

Her wish had involved him; he'd felt it. And his wish had escaped from him almost before he'd formed it, as though having a life of its own. And it had involved her.

What had begun as a lark had caught a current of air and flown beyond his control.

Brian held her one last moment then drew a thick sigh. "Well, I suppose you have to get back to the shop and I should try to get something written today."

"Yes," she agreed absently. "I suppose."

Rachel turned in his arms to look up at him, her dark eyes as startled as he felt. Then, as though she suddenly understood something that escaped him, she smiled and reached up to pull his face down. She kissed him with a tenderness that touched the vulnerable core of him no one else had ever reached.

He responded as gently, reverently, because passion had nothing to do with what they communicated. Wordlessly they spoke of generosity and understanding and the precious acceptance of a beautiful moment.

Brian led Rachel back to the car, each taking one last dubious look at the sky.

SEEKING EACH OTHER OUT in their free time became a habit for Brian and Rachel; trying to make that time together difficult for them became a habit of Davey's. Jessica already considered Brian a friend, but Davey had a less favorable opinion of the two female intruders in his life—they were in the way, and he was jealous of them.

"Monopoly's boring," he declared firmly on one such occasion. "And Scrabble is too much like school."

The four had just cleared away the dessert dishes. A large bowl of fresh popcorn stood in the middle of the table and Rachel pushed it toward Davey.

"No, thank you." He pushed it back.

Jessica glared across the table at him. "Then what do you want to do? Throw frogs in the bathroom?"

Davey looked at Brian as though the man had betrayed him. "Can't we watch the Trailblazers-Lakers game?"

"No," Brian replied for the third time, pulling the bowl toward himself. "We have guests who aren't interested in the Trailblazers and the Lakers. What about Clue?"

"No!" For the first time that evening, Jessica and Davey agreed.

"Hangman?" Brian suggested.

Davey looked disgusted. "If our guests aren't interested in the Blazers and the Lakers, they won't know the names of the team members we always use."

"Chinese checkers?" Rachel looked around the table. Davey rolled his eyes and Jessica began to object but was quelled with a look. Having been sniped at all evening by Davey, Jessica subsided in a pout.

"That's a dumb game," Davey said as Brian retrieved the game from the hall closet and opened it on the table. Ignoring the boy, Rachel reached into the box to sort the colored marbles and encouraged Jessica to help her.

"I want to watch the Blazers," Davey insisted once more.

Finally at the end of his patience, Brian put the empty box aside and turned to Davey, his expression firm. "I'm not going to turn the television on. If you want to watch the game, you'll have to go home to do it."

Davey's dark eyes reflected pain and then anger. Pulling himself together with an almost pitiful dignity, Davey took his jacket off the back of his chair.

"Thank you for dinner," he said to Brian.

Brian nodded. "You're welcome."

"See you later," Davey said glumly.

He left quietly by the sliding-glass doors.

"I'll be right back. I want the blue." Jessica skipped off in the direction of the bathroom, and Rachel and Brian turned to face each other in the evening's first peaceful moment.

"I'm sorry," Rachel said.

Brian shook his head. "You didn't do anything."

"Well. Jess wasn't being a model of nobility."

"The way Davey kept picking on her, I don't blame her."

Rachel sighed. "He's jealous of us."

"I know. I can even understand it. But I won't do him any favors by letting him be selfish and rude."

"But you're all he has."

"I know," he said again. "And that's all the more reason. You ready, Jess?" He smiled at the child as she took her place across from him.

"I'm ready," she said, kneeling on her chair to see better. Then she added with an impish grin, "I should warn you that I'm good at this."

Brian leaned toward Jessica and said seriously, "And I should warn you that if I lose, there are no seconds on dessert after the game."

Just as seriously, Jessica replied, "Mom brought the dessert."

Rachel laughed and Brian turned to her with a look of pained forbearance. "You had to have a kid that's smarter than me. Could we get started?"

BRIAN LET HIMSELF into Davey's house with Mrs. Callahan's small requirement of groceries. He had thrown in a box of Davey's favorite cookies and a jar of the strawberry jam the boy used by the tablespoonful when visiting him. He put the groceries away, then found the old woman dozing on the living-room sofa. She was small and frail and hardly formed a shape under the old quilt that covered her.

Brian touched her arm. "How are you today, Mrs. Callahan?"

The old woman awoke and smiled, patting his hand. "Just fine, Brian. How's the book coming?"

Brian sat on the edge of the coffee table. "I've had a few distractions lately," he admitted. The woman was sharp, despite her age, and he found her fun to talk to.

She nodded knowingly. "The pretty but pesty balloon lady and the dorky girl."

Brian laughed at the description that must have come from Davey. "The lady is pretty and not at all pesty," he corrected. "And the girl is really a sweetheart."

Mrs. Callahan laughed, the sound surprisingly young. "Davey thinks no one is good enough to keep company with you—except him, of course." She folded small, bony hands at her waist and said, as though the thought had just struck her, "You know, Davey has an uncle somewhere from his mother's side of the family. In the East, I think. My daughter-in-law's older brother. I've been thinking about seeing if I can find him."

Brian studied her closely, mistrusting her casual tone. In the two years they'd been neighbors, Mrs. Callahan had always looked as though a strong breeze could blow her over. But he thought he'd seen a change in the last few weeks, a real frailty about her that hadn't been there before.

"Are you sure you feel all right?" he asked.

She sent him a bright, toothless smile. "Well, I've had to quit my aerobics class and I'm thinking of selling my Nautilus..."

"Will you behave yourself," Brian scolded, laughing. "Has the county nurse been to see you this week?"

"Twice. I like her."

"What does she say about your health?"

Mrs. Callahan shrugged philosophically. "What we all know; that I'm old. I don't think I'm in any immediate danger, but I have to think about Davey's future," she said, sobering. "I want Davey to be with someone who'll care. He's a special boy, but not very easy to understand."

She smiled again, reaching out to rest her hand on Brian's knee. "You're so good to him, but he can't pester you forever. I'm going to ask my attorney about trying to find Davey's uncle." She sighed wearily, as though the conversation was suddenly becoming a strain. She pointed to an upright piano that stood in the corner of the room. "I left the grocery money there for you. I'd appreciate it if you'd take it this time."

Brian got to his feet. "Can I get you anything before I leave?"

Mrs. Callahan gave one slow shake of her head, already dozing off again.

Brian left the money and passed through the kitchen on his way out, encountering Davey, who was just coming home from school. The boy gave him a spontaneous smile. "Hi!"

"Hi!" Brian replied. "Have a good day?"

Davey shrugged, then apparently remembering the previous evening, he frowned. "I'm sorry about last night."

"They're my friends," Brian said.

Davey nodded. "I know. It's just that . . . they're there all the time."

"So are you." Brian smiled to soften the gentle criticism. "But they don't mind. Unless you act like you did last night."

The boy turned away from him and dropped two school books on the counter. "I never get to talk to you anymore."

Brian studied Davey's thin but well-formed back and noted the slump in the shoulder that meant genuine distress. Since he'd met Rachel, he and Davey had lost those man-to-man times he had vowed he'd make time for when he first discovered how lonely the boy was. It was a commitment he couldn't shirk simply because he was on a deadline and there were other demands on his time.

He went to lean against the counter and face Davey. "Have you got something you need to talk about?"

Davey looked up at him, his dark eyes vulnerable. "Lots of things," he admitted. "But nothing special, I guess. But I miss watching the games with you and yelling at the referees and eating popcorn with butter on it." Davey frowned and gave Brian a look of very masculine frustration. "How come Rachel never butters the popcorn?"

Brian laughed and pulled the boy to him, giving him a quick, strong hug. "Because women are always watching their weight and butter has a lot of calories. Look..." He held the boy at arm's length with a hand on each shoulder. "Rachel and Jess are going to a baby shower or something tonight. Want to come to Seaside with me? There's a wrestling match at the convention center."

Davey brightened perceptibly. "Yeah!"

"All right. Let's ask your grandmother."

RACHEL AND BRIAN WALKED hand in hand on the trail that circled Cullaby Lake. It was a sunny Sunday and after days of rain and being cooped up inside, Jessica and Davey were racing along ahead, their voices loud, their spirits high. Since his conversation with Brian, Davey tried to be more cooperative, and Jessica responded by offering a fragile friendship.

As youthful laughter carried back to them on a pine-scented wind, Brian shook his head in surprise. "I thought this afternoon was going to be an ordeal but the kids have been pretty good." He stepped ahead of Rachel to leap over a hole in the path then reached back for her hands. "They seem almost to like each other today."

Safely across the hole, Rachel settled back into step beside him. "They do like each other," she said. When he angled her a skeptical look she laughed. "They get along as well as siblings would, and they spend almost as much time together. Kids'll fight. That's one of life's primary rules."

"They can sure cramp a relationship." Brian's grumble was intended as good-natured teasing and that was the way Rachel took it. He meant no criticism of his young neighbor and no complaint against Jessica. It was simply that conducting a romance—or a friendship—with children constantly in attendance was challenging. Although Rachel wasn't entirely convinced that he wanted their relationship to develop beyond where it stood, anyway. Of course, she wasn't sure what she wanted, either.

"So, how's the book coming?" she asked, deliberately turning her thoughts in another direction. "Did you get a lot done this week?"

Brian pulled Rachel into his shoulder, putting a hand out in front of her face as they passed a gnarled and thorny bush. "Some. I'm not quite on schedule, but I'm catching up."

"Are we responsible for your slackened pace?" Rachel asked. She indicated herself and the children running back toward them.

He gave her shoulders a squeeze as though to absolve her of responsibility. "You just don't work as hard or as single-mindedly when there are other people in your life. It's one of the facts. Like kids fighting. That's probably why a lot of writers are divorced or never marry, or write in seclusion and spend only part of their time with family and friends."

"Fortunately, you prefer a solitary life-style," she said, trying to sound casual, nonjudgmental.

He was silent a moment as the kids came screeching to a halt in their path. "Hm," he said, a touch of irony in his voice. "Fortunately."

"Oh, Davey!" Rachel exclaimed in distress as the boy pulled a pitiful wet bundle of black-and-white fur from inside his coat. "What happened?"

Instinctively, Rachel reached for the animal, having to hold it closely to see that the skinny, soaked creature was a cat. It lay still in her arms, except for a shiver, and its meow was almost inaudible.

"Can we take it home, Mom?" Jessica demanded, coming to stand beside her mother and lean over the cat. "Mom, can we? We can't just leave it here. Can we?"

"It's mine!" Davey said angrily. "I found it!"

"But your grandmother won't let you have it," Jessica shouted back. "You just said so."

"It's mine." Davey took the animal gently from Rachel and held it against his chest, draping his jacket front over it. Jessica followed the cat, standing in front of Davey and reaching a hand in his coat to pet it. The boy allowed that, as long as she didn't try to take it from him.

"Mom?" Jessica looked at Rachel again, demanding an answer. Her eyes were wide and distressed.

"Honey..." Rachel cast a guilty look at Brian. "Our lease says we can't have pets. I'm sorry."

"Well, we can't leave it here," Jessica said, on the brink of tears. She sat on a stump and folded her arms stubbornly. "I *won't* leave it here."

"Davey, will you let me see it?" Brian reached two large hands out, and the boy placed the cat in them without hesitation. Brian drew it close to his wool jacket and stroked the wet coat carefully. Rachel saw his long fingers massage gently just before the hind legs.

"Is he gonna die?" Davey asked in a hushed, horrified tone.

Brian shook his head. "I don't know, Davey. It's pretty scrawny. Somebody either lost or abandoned it out here. Might have been without food for quite a while."

Jessica stood to plaster herself to Brian's other side. "But it's talking."

As though on cue the cat meowed.

Brian looked down at Jessica and smiled softly, a smile that stalled Rachel's heart. "Yes, she's talking."

Jessica's eyes widened. "She?"

Davey looked down at the pitiful hunk of fur then up at his friend. "She?"

"It's a female," Brian said, his hand stroking gently down her back, pausing again in the same spot in front of her hind legs. He glanced at Rachel, his expression reluctant but defeated. "And she's pregnant."

Rachel saw the delight on the two young faces, followed instantly by despair. For the first time since Rachel and Brian had been seeing each other, Davey and Jessica shared a common thought.

Davey took the cat back from Brian and he and Jessica sat together on the stump Jessica had occupied earlier in protest. "I'm not leavin' her," Davey said firmly. He looked up at Brian, his dark eyes unafraid. "I'll stay with her and find her some food. Tell Grandma."

Jessica looked at her mother mutinously, prepared to endure the vigil with Davey.

Brian looked down at Rachel and she watched a score of emotions cross his teal-blue eyes—impatience, frustration and sympathy among them. Then humor seemed to settle there and he smiled down at the children. "Don't you think she'd be more comfortable in a box behind the stove at my house?"

Davey and Jessica stood simultaneously, Davey's coat still shielding the cat. The boy looked up at the man as though the resolution of the situation was still uncertain.

"You mean take her home? To your place?"

"Yeah."

Davey held the cat a little closer. "She's mine."

"I know."

"You'll let me keep her there?"

"Yeah."

"How long?"

Brian shifted his weight, his manner still patient. "Until the kittens come. Then we may have to make other arrangements."

Davey nodded soberly. His brown eyes filled and his bottom lip twitched dangerously but he bit down on it, angling his chin. It amazed and pained Rachel that a child could have such control.

"Thanks."

"Sure."

As Davey started down the trail and back to the car at a hurried pace, Jessica, never one to exercise control, leaped at Brian with a whoop of delight. He caught her as her legs wrapped around his waist and she planted a big, noisy kiss on his cheek.

"Thanks, Brian!" she squealed then wriggled to be set free, chasing down the trail after Davey.

Rachel and Brian stood in the middle of the overgrown trail, weak sunlight filtering through the damp growth, the sound of the children's footsteps receding. Brian closed his eyes and shook his head. "What have I done? A pregnant cat! Kittens! Davey will be over all day—every day!"

Rachel reached up to pull his head down and kiss him. Her heart was filled with affection for him. She cleared her throat and laughed softly.

"I hate to tell you, fella, but you just did a very selfless, very... parental thing."

He groaned. "Oh, God. Why didn't you stop me?"

"Because you were so glorious." She tucked her arm in his and began to lead him down the trail. "Do you know how few fathers would have done such a sweet thing?"

"I'm not a father, Rache, I'm just a neighbor. Oh, God. Kittens. Why did you let me do it?"

Rachel laughed with him as they walked back to the car.

As Brian rooted through the trunk for something with which to dry the cat, Rachel remained standing outside the car, looking in at Jessica and Davey huddled over their shivering charge. And suddenly the warmth and the humor in the situation left her and she saw only the sadness.

Poor abandoned cat, she thought, probably discarded because kittens would make demands on its owner and pets were supposed to be fun and not trouble.

Demands were beginning to surface in this relationship she shared with Brian and they in turn shared with the children. Because of all the time they spent together, they were beginning to behave more like a family than friends; and because of the agreement made in the duck shack, that very closeness would prevent them ever knowing what it would be like to become lovers. Their relationship would have to stop before each became bound beyond what had been agreed.

Still smiling from the lighthearted walk back to the car, Brian handed a scrap of towel into the back seat then turned to pull Rachel into his playful embrace. But she went stiff in his arms, flattening her palms against his chest.

He looked down into her grim brown eyes and frowned. He put a hand to her face and she turned away.

"What's the matter?" he asked.

Rachel searched his gaze for a moment, wondering if she could explain. But there was already confusion in Brian's eyes, and that seemed like a poor platform from which to launch a discussion on the complexities of a modern relationship. She simply shook her head and pulled out of his arms. "We'd better get the cat home."

PENNY ARRIVED AT WORK one morning with a distinctly green complexion. It was the week before Valentine Day, and Rachel had enough orders to keep a staff of four working full time.

"What's the matter?" Rachel asked in concern while filling a giant heart-shaped mylar balloon with helium. The words "I Love You" in white script grew out of the inflated balloon.

"Nothing," Penny insisted. "I'll be fine."

"You're green."

"I'll be fine as soon as I've had my coffee."

But the coffee and the clerk did not remain together long enough. Rachel patted Penny's now paper-white face with a cold washcloth. "I'm calling your sister, Carole," she said. "You're going home."

When Brian called at noon to invite Rachel to lunch, she explained her predicament. "I won't have time to eat it, much less go out for it." The phone cradled on her shoulder, she was cutting lengths of ribbon. "This is one of the busiest weeks of the year and I just sent Penny home sick."

"How are you going to handle things alone?" Brian asked.

"I'll think of something, but I probably won't see you until it's over." The bells over the front door jingled merrily. "Here's a customer. Got to go. Thanks for the lunch invitation, Brian."

A half hour later Rachel hurried into the front of the shop as the bells announced another customer. Alicia Tate walked in, pulling her cloak off as she strode behind the counter. She handed Rachel a small paper sack that smelled of something delicious.

"I understand you need an extra pair of hands for a few days," she said, finding an empty cubbyhole and stuffing her cloak and purse into it. She straightened, wearing an emerald knit sweater and slacks. "I don't know a thing about balloons, but I did clerk in a department store before I met Brian's father. That's a burger and a Coke, by the way. Eat while you have the chance."

"Oh, Mrs. Tate—" Rachel began to protest.

"Alicia."

"Alicia. I couldn't ask you—"

"You didn't. Brian did. And the dear likes to have what he asks for. He called me right after he talked to you. He's waiting for a phone call from his editor then he'll be down to make deliveries for you.''

"Oh, but—'' Rachel began to protest again, but the telephone rang and Alicia went to answer it.

"Ballooney-Tunes,'' she said in a lyrical voice. "Blowing things up is our business.''

"*Inflation* is our business!'' Rachel whispered.

Listening to the caller, Alicia indicated with a nod that she'd get it right next time.

By closing time Rachel felt as though she'd either lost control of the situation, or things were going so smoothly that the crisis she had anticipated had failed to materialize. When Brian came in from his last delivery, Rachel locked the door after him and turned the sign from Open to Closed.

He looked around at the empty shop. "Where are Jess and my mother?''

"Picking up pizza.''

"Everything done?'' he asked.

She checked the day's order sheet. "Everything. How'd you do with that last delivery at the bank?''

He rubbed the knuckles of one hand on his chest, then studied his fingernails. "Our subject was in the employee's lounge on a break when I arrived. There was a room full of ladies and I was pretty wonderful. When I was finished she hugged me.''

Rachel leaned against the counter and narrowed her eyes at him. "I'm sure you did nothing to encourage her.''

He shook his head. "Didn't have to. She didn't seem able to help herself.'' Looking painfully modest he added, "I think it was bigger than both of us.''

Sighing, Rachel shook her head. "I could almost believe that if I hadn't taken the order. It was from her husband, who adores her. And whom she adores. I served on a PTA committee with both of them.''

Undaunted by having his story questioned, Brian asked sincerely, ''Then why did she want to know what I was doing tonight?''

''You're having pizza with your mother, Jessica and me tonight.''

He was silent for only an instant. ''Fortunately that's what I told her.''

Rachel straightened and started to walk away. ''Good thing.''

''Broke her heart,'' Brian murmured.

Laughing, Rachel spun around, aiming both fists at his chest. ''You crazy—'' He caught her wrists and led them around his waist, enclosing her in his embrace as he laughed with her.

He held her close, his mood altering subtly from laughter to something more serious. Rachel leaned back in his arms to look up at him and found mystery in his eyes.

''What is it?'' she asked.

He shook his head, smiling. ''I'm not sure. It feels a little like a cardiac arrest, but I think it's just a Rachel attack.''

She tried to look affronted. ''I'm making you ill?''

''Sort of.'' He sighed and ran a hand idly over her hair. ''Every time I have you in my arms I suffer palpitations, shortness of breath and a sort of pain . . .'' He touched a finger to the middle of his chest. ''Right here.''

Delighted by his admission but a little afraid of it, Rachel suggested softly, ''Maybe you need a doctor.''

He shook his head in denial. ''I think what I need is you.''

Though Rachel didn't move, Brian sensed her withdrawal and knew she wasn't ready to hear that he needed her. She was ready to be his friend, to be his companion in the day-to-day things for which each of them had admitted needing a partner of the opposite sex. But she wasn't ready to be his lover, and that was why he needed her.

He needed her as a lover not because it was all he wanted from her, but because it was the one part of her he didn't have and something possessive inside him, something he had never suspected was there, wanted to know her completely. She was becoming daily sustenance to him and he felt himself growing hungrier every day.

But during the past few weeks he had come to the conclusion that either she didn't need him in the same way, or she refused to acknowledge that need. Then he would remember that desire he would see in her eyes and could not convince himself that the need wasn't there. So she had chosen to ignore it. But why? She seemed to have come to terms with her first marriage and adjusted to widowhood. She had seemed open-minded about a relationship—a friendship—had suggested it herself. Why then the sudden withdrawal when they were at the point of turning a corner in their relationship? Apparently her suggestion that "it could be intimate, or not" had left an option open to her that he had ignored.

He borrowed a page from her book and decided to be candid. He folded his arms. "I'm not sure you're ready to hear this."

Unconsciously she squared her shoulders and folded her arms. "Just say it."

We look like two sumo wrestlers in the greeting ritual, he thought absently. She looked annoyed. She knew whatever he had to say would ruin the sweet complacency of the relationship they'd shared during the past month. But, hell, he was upset, too. Complacency wasn't what he was after.

"Okay." He paced across the floor as far as the storeroom door. Then he turned to face her. He dropped his arms and put his hands in his pockets. "Has it occurred to you that this relationship is going nowhere?"

For an instant her dark eyes registered surprise, then they sent him a knowing look. "You mean it's not going to bed."

"Cheap shot, Rachel," he replied with quiet frustration. "That isn't what I mean and it won't help the situation to pretend that it is."

She walked around the counter to sit on a corner of the small table where the telephone stood. It was strewn with curly lengths of ribbon, order sheets and cards. "Please explain what you do mean." Her voice was imperious.

"I mean that it's not developing," he said, finding a level tone of voice and determined to hold it. "We're not developing. We kiss and hold each other like a couple of kids necking, or we eat and work together like an old retired couple with nothing on their minds but companionship."

As he suspected, rather than choosing to deal with the complaint he expressed, she chose to take exception. She folded her arms again and swung a foot back and forth. "Great," she said, shooting him a dark look. "I remind you of a teenybopper and an old lady. You're such a flatterer, Tate."

"You're the one with a thing for honesty." He moved to the end of the counter closest to her and leaned an elbow against it. "Can you deny that it's true?"

"You agreed to be friends!" she said in an accusatory tone.

"I agreed to be friends and see what developed," he corrected.

She lowered her head and toyed with the pleat in her skirt. "Maybe there's just nothing to develop."

He straightened away from the counter in disgust. "Oh, Rachel!" In two strides he was at the table. Taking her hands in his, he pulled her to her feet. She looked at him with anger and mild alarm. He took her place on the corner of the table. "Kiss me," he said.

"What?" she demanded impatiently.

He took her arms and pulled her closer. Then he put his hands on his knees. "I won't even touch you. And I won't kiss you. You kiss me."

She sighed and folded her arms again, looking obstinate. "Why?"

"As a favor," he said evenly. "I've done a few for you today."

Rachel dropped her hands. "Generous of you to call it to my attention. But why would you want to be kissed by a teenybopper or an old lady?"

"Rachel Bennett," Brian grumbled, "you have more mouth than any three people I know."

With an arched eyebrow she put both hands on his shoulders. "I thought that was what was required here." And she lowered her mouth to his, intending to be chaste and quick. But the interesting texture of rough mustache and warm, pliant lips always intrigued her, and she found it impossible to simply pull away without exploring just a little. She rubbed her lips against his, felt them part slightly and expected him to take advantage. But he didn't. He remained passive and still.

Something in her responded to the challenge. Standing over him she had a slight height advantage and she used it, bringing her hands along his shoulders and up his warm, strong neck to his ears. She was aware of the wool of his sweater and the soft cotton of his shirt collar then the wiry texture of his hair. She leaned into his thigh and applied more pressure to his mouth. His lips parted farther and she sought his tongue, teasing it until it responded and their mouths and arms locked together. Feeling satisfied, she drew back. And it wasn't until she looked into his mischievous eyes that she realized she had proven his point and not her own.

She clasped her hands around his neck and sank onto his knee. "That was disgustingly easy for you," she said with ill grace.

He smiled, his arms going around her waist. "The truth can always be proven. Well, now I've made my point. What's yours?"

She was silent a moment. "I'm not sure you're ready to hear this."

"I'm braced."

"Okay." She drew a deep breath and said with a candor she was far from feeling in light of what she had just proven to him, "I'm not sure what to do about it, but I'm beginning to feel whiny and clingy."

"Whiny and clingy..." he repeated as though trying to interpret what she meant.

"Like Priscilla," she reminded him. "You have a tendency to hate that."

"Ah, yes." He nodded understanding.

"I was beginning to think maybe the thing to do was back off."

He tightened his hold on her, feeling more protective than frightened. "That would be cowardice."

"Maybe it would just be wise." Rachel sighed and leaned her forehead against his temple. "I don't want to hurt you and I don't want to hurt Jess. And I'm not too wild at the prospect of hurting myself."

Brian raised his head and looked into her eyes. "Are you afraid I'll be no better for you or to you than Jarrod was?"

She punched a fist lightly against his chin. "Just the opposite. I suspect how absolutely outstanding life with you could be. I just don't want to taste it and then..." Her eyes were filled with apology, but she made herself say it. "And then be denied it."

"Then aren't we fighting on the same side?" he asked gently.

She shook her head regretfully. "I don't think so. You want to round the corner and explore farther. So do I, but what if we find love there? Not a relationship or a friendship, but the real thing. What then?"

"Then we have a problem," he admitted. "But we don't have it yet."

Rachel sighed and got to her feet. "I have a child, Brian. I have to think ahead and avoid a problem if I can."

He looked up at her, his gaze steady and stubborn. "Backing off is not the answer."

"We agreed not to be a threat to each other, remember?"

"Seems to me," he pointed out quietly, "that you said, 'If intimacy develops—fine.'"

She nodded, her expression rueful. "But if I get clingy, that will threaten you. If you draw back, that will threaten me. It'd break the agreement."

"Okay." Brian got wearily to his feet, looking grim and unconvinced. "In deference to Jessica and the agreement we won't turn any corners—yet. But I don't think anybody ever got through life by standing still. I doubt it's even good for kids.''

Before Rachel could comment on that the telephone rang. It was Alicia. Rachel held the phone against her chest. ''Your mother wants to know where we are.''

''We're here.'' He joked, but with ill humor. ''She called us here, didn't she?''

''Brian says...''

''I heard him.'' Alicia forestalled Rachel's explanation. ''Smart aleck. Jessica and I have the pizza ready. What are you two doing?''

Brian, still near the phone, said airily, ''Tell her we're fighting about whether or not to go to bed.''

Glaring at him, Rachel put a swift hand over the mouthpiece then put the receiver to her ear. ''He said to tell you we'll be right there.''

Alicia laughed. ''That's not what I hea—''

''Five minutes,'' Rachel promised and hung up the phone. ''That was nice,'' Rachel scolded, reaching inside the storeroom door for her coat. ''Now your mother's going to think that I'm...that I'm...''

Brian helped her into her coat, pulled her hair out of the collar, then turned her to face him. His eyes were smiling and serious at the same time. ''What *are* you doing to me, Rachel?''

I'm trying to love you, she thought wearily, but you're not making it easy.

Rachel caught his coat sleeve and pulled him toward the door. ''I'm taking you to your mother's for pizza.''

''She never has any beer,'' he complained. ''What's pizza without beer?''

''You don't need beer.'' She pushed him out onto the sidewalk, closed the door and locked it. ''You have to be to work on time in the morning. Your first delivery is to the Cannon Beach Athletic Club.''

Brian groaned. The thought of himself, with a handful of heart-shaped balloons, walking into the club where all his friends worked out, did nothing to buoy his spirits.

Chapter Six

"Close your mouth, dear," Alicia recommended, polishing the glass top of the counter. "You look as though you've never received flowers before."

Rachel continued to stare at the dozen long-stemmed, bloodred roses in a tall crystal vase. She shook her head in wonder. "It's been a very rare treat. Particularly roses."

"I wonder who they're from," Alicia teased.

Rachel, reading the card that accompanied the bouquet, chuckled to herself, then read the message again. She looked up at Alicia and grinned. "Bad poetry. Does that give you a clue?"

Alicia rolled her eyes and spritzed a corner of the counter she had missed. "If Brian's adoring fans knew what really goes on in his mind . . ."

Rachel carefully picked up the vase. "I'm going to put these on my desk. Things get too frantic out here to risk leaving them."

As she disappeared into the back room with her fragrant burden, Alicia polished around the card Rachel had left on the counter and read out of the corner of her eyes: "Rachel, roses are fuchsia, violets are yellow, the world's in confusion, but I'm still your fellow."

Wincing, she muttered to herself, "Good grief. To think that I raised him."

When Brian returned from deliveries half an hour later, Rachel was standing at the helium tank filling a large silver heart-shaped balloon. She smiled at Brian over the burgeoning shape. "Violets are *not* yellow."

"I know." Brian acknowledged his distortion of the truth. Leaning across the counter, he watched her pull the balloon off the cylinder and heat-seal its stem. "But somehow, 'Roses are fuchsia, *bananas* are yellow,' just wasn't in keeping with the spirit of the message."

Rachel took a length of red ribbon and tied it onto the stem. "The world is in confusion?" She glanced at him, gently taunting. "Or our relationship is in confusion?"

Brian reached for a bell in the small box on the corner of the counter and handed it to her. "Not in confusion," he corrected. "Just not in conformity. I'm taking you to dinner and to the Coaster Theater tonight."

The bell attached to the bottom of the ribbon, Rachel let the balloon go. It bobbed beside her. "But Jessica..."

"Mom's going to watch her. It's the day before Valentine Day, and I think we should do something romantic. You'll probably be too tired to move tomorrow."

Pleased at the prospect of an evening alone in his company, even if they didn't know where their relationship was going, she leaned across the counter toward him. "What's on the bill?"

Their faces were inches apart and his eyes slowly roved her features. "An actor from Portland," he replied in a distracted tone, "is going to read Keats."

"Oh..." Rachel made a soft sound of approval. "I'd love that."

Brian pinched her chin then pulled her closer to kiss her. "I knew you would."

Rachel smiled and Brian felt his spine go soft. "That's almost thoughtful enough to absolve you of guilt for your terrible rhyme." She took hold of the heart balloon's ribbon and handed it to him, suppressing a longing for more of his gentle courting. "Meanwhile...here. And there are four more deliveries waiting for you in the back."

IT WAS COLD AND DARK. The crisp night sky shone with a frosty moon and a swath of stars stretching from one horizon to the next. Huddled together against the cold, Brian and Rachel walked home from the theater along the beach, arm in arm. The decision not to drive to the theater had been made as a concession to the romantic evening.

Brian tightened his grip on Rachel, who was unusually quiet. "Didn't you enjoy Keats?" he asked.

She sighed and leaned into him as the night wind swirled around them, smelling of salt and pine and the wonderful freshness of winter. "I loved it. He's always made me feel moody. He was such a tragic figure, dead at twenty-five of consumption and unrequited love. I guess the drama of all that appealed to me when I was in high school and..." She smiled up at Brian in the moonlit darkness. "I guess I never outgrew it. And he could be so funny. Do you remember the poem about the cat?"

"I do." Brian looked up at the moon, his eyes slitted against the cold wind. "But my favorite verse was the one about the maid."

"The Devon Maid."

"Right. Something about..." He stopped their slow progress on the sand and thought a moment. "Lying in the heather side by side."

Rachel nodded, picking up what she could recall of the quote. "'And we will sigh in the daisie's eye, and kiss on a grass green pillow.'" She paused, and the wind and the sound of the surf seemed to soften. "Isn't that beautiful?"

Silence fell as Brian's hands framed her face. "You are beautiful," he said. "In the spring we're going to look in that daisy's eye in that field in Jewell I was telling you about. But, right now..." His voice softened as his mouth lowered to hers. "I can't wait that long."

Rachel reached her arms around his neck, feeling his heartbeat, despite their winter clothing, as he pulled her into his embrace and kissed her. His mouth was cold from the night air but raised such a warmth in her that the stretch of star-bright, windy beach became the sunny setting of Keats's poem. Reality and all its attendant problems fled and they were alone on a grass-green pillow, two hearts in tune with spring and the moment.

Brian finally drew away and, tucking Rachel under his arm, started across the sand to the street that led to her duplex. In the darkness he frowned over the fact that his heart was beating fast and he found it difficult to draw an even breath.

WHEN RACHEL LOCKED THE DOORS the night of February fourteenth, she had filled one hundred orders more than the previous year—and she was the same shade of green Penny had been.

"You'd better get her home," Alicia told Brian, helping Rachel on with her coat. "Let Jessica spend the night with me so that you can rest completely. We'll come by in the morning to get her changed for school."

Rachel wanted to insist that she would be fine, but the words wouldn't come. The muscle pain had begun this afternoon and she now felt weak from it. That, coupled with a swiftly building nausea, had her longing for her bed. She put a hand to her head and frowned at Jessica.

"Honey..." she began, trying to call to mind the details she was sure she should be concerned about if Jessica was going to spend the night away from home.

"I'll be fine, Mom," Jessica assured her. "You look awful, though. I've got my key, don't worry."

Then they were all standing outside in the fresh air and Alicia and Jessica went off together and Brian bundled her into the Porsche.

Rachel was aware of the movement of the car, because it seemed to have a direct relationship to a disturbing movement in her stomach. She shifted fitfully in her seat, thinking longingly of her bed, of how good it would feel to slip in between the sheets and fall asleep. Her head hurt abominably and the simple act of sitting up seemed to become monumentally more difficult as the minutes passed. Her shoulders hurt, her knees hurt and everything in between was alarmingly uneasy.

The drive home seemed to take forever, but the car finally stopped and Rachel forced herself to lift her head from the headrest. "I do not have Penny's flu," she told herself emphatically as she mustered the energy to open the door and pull herself to her feet.

But when she finally managed to pull herself erect, she thought in confusion that perhaps she did have the flu after all. Or why would she be hallucinating that she was looking at Brian's home and not her own? She dipped her head to ask Brian, but he wasn't in the car.

Suddenly firm hands turned her around and lifted her. "Come on, Rache," a masculine voice said. "I think you're down for the count."

"Brian," she said groggily. "You were gonna take me home."

"I did." He strode up the porch steps, bracing her on his bent knee while he put his key in the lock.

"I don't live here," she felt obliged to point out as he kicked the door open and walked through.

"For the next few days you do," he said. He flipped a light on and she hid her face in his shoulder as her eyes ached in protest. "My house is closer. I don't think you'd have made it another five minutes to yours. And I think you're going to need looking after for a few days anyway."

They were climbing stairs, walking into a dark, cool room. "I think I'm...I'm sick," she agreed weakly as he sat her down on a soft bedspread. She began to slip backward and he held the front of her jacket, slipping his hand inside and around her back to hold her upright while he pulled the sleeves off. In a moment of surrealistic lucidity she smiled at him. "I want to undress you, too. But ... I don't think I can do it."

He laughed softly, tossing her jacket aside. He eased her back onto the spread and unzipped and unbuttoned her jeans. "Just hold the thought until you're feeling up to it. I'm going to put a pair of my pajamas on you. Lie still."

Brian pulled a pair of burgundy, ski-style pajama bottoms up her long, slim legs. He forced himself to operate with clinical detachment but he didn't find it easy. Sitting beside her, he lifted her up again to pull her sweater off and the soft pajama top over her head. Then he reached under it to unfasten and remove her bra. Amazed at his own strength of character, he tossed the flimsy thing in the pile with her other clothes, put her arms into the sleeves, and pulled her up to the pillow, bringing the blankets up to cover her.

Rachel turned into the pillow with a sigh. "Everything hurts," she complained woefully. Then she turned to look up at him in concern. "Brian!"

"What?"

Her eyes were dark and bright and brimming with confusion. "We're supposed to be backing off, not going to bed together."

"You're going to bed," he pointed out patiently. "I'm just sitting on it."

She frowned, trying to remember. "You took my clothes off."

He nodded. "Right. But I put pajamas on you."

Rachel held up a sleeve that had been cuffed back several times and plucked at the unfamiliar fabric. "It's a puky color."

Brian laughed in agreement. "They were a gift from my Aunt Maggie."

"Doesn't she like you?"

Shaking his head, Brian put Rachel's arm back under the covers and pulled the blankets up once more. "Go to sleep, Rachel. I'll be nearby. Call me if you need me."

She looked at him, her large eyes pleading, and reached out for his sleeve. "Can't you stay with me?"

Brian felt a silent groan rising in him. "I have to call the clinic and my mother." He disengaged her hand from the cuff of his jacket and put it back under the covers. "Stay under the blankets," he said firmly, "and lie still. I'll be back in a little while."

A brief conversation with a doctor on the clinic's night staff confirmed that Rachel had the flu. The mild delirium Brian described was probably a result of the bug hitting at a time when she was exhausted by long hours and hard work. Bed rest was the only known cure, along with warm 7-Up to help her nausea; otherwise the illness would have to run its course.

Alicia praised her son for taking Rachel home with him and promised to look in on them in the morning. She assured him that she and Jessica were having a wonderful time and that she would gladly look after the child until Rachel was feeling better.

Brian hung up the telephone, looked a little disconsolately at the black eye of his computer screen, which he hadn't even turned on in nearly a week, then hurried back down the hall to his bedroom in response to a groan from Rachel.

Rachel was up and down all night and most of the morning, the painful symptoms causing her to toss and turn. Finally worn out, she drifted off to sleep in the afternoon.

At that point, exhausted himself, Brian climbed in beside her, settled her comfortably in his arms and closed his eyes.

The sounds of wind and rain woke Rachel the following morning. Surfacing slowly from her deep sleep, she could hear a storm raging outside, driving splashes of rain against the window with the force of a hose. She rolled from her stomach onto her back, feeling mildly headachy and faintly uncomfortable.

She sat up gingerly, a hand to her head. The room was white with heavy oak furniture and completely unfamiliar. Where was she? She tried to think.

The movement of her arm as she pushed her hair aside caught her attention, and she studied the cuffed sleeve of the unfamiliar pajamas, thinking that someone had told her whose they were.

"Puky color," Brian said from the doorway. "I know. But it was the best I could do on such short notice. How are you this morning?'' He came into the room with a small tray and put it on the bedside table. Then he sat on the edge of the bed and looked into her face. Her eyes were still soupy, but her cheeks had the faintest tinge of color.

''Brian,'' she said in wonder. Then she had a vague memory of strong hands putting her to bed, helping her to the bathroom. She waited to feel embarrassed about that and was somewhat surprised to find that she wasn't.

But a score of other concerns crowded to the forefront of her mind. She threw the blankets aside and tried to swing her legs out of bed. But Brian's hand landed on her knee with firm but gentle pressure, aborting her escape.

''Jessica is at my mother's and Penny's well again and at the shop. There's nothing to be concerned about.''

Rachel frowned, having trouble assimilating what he'd told her. Her head still hurt and she rubbed it absently through the tumbled crown of her hair.

''Penny's at work on Sunday?''

He smiled. ''It's Monday. You slept through Sunday.''

He took advantage of her momentary silence by handing her a glass of amber liquid. She studied it suspiciously. It was either an awful lot of brandy or he made very weak tea.

''Apple juice.'' He pushed her hand gently toward her mouth. She drank it slowly and found it deliciously cool and refreshing as it went down. But the simple act exhausted her.

Brian put a hand behind her head and eased her back to the pillow. ''Good,'' he said softly. ''Go back to sleep and we'll try to get some food in you when you wake up again.''

''But—'' She wanted to protest but she wasn't sure what.

"Shh," he insisted.

It was so much easier to burrow into the pillow and comply.

When Rachel awoke again it was to the sound of Jessica's voice. "Mom?" And she opened her eyes to the warming sight of her daughter dressed in her Sunday best.

"Hi, Jess." Rachel smiled and laboriously pushed herself up to a sitting position. "You look beautiful. Where are you going?"

"Brian's taking me to school for the Winter Review."

"Oh, God!" The Winter Review! How could she have forgotten? Jessica had been rehearsing the songs for weeks. Rachel swung her legs out of bed. "Jess, I forgot..." she began to apologize, groping with her toes for slippers. "Just... just give me a minute..."

"No, it's okay." Jessica tried to push Rachel back to the pillows. "You're sick. Brian's coming 'cause he has to go with Davey anyway."

Rachel pushed against her daughter. "I've got to—"

"You don't have to do anything." The calm authority of Brian's voice interrupted Rachel's protest. "You're not well enough to go anywhere." He pushed her back to the pillows and held her there, waiting until her feeble struggles subsided.

Rachel finally lay still, her heart thumping and her head spinning from the sudden exertion. Much as she hated to admit it, Brian was probably right.

"I was planning to go with Davey," Brian went on, freeing her arms and sitting on the edge of the bed. "It's no trouble to keep an eye on Jess at the same time. I'll take good care of her; don't worry."

He was wearing a gray suit and looked fresh and handsome, while she felt like the bottom of the clothes hamper. She pulled her blankets up a little higher and forced a smile for Jessica. "Have you got everything?"

"Yes. And I remember all the words, too. I even figured out that tricky part I kept doing wrong."

"Good. I'll be thinking about you. Bye, sweetie."

Jessica would have come to hug her, but Rachel shooed her off again. "No, I don't want you to catch this."

"Everybody at school's got it. Bye, Mom. I love you."

"Bye, Jess. I love you, too."

"Feeling worse?" Brian asked when Jessica was out of earshot.

"Just sorry for myself," Rachel admitted. To her horror a tear spilled over and she brushed it away with the back of her hand. "I never miss these school things. They're one of the real bonuses of being a parent."

"Ah." The sound was soft and filled with empathy. "I'm sorry. I promise to tell you about it in detail when we get home. Will that help?"

She forced a smile. "Yes. You'd better go or you'll be late. Thanks for taking her."

"Don't be silly." Brian leaned down to kiss her and she shrank away, pushing at his shoulder.

"You'll catch the flu!" she said in concern, pulling the blanket up over her mouth. "And I'm sure I look like Typhoid Mary."

With an amused roll of his eyes, Brian pulled the blanket down and kissed her soundly. "I had it just before Christmas," he said. "And I've always had a thing for Typhoid Mary. And don't give my mother any trouble."

Rachel frowned. "Your mother?"

"She's going to sit with you while we're gone."

"I'm sure she wouldn't think of giving me any trouble." Alicia Tate walked into the bedroom with a tray bearing two steaming soup mugs. "Run along, darling.

I'm going to spend all evening telling Rachel what a brat you were as a child and what misery you caused me.''

"Really?'' Brian looked unconcerned as he walked to the door. "And who's going to fix your faulty water heater? Or are you going to go in for cold-water showers, like the Scandinavians?''

With her back to her son, Alicia gave Rachel a grimace that indicated she'd made a serious miscalculation. Rachel kept a straight face with difficulty.

"He was the sweetest little child,'' Alicia said, without turning around, perching on the edge of the bed and handing Rachel a mug of hot soup. "Just as cute as a bug's ear and with a disposition that made all my friends green with envy. *Their* children were so ordinary.''

"Don't overdo it, Mom,'' Brian called from the door.

Alicia winked at Rachel. "No, dear.''

Once the door closed behind Brian and Jessica, Alicia spent the evening telling Rachel about her son, just as she had threatened. But her story was full of praise rather than criticism.

"No woman could have asked for a better son,'' she said, putting the tray with their dinner things on the floor and sitting in a chair beside the bed, her slippered feet crossed and resting on the edge of the mattress. "He was a pretty good kid. We had the usual problems with youthful wildness, but he grew out of that in college, got good grades and landed the job with the *Daily News* almost immediately. I'm so glad his book has been a success.'' Alicia smiled at Rachel. "I think he's finally ready to settle down, though he won't admit it.'' The smile became conspiratorial. "I think you'd be perfect.''

Rachel had to laugh at Alicia's unabashed forthrightness. "I'm afraid not. He told me he doesn't want to be a father. I have a daughter.''

"With whom he is simply wonderful." Alicia frowned. "Almost as good as he is with that little character from next door. Hmm." Alicia leaned her head against the back of the chair and stared at the ceiling.

"Now before you go plotting," Rachel said with friendly firmness, "let me make my position clear. I'm not interested in getting married, either. He's a kind man; I'd have to be the first to admit that. But even in a friendship, he's . . . demanding."

Alicia sat up to study Rachel in surprise. "Would you want a man who wasn't? Who didn't care what you gave him emotionally?"

Rachel shrugged, running a finger along the stitching on the blanket binding. "I've gotten kind of used to not having to consult anyone when I have decisions to make."

Alicia nodded. "And have you gotten used to being sick with no one around to help you? It's a simple trade-off, dear. We give up some things and gain others."

"He told me that he sometimes has to get away for long periods of time. Usually without warning."

Alicia went suddenly still, her air of casual amusement dissolving. She lowered her feet to the floor and sat up in the chair. Rachel could almost feel her fighting against tension. Alicia looked at her hands then knotted them together, turning to Rachel.

"Did he tell you why?"

Rachel shook her head, a breath suspended while she waited.

Alicia thought a moment, then smiled, forcing herself to relax in her chair. She crossed one long leg over the other and folded her arms.

"There are two reasons, really," she said briskly, "both probably equally responsible, each very different from the other. One is simply a matter of heredity. My grandmother, who was born in Idaho, was married to a Blackfoot Indian."

At Rachel's little laugh, Alicia went on, "No, seriously, Rachel. And it was his habit to just take off when civilization encroached on his 'space.' When he felt crowded inside as well as out, he headed for the mountains and solitude. And then he came back. Sometimes a couple of days later, sometimes a week. But he always came back."

Rachel shook her head. "And his wife had to cope in the meantime."

Alicia shrugged. "She loved him."

"She was generous."

"He was worth it. I've always teased Brian about being a throwback to my grandfather."

Rachel relaxed against her pillows. "And the second reason?"

Alicia leaned forward, her arms crossed on her raised knee. "The second is less romantic and more painful. My first husband—Brian's father—was a brilliant businessman with a keen mind and lots of other qualities that attracted me. He loved me enormously..."

Alicia's voice broke and Rachel sat up in alarm. Alicia shooed her back, reaching to the box of Kleenex by the bed. "It's all right. I'm fine, really. I just try not to think about it anymore because it's so sad. Anyway..." She sniffed and dabbed at her nose. "He loved me very much and I loved him, but..."

She shook her head and Rachel saw the pain in her even as she tried to shake it off. "We had this beautiful son, and...I know he wanted to love him, for me, but he seemed only to see Brian as something between us, something that took my time from him. Children are so smart. Brian wasn't very old before he realized his father didn't like him around. He didn't understand why, of course, and, trying to spare him the rejection, I kept making up excuses. He soon learned to disappear when his father was around; it spared him the coldness of being ignored or bearing the heat of anger because he was in the way."

Rachel thought back to the night she had been at Brian's house, studying his mother's watercolors and asking him about his father.

"But he talks about him in a caring way."

Alicia smiled. "He must have been talking about Ben Tate, my second husband. Brian's natural father was killed in a plane crash when Brian was ten. Two years later I married Ben. He loved Brian, but the adjustment was hard for both of them. Brian was at a difficult age, and Ben was determined that for their relationship to be solid, Brian would have to respect him as a man. They clashed often and noisily. Again, Brian found renewal in being able to be by himself for a while. We had a cabin outside of Idaho City and we used to let him go there by himself, even when he was still in high school, because I understood how important it was to him to get away to pull himself together." Alicia drew a deep breath and smiled. "Ben and Brian turned out to be great friends. Ben adopted him eventually, when Brian felt ready. Brian was devastated when Ben died."

Rachel reached over to pat Alicia's hand on the arm of the chair. "Brian is such a wonderful man. How strong and loving you are to have pulled him through all that with his self-esteem intact."

Alicia squeezed her hand, then blew her nose and dried her eyes. "He's the wonderful one. He came to be with me when Ben was ill and, mercifully, was with me when he died. I'd have blown my mind without him the past two years. He teases me and bullies me and lets me pamper him so that I have other things to think about besides what sometimes becomes an awful loneliness.''

"Now, when you came to sing me Brian's tune,'' Rachel reminded Alicia, handing her one last Kleenex then pulling the box away, ''you asked me to consider my answer carefully because you were in the middle of an affair.''

Alicia rolled her eyes and laughed softly. ''I also told you I had all my own teeth. Don't believe everything you hear.''

She and Rachel laughed together, then Alicia became suddenly introspective and she began to play with the fabric at the hem of her skirt and a small thoughtful smile began to form. ''Well, there is a gentleman on the city council...''

''Tell me!'' Rachel insisted, curling up comfortably to listen.

When Brian came home with the children he was greeted with the sound of raucous laughter coming from the bedroom. While Jessica ran ahead to tell her mother about the evening, Brian settled Davey at the kitchen table with milk and cookies then followed the high sounds of feminine hilarity.

''Our class did the best!'' Jessica was saying when he reached the threshold of the room. The child was facing her mother, who was watching with rapt attention, her cheeks pink, her smile quick and bright. She's better, he thought with sincere relief. Then his eyes registered regret. She'll be leaving.

''Even Brian said we were best. We sang—'' Jessica, flushed with excitement, launched into a long litany of numbers then collapsed in giggles. ''Mrs. Johnson almost fell backward off the stage. You know how she directs so hard...'' Jessica made elaborate Arthur Fiedler movements with her hands. "Well, she stepped backward a little too far and almost fell into the front row. She went like this—" she flailed her arms frantically "—and Mr. Gordon came to her rescue. Then we had dry chocolate-chip cookies and watery cocoa. I'm gonna sleep on the sofa because Alicia has to work at the hospital tonight."

The swift change of subject caught Rachel by surprise and she shook her head insistently. "Really. We'll just go home tonight. I'm doing fine and—"

"No," Brian said firmly, advancing into the room. "You are better, but you're not well. You've hardly eaten in three days. You'd fall on your face if you tried to take a step."

"She'll be fine on the sofa," Alicia said bracingly. "I volunteer at the hospital a couple of nights a week. I tried to get someone to cover for me tonight, but I couldn't. Brian doesn't mind. Do you, dear?"

"Of course not. Jessica can walk to school with Davey in the morning. He's always here for breakfast, anyway."

Rachel wanted to resist but she was tired and she knew it would be hopeless. And her daughter looked tired despite her excitement.

Jessica kissed Rachel, then Alicia, and skipped off, calling back, "I'm going to see how Susan Sophia is doing before I go to bed."

Alicia frowned. "Susan Sophia?"

"The cat." Brian laughed. "Jessica thinks of her in grand terms. Davey calls her Sue."

"Well, darlings. I'm off." Alicia stood, smoothed her skirt and moved toward her son.

"I know you're off, Mother, but I wouldn't be so boastful about it."

Alicia hugged him then jabbed him viciously in the ribs with her elbow. "Don't get smart with your mother. She's getting old. One appreciates kindness in one's twilight years. Good night."

Brian laughed, rubbing his side. "Night, Mom."

"Are you sure it's all right about Jessica?" Rachel asked as he sat on the edge of the bed. "You're on a deadline with your book and I know you can't have accomplished anything the whole time I've been here—"

Brian cut her off deftly with, "Do you want to hear about the Winter Review, or not?"

Subsiding, she leaned against her pillow and folded her arms. "Tell me everything."

"Mrs. What's-Her-Name did almost fall backward off the stage; that was the highlight of the evening." He laughed reminiscently as he pulled his suit coat off and tossed it onto the chair. He pulled at his tie and unbuttoned the top button of his shirt. "Davey laughed so hard he couldn't continue to sing. It was embarrassing. Course Jess and the other kids weren't exactly stoic. Even the parents were having a tough time. The first graders are ready for Radio City Music Hall. They had these wonderful gestures and this great choreography..." He twirled his hands and did a sort of Hawaiian sweep to the side that made Rachel burst out laughing. Then he tapped her knee to get her attention. "Jessica was wonderful. You didn't tell me she had a solo."

"Was she nervous?"

He thought about it. "No, I don't think so. She had just the right blend of confidence and humility that grabs an audience by the heart and doesn't let it go. And it doesn't hurt that she has a beautiful voice. I was very proud of her. Even Davey applauded for her."

"Well..." Rachel said softly.

The bedroom was dark, except for the small light on the bedside table. It had been dark for hours, of course, but somehow with Alicia sitting beside her she hadn't been aware of it. The shadows darkened Brian's face and the weak light shone in his eyes and glinted off his hair. He looked dangerous, leaning on an arm braced on the other side of her legs, and she felt very vulnerable. Rachel tugged on the blankets that had fallen to her waist.

"Thank you for taking her."

He inclined his head in a careless gesture. "I told you I had to take Davey anyway."

She smiled at him, observing his suavely sexy appearance and considered the very unsophisticated, unsexy atmosphere in which he had spent the evening. "Tell me again how kids get on your nerves."

"They did get on my nerves." He grinned and got to his feet. "I just managed to have a good time anyway. I'm that kinda guy."

"Well, in the face of such nobility—" Rachel scooted down in the bed "—I'm going to sleep."

Brian reached down to lift her head and resettle the pillows under it. At his touch, sensation raced down Rachel's spine and outward to soften and warm her body. He looked at her for one long, nerve-racking minute, then leaned down and kissed her lightly on the lips.

"Don't worry about Jess in the morning, I'll see that she gets off to school. Good night."

There was a soft click and the room was bathed in darkness. Rachel lay in the shadows telling herself scathingly that she should have insisted on going home. She was better—a little weak, but definitely better. She missed the comfort of her own bed, the familiarity of... She turned over and punched her pillow. No, she didn't. She didn't miss a thing about their small duplex. She liked it here, with Brian. Though the conditions had been strange with her ill and him tending her, she liked seeing him during the day when he took a break from work, and hearing his voice when he was downstairs with the kids. She enjoyed the closeness.

An alarm sounded inside her. Propinquity without commitment wasn't healthy—particularly if a child was involved. Well—she shifted her pillow again and sighed— Brian wouldn't want it anyway, so it didn't matter. Tomorrow, she would go home, and they could go back to their curious friendship. They had made an agreement and she wouldn't be the one to break it.

Chapter Seven

Quiet. Bleak daylight filled the room, but there was no sound. Rachel turned her head to glance at the clock on the bedside table. Eight o'clock. This was frantic time. Jessica should be chasing down her shoes, making sure she had lunch money. Someone should be reminding her that it was time to stop watching cartoons and start brushing her teeth.

Rachel leaped out of bed, certain that Jessica had slept in after her late night, and Brian, not accustomed to having a child under his roof, had simply forgotten to set his alarm. She was in the middle of the living room before the suddenness of her movements caught up with her and made her head spin like a plate on the end of a balancing pole. She put a hand up to her forehead and took a moment to steady herself.

A firm hand took hold of her arm and guided her to the sofa.

"You've got to move a little more slowly," Brian warned her gently. He placed a scratchy afghan around her, pushed her gently back into the corner of the sofa, and put her legs up on the soft cushions.

Rachel heard the crackle of a fire and opened her eyes to see snow flurry past the window.

"Snow," she said softly, momentarily distracted by the sight. It didn't come every winter in Cannon Beach and even when it did, it often didn't stick. There had been lots of snow in Kansas and she had missed it.

"Better?" Brian was sitting at the other end of the sofa, rubbing her cold bare feet in his warm hands.

"Did..." She wanted to sit up but that would mean pulling her feet away and his ministrations felt so delicious. "Did Jessica get to school?"

"Yes. She left with Davey about fifteen minutes ago."

Rachel looked at him in surprise. "Early?"

"I gave them money to stop at the bakery on the way. Stay still. I'll get your slippers."

Brian was back in a minute with a pair of blue scuffs— her blue scuffs.

"We stopped by your place last night on the way home from the revue," he said, reading her mind. "We picked up a few of your things, too. I imagine you're getting pretty sick of my Aunt Maggie's puky taste in pajamas."

He also carried a pillow off the bed, settling it under her head, then straightening the afghan.

"Okay, this is the last meal you're getting in bed," he said, looking down at her, his hands resting lightly on the hips of his jeans. "Scrambled eggs and toast? French toast? An omelet?"

He looked deliciously fresh, and now that moving around a little had her blood flowing, she was beginning to realize that she was almost herself again.

Knowing Penny was efficiently taking care of the shop and that Jessica was safely on her way to school left her feeling relatively carefree. She realized with a pleasant start that it had been a long time since she'd been so free of responsibility. The freedom made her a little giddy.

Rachel leaned back against the pillow and flung an arm out behind her in dramatic abandon. "Oh, I think eggs Benedict would be nice," she ordered in an affected voice, "with toast points, of course, and a glass of *Chateau Neuf du Pape*. Chilled, please."

"Right," Brian replied. "On your head or down your shirt?"

She lowered her arm, pouting. "I thought you could float a peach in it."

He laughed. "You being the peach?"

She looked away from him, her manner that of displeased royalty. "You've just forfeited your gratuity, my good man."

Brian sank down beside her on the sofa. "Look, lady. I'm just a poor working stiff. We're outta hollandaise sauce and you can't float a peach in Bud Light. Now have a heart."

Rachel heaved a long-suffering sigh and faced him squarely. "The atrocities one has to put up with among the unenlightened. It's so upsetting. Very well, my good man. French toast it will have to be, if we must be so pedestrian. With strawberry jam, please, and powdered sugar." She raised her chin in a questioning angle. "You do have those, I trust?"

Brian studied her, fascinated and a little frightened by his own vulnerability. Her eyes were full of warm affection and a wonderful insanity, and it occurred to him—not for the first time—what an effect those qualities could have on a man's life. Even with snow flurries waltzing by the window, he couldn't remember a sunnier day.

Grasping her wrists, Brian pulled Rachel to a sitting position, then into his embrace. He laughed softly. "Good to have you back, Rachel. And in such good form, too."

"Well..." Her arms wrapped around his neck, she planted a gentle kiss on his cheek. "Thanks for taking such good care of me. And Jessica."

"It was my pleasure," he replied gallantly.

Rachel leaned back to look into his eyes. "Now, that has to be a fib."

"Oh?"

"We were a lot of trouble. Don't—" she stopped his denial with a hand over his mouth "—try to say we weren't. We were definitely a demanding family, with me sick, and Jess needing someone to take her to the Winter Revue, then get her off to school."

He removed her hand and kissed its palm. "On second thought, maybe you *were* a lot of trouble," he said with a grin. "You can redeem yourself by setting the table."

"Right." Rachel accepted his hand up. "And I'm starving."

"But you're still not getting eggs Benedict," he said, leading her off to the kitchen. "That *would* be a lot of trouble."

I'm going insane, Brian thought with a sense of mild panic. He whipped eggs and milk and a little vanilla in a bowl and watched the woman moving around his kitchen table. She looked so right there. She felt so right in his arms. Worse than that, she felt so right inside, deep in his heart, where he really knew if something was good for him or bad. I don't want her to go. He allowed himself to form the thought then forced himself to look at it and analyze what it meant. Love? he wondered. It couldn't be. He'd been alone so long it was probably just ... comfortable to have someone close at hand all the time, someone who needed him and made him laugh and laughed with him. That was it.

Permanent exposure to what had seemed so appealing the last few days would make him antsy. He'd want to take off for a few days, or maybe longer. She'd get angry and it would be all over. Why put himself through that? In a couple of days, after she'd had time to gather her strength, she could go back to her place and leave him in peace. He had a deadline in six weeks, for God's sake, and because of her he'd been losing ground on a daily basis.

She turned to smile at him, and the whisk stopped dead in the bowl, as though it were mechanical and he had turned it off. He seemed unable to function when she looked at him like that.

"Where's the powdered sugar?" she asked.

He tilted his head toward a cabinet, then turned away from her to dip bread in the batter. "Try that cupboard. If there is any it's probably way in the back."

He's upset, Rachel thought, watching the deliberate way he'd turned his back on her. She couldn't blame him, of course. She and Jessica had turned out to be a heavy burden on his time when he could least afford it. He'd spent almost a week helping her at the shop and spent so much time catering to her during the past few days, she was sure he'd had no time for himself or his book.

He didn't want family responsibilities. He'd made that clear more than once, and finding himself faced with almost several days of a reasonable facsimile thereof, he was probably irritated and annoyed, despite his insistence that caring for them had been no trouble.

But on the other hand, he hadn't acted annoyed. Rachel found the powdered sugar and took it to the table, her motions automatic as her mind remembered his embrace. The sweetness of his hug had felt as though their differences were beginning to blur, and that those things that they held in common were beginning to merge and strengthen the flimsy underpinnings of their relationship. But perhaps she was wrong. Rachel poured coffee, feeling glum and strangely out of sorts. Brian brought a platter of French toast and two plates to the table. Looking into Rachel's dark eyes, he mistook moodiness for the remnants of illness. "You'd better get back to bed after breakfast. You're not as strong as you think you are."

She gave him a dry glance as she brought her coffee cup to her lips. "Isn't that true of a lot of things?"

He sat opposite her, an eyebrow arched in confusion. "Pardon me?"

She shook her head and helped herself to a piece of the soft, steaming, golden bread. "Never mind. Pass the powdered sugar."

"BRIAN, I'VE *GOT* to go home." Rachel was folding her few changes of clothes into the paper bag in which Jessica had packed them the night of the Winter Revue. "You talked me into staying two more days to rest up, but now I've got to go."

"But it's Saturday," he pointed out reasonably. He was pleased that he sounded reasonable—he felt desperate. "We always do things together on the weekends. Why not just stay until Monday morning?"

Her nerves taut, her mood uncertain, Rachel turned to him impatiently, slapping her blue scuffs into the bag. "Brian, you know why."

He did. They'd been dancing around the reason for weeks, particularly during the past few days, which they'd spent together under the same roof. He took hold of her shoulders and pushed her down onto the edge of the bed, angling his body to sit beside her. "Yeah, I know," he said gently. "Why don't we talk about it?"

She put her hands up to block his hold but he held firm. With resignation in the angle of her shoulders she folded her arms. "Talk about what, Brian?"

"I don't want you to go."

She nodded, her eyes resting sadly on his. "I know. I don't want to go. But I can't stay."

"You've enjoyed being here," he challenged, retaining his grip on her arms when she tried to pull away again. "You've relaxed; I've seen it happen. And I've liked having you here. It's such a nice surprise to look up and find you there—like a gift." His hands moved to her face and he rubbed his thumbs gently across the flush on her cheekbones. "Stay, Rachel."

Like a gift. That was precisely how it felt. Rachel felt the resolution she'd mustered up this morning soften and prepare to dissolve as her mind played his words over and over. "It's such a nice surprise to look up and find you there . . ."

But she forced herself to remember Davey's feelings. He was unhappy with Rachel and Jessica around all the time. The boy needed Brian now, needed to know that this relationship he'd formed with him was solid—Davey didn't need to share him right now, to feel like an intruder where he was becoming so comfortable. And there was Jessica. She wanted solidity for her daughter, security without threat of eventual separation.

Rachel took hold of his solid wrists and pulled them firmly down. "I know how you feel," she said gently. She had intended to be firm but somehow the feeling wouldn't be expressed that way. "I know how I feel. There's something very precious here. And if it was just us, I think I'd take the chance. I'd stay with you and let whatever would happen, happen." She sighed and brought one of his hands to her lips. "But you need space, Brian, and I need...I need a perimeter. I need it for my child and I need it for myself. I lived an unstructured, disordered life when I was married to Jarrod and I hated it. There is no amount of money and no applause that could make it worth it for me."

He frowned at her, as though trying to interpret what she meant. "Writing's not a nine-to-five occupation."

She shook her head. "I know that. And I don't mean that life has to fit into a workaday slot. But children need routine. And I have a business; I need routine. You'd probably get really bored with that and have to go 'walk-about' or whatever it's called..."

He smiled at that and she swatted his arm. "You know what I mean."

He caught her hand and held it between his two. "Yes, I know what you mean. But I have to do that for my work, and sometimes I have to do that for me." He looked grave, unyielding, and she felt the beginnings of despair. "But I'd come back."

"I know." Rachel stood and walked across the room, taking a few of her personal things off the dresser. "But I'd worry in the meantime. I'd need you with me, Brian, secure in our little fenced cottage."

Brian leaned back on the mattress on an elbow and watched her put her things in the bag.

"So, what do we do now? Have we gone as far as this...this friendship is likely to go? Is it over and do we part? Or do we just go back to the way it was, meeting for dinner and weekend hikes?" His voice was challenging, cynical. She looked down into his eyes and knew, as he did, that it would no longer ever be enough for either of them. It was time to turn a corner, or turn away.

"We can't go back to that," she said, carefully lining up the seams of the paper bag then folding the top down as though it were some giant picnic lunch.

"You're right," Brian confirmed.

She put the bag on the floor by her purse and took her jacket out of the closet. She gave him a small smile and sighed. "And I don't think there's any going forward. Will you take us home or shall I call a cab?"

A light rap on the bedroom door announced Jessica. She poked her head around the door, here eyes large and unhappy.

"I'm ready," she said. A plaintive meow almost drowned out the sound of her voice. Rachel went to the door and pulled it open. A complaining Susan Sophia was draped over Jessica's arm. In two weeks she had fattened up considerably and her coat had become shiny and thick. She looked as though she would deliver her kittens at any moment. Jessica looked at Brian. "Can I feed her, Brian? I think she's hungry."

"Sure, Jess."

Jessica turned away without looking at Rachel, her thin face grimly set.

Rachel turned to Brian with a sigh. "She used to like me until you came into our lives."

He got to his feet and shook his head at her. "She doesn't understand why you won't stay long enough for her to see the kittens born. I don't either."

"We've just been through—"

"I know. But all you've got is arguments why it won't work. Why not try and see if it will?"

Rachel shifted her weight to one hip and looked him in the eye. "Brian, will you marry me?"

He considered her a moment, then laughed softly. "I have things to do today."

"In other words, no. There you have it." She picked up her purse and bag and threw her jacket over that arm also. "I'm not going to live with you, learn to love you beyond anything and have Jessica do the same, then one day have it all fall apart."

"How do you know it will?"

"It will. It has no structure, no walls, no perimeter. I'd hate it."

Brian caught her arm, as she would have walked out of the room, and pulled her back. "You'd rather be confined—imprisoned—with no way out?"

"It isn't prison," she said insistently. "Wild roses need a trellis to climb on, there's no warmth without a fireplace to confine the fire and a draft to draw up the air, traffic needs a road to follow, even birds have an established route, Brian."

He smiled, an unexpected smile she had to steel herself against. "That's staid thinking for a woman whose business is something as ethereal as helium-filled balloons."

Rachel sighed and looked into his eyes. "It's an ethereal business with strings attached—the ones that hold the balloon. The balloon is beautiful and whimsical and gives a lot of pleasure, but without the string it would fly away. And then what good would it be to anyone? That's why there's only one wish balloon in a bouquet. You have to hold the other eleven to enjoy them."

Brian called up all sorts of arguments, none of which seemed worthy of the one stated. Frustrated, he brought up the only one he thought she'd have trouble refuting.

"I thought you didn't want to get married again," he said.

She laughed softly and punched him lightly in the ribs. "That was before I met you." Unable to look at him, Rachel went to the kitchen in search of Jessica. The child was sitting on a kitchen chair, bent over, watching Susan Sophia crunch her Friskies as though it were her last meal.

"Got everything?" Rachel asked brightly.

"It's by the door," Jessica replied without looking up.

Rachel braced herself to turn around and thank Brian for all he had done for them when the kitchen door burst open. Davey ran into the room and Rachel knew instantly something was wrong when the door didn't slam behind him. He was ashen and his mouth was working unsteadily.

Brian went to him, taking his arms as the boy reached out to him. Davey swallowed and said in a constricted voice, "I...I think something's wrong...with Grandma."

"Stay with Rachel," Brian ordered quietly then went out the door at a run.

Rachel gently eased Davey into a chair, worried about his pallor. She poured him a cup of hot chocolate and he drank it slowly, going to sit on the floor beside Susan Sophia. He stroked her while she ate, and she stopped occasionally to nuzzle his knee before going back to her bowl.

Jessica, for once, didn't try to compete for the cat's attention. She sat near Rachel with a glass of orange juice, her big eyes watching the window through which the back door of Davey's house was visible.

Within fifteen minutes the shrill sound of an ambulance could be heard, growing louder as it pulled into the driveway between the two houses. Rachel and Jessica watched through the window while two white-garbed young men ran into the house. Davey continued to stroke the cat.

Five minutes later one young man ran out to the ambulance for the stretcher, and five minutes after that, Mrs. Callahan was brought out, tiny and still. Jessica shrank against Rachel, who rubbed her small shoulder, grateful that Davey had chosen not to watch.

Brian sprinted between the houses and into the kitchen. Seeing Rachel and Jessica but no Davey, he frowned until Rachel pointed to the boy on the floor near the cat. Brian closed his eyes for a moment then got down on his haunches beside Davey.

"I'm going to the hospital with her, Davey. I'll call you when I know anything."

Davey gave Susan a long, slow stroke. "Yeah," he said quietly. "Okay."

Brian put his cheek to the boy's head for a moment, holding him close. "It's going to be okay."

"Yeah," Davey said.

Brian got to his feet and turned to Rachel. Before he could say anything she reached up to kiss him lightly on the mouth. "I'll stay. Don't worry. Call us when you can."

FOR SOMETHING TO DO, Rachel had located ingredients for meat loaf and a salad and was pressing the meat mixture into a pan when she heard the sound of Brian's truck in the driveway. Night had fallen and darkness lay over the neighborhood, the lights of Cannon Beach sparkling from several blocks up the road.

Rachel met him at the door and knew the moment she looked into his face that Mrs. Callahan had died. Death left a mark on those who saw it; she had seen it in her own reflection after she had identified Jarrod. And Brian wore that look now, a sort of resigned disbelief.

Rachel put her arms around him and held him for a long moment, then he pulled away. "How's Davey?" he asked.

"Calm," she replied. "I don't think I've ever known a child so controlled."

Brian nodded. "Ugly, isn't it? I think he's just never felt safe enough to let his guard down."

"So what happens to him now?"

Brian went to the refrigerator and poured a glass of wine. He looked over his shoulder at her. "Want one?"

"Please."

"The head of Children's Services in town is a friend of mine. Davey will stay with me while they search for family. Mrs. Callahan once told me that Davey's mother had a brother in the East. She was going to have her attorney try to find him, but I don't know if she ever got to actually doing it. Anyway, my friend is going to try to check that out. Apart from that, I don't think there's any other family." He took a sip of the wine. "Where is he?"

"In the den with Jessica. Just send her here to me." Rachel indicated the dinner preparations on the counter. "I don't know if anyone will feel like eating, but I thought I'd fix something."

Brian studied her for a long moment. "I suppose some attempt at normalcy is all we can do."

She nodded. "Right."

As Jessica reluctantly left the den, turning back to give Brian and Davey one sad-eyed look over her shoulder, Brian turned the television off and sat beside the boy on the love seat. He noted Davey's pallor and his eerie calm and thought with a sense of panic that he didn't know how to do this. He had had the same feeling of panic not so long ago, when he told his mother that Ben had died.

She had wept and clung to him, and he had been able to deal with that. This child was completely dry-eyed, emotions carefully closed off because a lifetime of losing those he loved had taught him that it was safest.

This requires a psychologist, Brian thought helplessly. Someone who knew how to say the right words so that the trauma didn't last forever. But there was no psychologist; there was no family. There was only him, and because he had no knowledge of how to do this, he tried to relax and let instinct guide him.

Brian pulled Davey close to him and put an arm around his shoulders. The boy didn't resist, but neither did he take advantage of the closeness. He remained still, his arms folded.

"Your grandma's gone, Davey," Brian said gently, holding him, waiting for a reaction. He was not surprised when there was none, just the expellation of a sigh.

"I thought so. Are we gonna have a funeral?"

"Yes. On Tuesday."

Davey looked up at him. "My dad didn't have one, you know."

Brian tried not to look startled. In all the time he'd known Davey, he'd never mentioned his parents. Mrs. Callahan had told him a little but he and Davey had never discussed it. "He didn't?"

Davey shook his head. "He was a pilot in the Air Force. In Texas. He crashed. I was just little. They had something in church, though."

"Probably a memorial service."

"Yeah. That's what Mom said. She just went away." Davey looked into Brian's eyes, his own dark ones filled with a grimness that was startling to see in a child. "They don't have funerals for that. It feels like they should, but they don't. You just—" he shrugged bony shoulders "—move in with somebody else. Grandma." He said the word with the barest catch in his voice and Brian prayed that finally there would be some purging emotion. But

Davey squared his shoulders and asked evenly, "What happens now? I think we've run out of people."

Brian held him close, resting his cheek on the boy's head to hide his own distress. "A man named Greg McCloskey, a good friend of mine who works for the county, is going to see if he can find your uncle. Until he does, you're going to stay with me."

He felt the child's head nod against his chest. "Okay. Thanks."

Brian pulled him away and holding the small shoulders in his hands, he said quietly, "You know, it's okay to be upset. If you want to cry or scream or throw something, it's all right. Anyone would feel that way. It's hard to lose someone you care about."

"I'm not upset," Davey replied calmly. "Grandma was real tired. I don't think she wanted to be here, anyway. She wanted to be with grandpa and my dad."

Brian nodded, wondering with a flash of anger that went a long way toward restoring his emotional equilibrium, what kind of woman his mother was that she could have ever walked away from this boy.

"Okay," Brian said briskly. "I thought I'd go next door and get some of your things. Do you want to come and show me what you need, or would you rather stay here? Rachel and Jess are fixing dinner. They could probably use some help."

"I'll come with you."

DINNER WAS AN UNEXPECTEDLY normal affair. It might have been a little quieter, but not unlike many of the other dinners the four of them had shared during the past six weeks.

After dinner Brian took the children to the video store to select a few movies to keep them occupied over the weekend. Rachel cleaned up and baked peanut-butter cookies.

Davey seemed as excited as Jessica over the new Star Trek movie and Rachel settled them in the den with cookies and milk. Normalcy, Brian had said. A little boy who showed no grief at the loss of a grandmother he'd lived with for the past two years wasn't normal, but perhaps if they could establish some semblance of order in his world, the problem would work itself out.

Rachel found Brian stacking wood in the cone fireplace. "Cup of coffee?" she asked.

He was stuffing twisted shafts of paper into the carefully stacked pile. "Sounds good."

By the time Rachel returned with two steaming mugs of strong coffee, the fire was crackling merrily and Brian was sitting cross-legged on the carpet in front of it.

He took the small tray from her with the mugs of coffee.

"No cookies?" he asked, obviously disappointed.

Rachel stopped before settling herself next to him, one knee on the carpet. "They're peanut butter, Brian. Children's cookies."

He smiled. "I know. I had one of the kids's when I set the movie up for them. I like them."

Rachel rolled her eyes and went to the kitchen then returned with a plate of cookies. "The small ones are a little hard. I'm not used to your oven."

Brian took a small, crisp cookie and dipped it in his coffee. "Good for dunking. Mmm." He made an enthusiastic sound of approval. "You have hidden talents, Mrs. Bennett. How come you never made cookies before?"

She took a cookie from the plate and broke it in half, dunking it as he had done. "Mothers always make cookies when children are upset. It's in the parents's handbook somewhere.'' The soft, dunked part of the cookie broke off and plopped into her coffee. She studied it in dismay.

Brian laughed softly. ''The trick with dunking is that you put it right in your mouth. You don't pause to philosophize or you end up with sludge in the bottom of your cup. Here, I'll get you another.''

Brian was back in a minute with a fresh cup of coffee.

Rachel waited until he had settled himself again just inches from her in front of the fire. She took a sip of her coffee and wondered warily if what she was about to propose was the right thing. Whether it was or not, she had to do it, so she supposed it didn't matter. However things turned out, she would live with them.

''I've got a proposition for you,'' she said quietly.

''I'll take it,'' Brian said, without looking away from the fire.

She sighed and turned to face him. ''Not that kind, Brian.''

He turned, too, swiveling on his derriere to sit facing her. His eyes were firelit and unfathomable. ''What kind, Rachel?''

''I'll stay and help you with Davey.''

For a long moment Brian said nothing. He sipped at his coffee and then set the mug on the carpet in front of him, fingers tented over it protectively. ''Why?'' he finally asked.

Surprised at his reaction, Rachel replied a little sharply, ''Because you're within about five weeks of your deadline and having a child around continually is a little different than having him drop by once in a while. You'll have to cook for him, wash his clothes, see that he bathes and know where he is and . . .'' The details were endless, and she frowned at him, frustrated that he didn't seem to grasp the scope of the job he had taken on.

"Thanks," he said, his eyes steady on hers. The fire-light danced in them and she saw herself reflected there, too. "But I don't want you to stay for that reason."

She gasped impatiently. "I'm trying to help. You've done a lot for Jess and me. The least I can do is come to your rescue when you need me."

He shook his head. "That's not a good reason, either."

Ready to strangle him, Rachel turned so that they sat knee to knee. She rested her hands on her crossed ankles and leaned toward him with annoyance in her eyes. "What is the matter with you? Just this morning you couldn't stand the thought of my leaving."

He moved his cup out of harm's way. "I don't want you to go."

"Then why—?"

"I want you to stay," he interrupted quietly, "because you want to stay. And not because of Davey, or some imagined debt. I want you to stay because you want to be with me."

Rachel dragged both hands down over her face then dropped them to her knees with a slap. "Brian, this is no time to have that argument."

"Rache, our problem exists whether I have Davey or not. A normal two-parent environment would be good for him now, but I don't know how long I'm going to have him. If you're staying because of him and you'd really rather not be here ... You could be stuck at my house for weeks, and we'd all suffer for it, because the harmony wouldn't be there. And that's what family life is all about, isn't it?"

"How would you know?" she demanded. "You're afraid to have one."

"I've watched you with Jess," he said, cutting off her flare of temper. "And I remember times with my mother and my... father."

"Your stepfather?" she asked.

His hand stopped as he reached for his cup and he turned to look at her, surprise in his glance.

"Your mother told me," she explained. She took a deep sip of coffee and looked him in the eye. "I find it hard to imagine a parent not loving you."

Brian put the cup slowly to his lips and Rachel recognized the gesture as a stall. He was groping for control. "So did I," he said after a moment. A self-deprecating smile quirked his mustache. "Not that I was that lovable a child. But I loved my real father so much I had a hard time understanding why he didn't love me. It wasn't until I was eight or nine that it occurred to me that I took his time away from my mother. It wasn't a sexual jealousy or anything like that, simply a selfish one."

"But your stepfather loved you," she pointed out quickly, hating that hurt she could see deep in his eyes.

He nodded, smiling. "Yes. Ben loved me. That took me a while to grasp, too. He was on my case so much, never let me get away with anything. At twelve, it's hard to recognize that for what it is. But I did eventually. I miss him a lot—even now."

Rachel nodded, turning to look into the fire. Missing family was something she could identify with. "I know what you mean. When my parents came out for Jarrod's funeral, they could only stay a few days. It was the first time they'd ever seen Jessica and they still managed to spoil her rotten. I'd like so much to take her back to Kansas and show them what a special little person she's becoming."

Brian studied her firelit profile as she stared somberly ahead of her. "What's stopping you?"

"Oh . . ." Rachel tilted her head to the side and the rich brown color of her hair seemed to ignite. "We telephone one another on holidays and we exchange letters and pictures, but getting plane fare together would require a bigger budget than I've got to work with. And I've always felt as though my decision to leave my family and go with Jarrod made me an outsider; as though I didn't belong anymore. And I had always been kind of a daddy's girl." She turned to smile at Brian but he saw pain instead of laughter in her face. "I know he was very disappointed in me."

"If he loved you," Brian said, "then he understood that you did what you thought you had to do. Even if it hurt him."

"Maybe," she said wearily. "Maybe the guilt I've felt all these years has made me paranoid, and when I talk to him on the phone, I sense things that aren't really there. I always feel like he's a little abrupt, a little cool."

Brian laughed softly. "Maybe he just doesn't want to run up your bill."

Rachel laughed with him and then reached up to clasp her hands around his neck. "Will you let me stay with you if I tell you that I like sharing this house with you because you have such a handle on life, even though you don't know you have?"

He appeared to pause to consider her question, frowning over the complexity of it.

"That despite your claims about not wanting children," she went on, "or the *prison*—" she repeated his word with a dramatic roll of her eyes "—of marriage, that I feel safe and warm with you, secure in how it feels to be with you even though we don't know where this relationship is going? Does that make any sense?''

Brian put his hands at her sides, rubbing gently up and down her rib cage. It felt so fragile under his hands. ''I doubt that it would to anyone else,'' he said with a smile that was amused yet curiously grave. ''But I think I'm beginning to understand you, and I admit with trepidation that it makes perfect sense to me. Come here.'' He stretched a leg out behind her and pulled her so that she sat between his knees, her shoulder tucked into his chest. He bent the knee behind her for support. And then he kissed her long and deeply. Rachel could feel the desperation in his hands.

She put her hand to his face and ran her thumb gently along his jawline. ''Are you scared?'' she asked softly.

''Me?'' He held her a little closer and laughed softly. ''Hell, I know I can survive for days in an ice cave, weeks in the desert and probably even months on a raft. I know what plants and berries to eat and which ones would mean death, I can treat my own snake bite and build a reasonable shelter in an hour. Scared? Me?'' He took her hand from his face and turned it to plant a kiss in its palm. ''Yeah,'' he said. ''Terrified.''

Chapter Eight

Rachel began to think of her "occupation" of Brian's house in the full military meaning of the term. If this was normalcy, she decided a week after Mrs. Callahan's funeral, family life was a veritable battlefield. Though she and Brian had done their best to establish a normal pattern of life at the beachfront house, the children seemed to have declared war—on parental authority as well as each other.

"It's testing," Rachel tried to explain to Brian late one evening after the children had gone to bed. It had been an unpleasant few hours with continual bickering, finally ended by the imposition of an early curfew. "They're both in a new situation and they're pushing against the rules to see how far they'll stretch."

Brian lay on his back in front of the fire, one knee bent, one arm behind his head. "Davey's spent a lot of time with me. He knows what my rules are."

"But now Jess and I are here and he's wondering if they still apply and if I'll enforce them, as well. And Jess needs to know that you won't let her get away with doing things I don't allow."

Brian ran a hand over his eyes. "Couldn't we just post an edict?"

Rachel, sitting beside him, laughed and leaned an elbow on his chest. "Violators will be shot or hanged?"

"How about just spanked and put to bed?"

"That's the easy way out," she chided.

He smiled. "You can almost see why parents resort to spanking, though, can't you? It's probably the only way you've got control of the situation."

His question was borne out the following day when Rachel arrived home from work. It was dusk, and a light, cold rain was falling steadily. She pushed through the front door and was halfway into the dark living room when the sound of shouting stopped her. The children were always screaming at each other, but this time Brian was shouting and she stopped in her tracks, wondering what had happened now.

"How many times have I told you, Davey, that you don't ride two on a bike?"

Silence greeted the question. Rachel shifted sideways in the shadows to view the tableau in the kitchen. Brian was standing in the middle, hands on his hips, glaring down at the children, his shoulders squared. Davey and Jessica were lined up against the dishwasher, side by side. They were wide-eyed and at attention.

"It was my idea," Davey said finally, his voice carefully quiet and respectful. "I asked her to come."

Brian directed his gaze at Jessica. "Then if you're going to play with him, Jess, you're going to have to think for yourself instead of following his suggestions." Brian drew a deep breath and went on more calmly. "Jessica, if your mother had come home and seen you careening down that wet hill on the handlebars of Davey's bike, she'd have had a heart attack."

Rachel felt her heart skip a beat as the image came to life in her mind, complete with a log truck crossing the intersection at the moment the bike reached the bottom of the hill, unable to stop.

"Don't you see," Brian continued, "that it doesn't matter whose idea it was? Had a truck or a car been crossing the intersection when you got to the bottom, it wouldn't have asked whose idea it was before it hit you. It would have simply killed you. Both of you!"

"My brakes work fine." Davey took a step forward then moved backward when Brian took a deep breath.

"The pavement was wet!" he said loudly, "and there is gravel all over the road at this time of year!" Both children fidgeted and looked everywhere but at Brian. "You were lucky today, but you might not be again. Now, if you can't see the danger, then the bike stays in the garage for the next couple of weeks so that you have time to think about it. Both of you."

Davey took another step forward. "Jess needs it to go to her tumbling lesson."

"It's six blocks," Brian said. "She can walk."

"I can't run errands for you anymore, like the post office and—"

"Yes, you can. *You* can walk."

Davey subsided, his feeble glare once more in evidence.

Brian stepped back. "Go to your rooms. Do your homework. I'll call you when dinner's ready."

Davey marched through the living room toward the bedrooms, ignoring Rachel. Jessica looked relieved to see someone she thought would be an ally and opened her mouth to explain. Rachel pointed to the direction Davey had taken. "Move it!" she ordered.

Her distress increased by her mother's apparent desertion, Jessica burst into tears and ran for the bedrooms.

Rachel went into the kitchen pulling her coat off, and directed Brian to a chair at the table. She poured two glasses of wine and handed him one, sitting across from him.

"God, these kids are going to turn me into an alcoholic," he said, taking a long swallow. The tension was leaving Brian but Rachel saw the fear in his face as he related the incident to her. She listened in silence, grateful she hadn't been here to see it. She'd have definitely had the heart attack he'd predicted.

"My instincts were right," Brian said, downing the rest of the wine and pushing the glass aside. "Now I'm sure I'm not parent material."

"You handled that beautifully." Rachel patted his hand.

He looked up at her in surprise. "I scared the hell out of them."

Rachel lifted a knit-clad shoulder. "That's how it works, my friend. In certain situations, kids are smart and they will usually see things your way if you explain. In matters of personal safety, they have no sense. So you yell at them."

He studied her as though assessing her evaluation of a parent's role. "I feel like a rat."

"Sure you do. That's how they fight back. You look into those big eyes and those sad faces and think to yourself the poor little dears didn't know any better. Then you remind yourself that those pretty little faces could be just a memory if it ever happened again. So you do what you have to to make sure that it doesn't."

Brian was leaning on his folded arms now, watching her, and she reached out to put her hands on the arm that was uppermost. Her eyes were dark with sincerity. "I'm glad you were here to scare the hell out of my daughter,

Brian. I'm glad you cared enough to do it. I don't know if I could have dealt with them so effectively.''

Brian unfolded his arms and caught both her hands in his. He laughed. "So, that's how it works?"

Rachel nodded. "That's the ugly truth. And it goes on and on, day after day, in big and little ways until you think it'll make you crazy. Then one day this child will do something noble and selfless that will make you so proud, or his or her arms will come around you and you'll feel all that energy and intelligence and basic goodness and know that you've brought it this far. It's heady stuff."

Brian heaved a deep sigh and brought her hands to his lips. Then he retained his hold on them. "How did I get along all these years," he asked in all apparent seriousness, "without you to explain life to me?"

Rachel shook her head. "I can't imagine. To think you managed to become one of this country's most widely syndicated columnists, won all those awards and wrote a best-selling book without me to guide you. Boggles my mind."

Brian squeezed her hands and stood with sudden decisiveness. "We need a break. If my mother is free to watch the kids, I'm taking you out."

"Where?" she asked in surprise as he went to the phone.

He stabbed out Alicia's telephone number. "Dinner and dancing. Wear something slinky." When she would have protested that it was short notice to expect his mother to be available, he held a hand up to silence her then spoke into the phone. "Hi, Mom. Listen . . ."

Alicia arrived thirty minutes later in the company of Tom Benedict, the councilman she'd told Rachel about. Tom was tall and white-haired and pleasantly portly.

"I wish you had told Brian you had plans," Rachel scolded, greeting them at the door while Brian finished dressing.

"I didn't," Alicia insisted. "Tom just dropped by as I was getting ready to come over. I didn't think you'd mind if he sat with me."

"Of course not." Rachel took their coats. "But I feel so guilty. You could have gone out."

"I wasn't going to take her out." Tom laughed. "I was going to sit on her sofa and feed her chocolates." He held up the box that had been tucked under his arm and added guilelessly, "Then I was going to seduce her."

"A man after my own heart," Brian approved, pulling on his coat as he walked into the living room. He extended his hand to Alicia's companion. "How are you, Tom?"

The man smiled broadly. "Great. Your mother's good for my health."

Alicia blushed as Brian arched an eyebrow at her before hugging her. "Thanks for coming, Mom. And remember your arthritis."

Turning to Rachel to divert attention from herself, Alicia asked about the children.

Rachel explained about the bicycle incident. "They're having dinner in their rooms because they're grounded. Lights out at nine o'clock. We'll be at the Shilo Inn in Seaside. I put the number on the board by the phone."

"We won't be too late," Brian promised, helping Rachel into her coat. "Feel free to eat or drink whatever you can find."

Alicia followed them to the door and waved them off. "Have fun. And don't worry about anything."

"Your mother was blushing," Rachel said. "And the gentleman looked distinguished but definitely roguish."

She had polished off paté and crackers, salad, lobster bisque, Veal Marsala, pilaf and sautéed vegetables. She was now nibbling daintily on a sprig of parsley.

Brian leaned back in the tufted booth and watched her lazily. He felt relaxed and unusually mellow. "Let's not talk about my mother or the kids."

Rachel smiled, twirling the remaining stem between her thumb and forefinger. "We could discuss my work, or your deadline."

"No."

"Well, let's see." She disposed of the parsley, chewing thoughtfully. "There's a zoning change proposed for the block north of town."

"Hardly stimulating."

"All right. Let's think national. The Iran-Contra affair is—"

"Absolutely not."

She nodded, reaching for his parsley. "You're right. International then. Ah…traffic in the Persian Gulf. Now there's a topic…"

Brian dropped his napkin on the table, reclaimed his parsley and tossed it on his plate. Then he was on his feet and leading her toward the dance floor. She was laughing when he pulled her into his arms.

"Well, what do you want to talk about?"

"I've heard of people getting silly on too much to drink, but too much to eat?"

Rachel let her body drift against his, finding a comfortable spot for her head in the hollow of his shoulder. "I didn't have too much to eat," she protested mildly. "I had just enough. In fact, I was looking forward to dessert."

He rested his chin on her hair. "You had more to eat than I did."

"You said you didn't want those two pieces of brochette."

"You had already eaten them when you asked."

Rachel twined her arms around his neck as they swayed to the moody music. She issued a sigh of complete contentment. "I guess I'm silly from the unexpected bonus of having time alone with you. I feel giddy and schoolgirlish—like I've recklessly defied a curfew to meet you on the sly." She raised her head to look into his eyes, her own dreamy and unconsciously provocative. "And you, of course, have turned your back on title and riches to pursue me."

"Bad move on my part," Brian said.

She straightened away from him, her arms still around his neck. "Why?"

"I'd need the riches," he replied gravely, "to keep you in food."

He laughed as she rolled her eyes, then he pulled her back to him, his arms enveloping her in muscle and warmth.

"This is supposed to be a romantic interlude," she scolded.

"My contention from the very beginning," he said, kissing her temple. "So let's talk about us. Did I mention how gorgeous you look in black and silver?"

He had complimented her several times on the soft black crepe with its splash of sequins on the fitted bodice, and the fluid sweep of the tea-length skirt. She was happy now that she had listened to Penny when they'd gone post-Christmas sale shopping and had succumbed to style rather than frugality.

Through the thin fabric she could feel the warmth of Brian's body, the roughness of his jacket, the smoothness of his dress shirt. Under her fingers, his hair felt thick and wiry.

He shifted his head as her fingers explored near his ear. "Careful," he warned softly.

"Sorry." She flattened her hands against his shoulders and held him close. "You look wonderful in a suit." She punctuated the compliment with a kiss on his chin. "But I think I like you best in jeans and that blue plaid flannel shirt you wear around the house."

He looked down at her, asking quizzically, "Why?"

"Because you wore them the day we went duck watching," she replied with a subtle sobering of mood. "And I'll always remember how I felt then. Safe. More than safe from outside harm. Safe within myself, as though I could be completely honest with you and you would make no judgments. As though all you would ever want from me was just what I had to give." She smiled suddenly as affection for him swelled inside her. "And because the blue takes the gray right out of your eyes and makes them the same color as a spring sky. And that reminds me of that poem of Keats's that you like so much."

Brian pushed her head back into his shoulder and felt tenderness and passion at war within him. "How does that go, again?" he whispered.

She spoke softly into his ear, her breath tantalizing him. "'And we will sigh in a daisie's eye, and kiss on a grass green pillow.'"

He remembered the lines perfectly, but he loved the way she spoke them, her voice dreamy and low. The sound of it brought to mind images of the two of them in that daisy-filled field in Jewell with the smell of new hay in their nostrils.

She looked up at him and smiled, and he saw it in her eyes—that look that said he was life itself to her. And he was finally able to admit to himself that she was that to him—the very air that filled his lungs, the essence that made him more than just six feet of blood and bone.

He stopped their lazy movements and looked down at her as he finally understood what his life was all about.

"I love you, Rachel," he said.

He felt her body stiffen in surprise; then a soft sigh left her as happiness blossomed on her face. Pleased with her reaction, he said it again. "I love you."

"I love you, Brian," Rachel whispered, feeling as though a key had been turned, a door opened. Love. At last.

He leaned down to kiss her and she said the words again, this time against his mouth, and the air around them seemed to echo with them as he held her. Then he pulled away, grudgingly remembering where they were. "I think we'd better go home."

They found Tom dozing in a corner of the sofa with Alicia asleep in his arms.

"Isn't that sweet?" Rachel tiptoed into the room.

Brian pushed the door closed and Tom awoke with a start. "Oh," he said, smiling without embarrassment. "Hi. Have a good time?" He stretched and rubbed Alicia's arm. "The kids are home, Allie."

Alicia awoke in a flutter, straightening her lavender sweater, fluffing her hair. Tom watched her with amused interest as she got to her feet and pulled Rachel into the kitchen to show her the muffins she had baked and to tell her that the coffee was freshly made.

"The kids turned their lights off at nine without complaint," she went on to report. "And we didn't hear a sound out of them. Well . . ." She went to the closet for their coats and gathered up her purse. "Good night, darlings. Call me any time. You should get out more."

"Good night." Tom turned at the door to shake Brian's hand and wave at Rachel. Alicia could still be heard talking as Tom followed her out.

"Thanks again," Rachel called. "She's in love," she said more quietly as she turned to Brian.

But he wasn't thinking about his mother at the moment. He closed the door, and the action seemed to take all the air out of the room.

Rachel felt her spine weaken as he put his hand to her back and pulled her close.

"It's time," he said, his eyes dark blue, "that we turn that corner."

For just an instant Rachel was afraid. Giving yourself to someone else was such a gamble, and the last time she'd done it, she had lost. Then she looked up into Brian's eyes. They were so full of love for her that fear evaporated and she was filled with the courage that makes a woman able to entrust to a man all that she is and hopes to be. She put her arm around Brian's waist as he pulled her close and led her toward the bedroom.

The room was dark and cool as they went into it without turning on a light. Brian closed the door behind him and stopped Rachel with a warm hand on the back of her neck as she moved toward the bed.

Responding to a need to simply hold her, he pulled her back against him, wrapping his arms around her, placing a kiss on the fragile cord of muscle at her neck as she tipped her head to the side. He absorbed the wonder of her quiet pliancy and the knowledge that she longed to be his as much as he wanted to belong to her.

Rachel grasped his arms and held, feeling muscle and tenderness, passion and simple, touching adoration. Needing to be held, she rested her head against his shoulder and let him rain kisses along her throat to the neckline of her dress. Then suddenly she needed more—much more.

Brian felt her shift expectantly and turned her in his arms, his hands working the zipper at the back of her dress. The soft fabric fell silently to the floor. Her fragrance filled his nostrils, floral and springlike, and a field of daisies danced behind his eyes as he tossed aside her bra, removed her slip and stockings and panties.

He became aware that she was pushing at his shirt and he shrugged out of it, his fingers sliding up into her hair, pulling her lips up to his as she unbuckled his belt, unfastened his slacks. He thought he would remember forever the feel of her fingernails skimming his legs as she pushed his pants to the floor.

He tossed the blankets back and pulled her with him to the middle of the bed. For a moment he simply lay in the cool softness, holding her against him, marveling at how satiny she felt, and how every soft inch of her was his.

Overpowered with sensations, Rachel pressed against him, feeling long muscles in his arms and legs, broad strength across his chest. His hands moved over her in long, possessive strokes, and she leaned into them as delicious sensation followed in the wake of his touch. She was sure she felt cells come alive, nerves awaken as a warm glow covered her from head to toe.

Brian's breath grew shallow as he reacted to the erotic power of her eagerness. The gentle delight with which her hands explored him and her kisses covered him acted on him like some heady potion.

Rachel shifted to receive him as Brian sent tiny kisses up and down her thigh, then nudged her legs apart with gentle insistence. His hand invaded, just toying with her at first, teasing so that sensations, new and almost frightening, began to build in her.

Brian felt her body constrict, and he hesitated, stopping to look down at her, brushing the hair from her face. He felt her curls against his palm, the warm, damp contour of her face.

"Are you okay?" he asked.

Rachel leaned a hot cheek against his shoulder and expelled a sigh. "It's been such a long time, Brian. Actually... this is new." She lifted her head and he pushed her hair back to see her face. Her eyes and her smile shone. "Jarrod and I were kids, and then we were enemies." She shook her head in wonder. "I've conceived a child, but I've... I've never felt this before, Brian."

Brian tilted her back into the pillows and leaned over her. He settled her head on his arm and his other hand on the slight convexity of her stomach. He noted in alarm that his hand was trembling and wondered at the responsibility he felt for her emotional and physical satisfaction. But he didn't stop to analyze it because her hand was stroking his chest, dipping dangerously low, and he wanted more than anything not to leave her behind.

"Then relax," he said, "and let me take you farther."

Rachel leaned against his naked length, letting her hand trail the line of his waist to his hip. She tried to focus her mind on stillness. His fingers probed to part her and she concentrated on relaxing against the instinctive resistance her body made. But his fingers moved in an insidiously delicious pattern and she felt as though something deep inside her, something he could not have reached, began to race toward him.

"Easy," he cautioned in a tender whisper. He kissed her mouth then planted a chain of kisses between her breasts. "Let it take a little longer."

In an attempt to comply she turned her attention to him, moved her hand to his muscular thigh, then along the inside of it, finally giving his arousal her total attention.

Easy, Brian thought to himself. Easy. Take your own advice. But—God—for a woman who had never been there, she was sending him over the edge faster than he'd ever gone before.

"Brian..." His name on her lips was just a whisper of sound, and if he was wary of interpreting it as an indication that she was ready, her firm grip on his forearms became confirmation.

He knelt astride her, pushing her tumbled hair back to look at her. She put her hands up to his face and gazed back at him, her expression a combination of passion and wonder. Then she pulled him down to her.

He entered her with care, trying to remember what she had said, what he had sensed—that it had been a long time since she'd made love. As long ago as Jarrod?

Rachel's body closed on him, as though taking back a part of her that had been missing. Basking in the beautiful feeling of two bodies joined as one, Rachel sighed, her body tightening as the sensation overpowered her. Her body seemed to open and close as though drawing in some life-giving element that drove her mad with desire.

She thought in awe that she'd been a prisoner inside herself for so long. But she knew now with the certainty born of discovery that love had given her a new dimension, a meaning to the word woman she had never understood before.

"Brian," she whispered.

Her entire body seemed to convulse beneath him. Brian had been prepared to let the experience be hers, to enjoy the still considerable satisfaction he felt from simply having his body joined with hers and to feel her passion and her discovery.

But Rachel was so beautiful, and his body went wild. It was a long time before they finally quieted in a tangle of blankets and sheet in the middle of the bed.

Brian pillowed Rachel's head on his shoulder and she tucked her arm around his waist. She held him as though afraid something might try to take him from her.

"Are you okay?"

"No."

"No?"

"Better than okay. Marvelous. Maybe even stupendous. You?"

"I don't think I've got an adjective for it," he said. "Twenty years of finding just the right words and you now see me at a loss."

Rachel was quiet a moment then she asked thoughtfully, "How can I ever tell Jessica what waits for her in the arms of the right man?"

Brian chuckled. "I wouldn't bring it up just yet. We've got our hands full as it is."

Rachel planted a kiss on Brian's chest then crossed her hands over it and rested her chin on them. "I love you, Brian. Does that still terrify you?"

He toyed with her hair, pulling a strand of it free from the mass and drawing it across her upper lip like a mustache. "It's a little hard to dredge up terror right now. I feel more . . . languid and content."

Rachel pursed her upper lip to keep the mustache in place. With an exaggerated French accent she asked, "Ah, monsieur. How will you feel in the morning?"

"No doubt very ooh la la!" he replied, laughing. He snatched the strand of hair in his index finger and tucked it behind her ear. "I love you, Rachel. Shall I show you again?"

Rachel giggled. "In French?"

He gave her a Maurice Chevalier laugh.

FOR THE NEXT WEEK, it looked as though life was establishing a satisfying pattern for each member of the foursome. Brian, now firmly established as father figure, got less guff and more cooperation. His book was progressing, and he decided, with a few sixteen-hour days behind the word processor, he might make the deadline after all.

Rachel went to work and came home, performing her duties at both places like any other woman in America. She had it at last, a loving man, children, a routine she could live with. But she always turned away at the thought that the loving man was not a husband, and that one of the children, one who was weaving his way into her heart where the essence of her motherhood lived, wasn't hers. But she went happily from day to day, holding tight to what she had.

It pleased her that Jessica seemed so happy. Rachel knew that she now loved Brian and the way he would catch her when she ran across the room at him, or swing her playfully around, or tickle her into giggling helplessness. She even took his occasional scoldings philosophically, telling Rachel with an accepting shrug that it was all part of having a father.

Davey appeared to find life more agreeable than he had for a long, long time, as long as no one brought up the search for his uncle. When Brian was around, Davey was his constant shadow. But when Brian was closed in his office or out on an errand, Rachel often found Davey close beside her on the sofa, or leaning against her as she worked at the stove. He was now cautiously affectionate with her and she tried not to embarrass him with effusion. He seemed also to have accepted and learned to cope with Jessica.

Even Susan Sophia adjusted sufficiently to give birth to three little rodentlike offspring.

"Mom!"

"Brian!"

It was a Sunday morning and despite the Oregon coast's distance from the San Andreas fault, an earthquake was in progress. Or so Rachel imagined. She should run to a doorway, she debated groggily, under a major support beam, but she'd really rather die in bed, and the children were smart enough to figure that out for themselves. In fact, they were the ones who explained it to her after a study their class did on earthquakes.

But there was Brian. She opened one eye and saw his head next to hers on the pillow. He was asleep. She put an arm across his head to shield him from debris and went back to sleep.

"Rachel," Brian said, his voice muffled. "I can't breathe."

She sighed and moaned a little, patting his nose. "I'm shielding you from debris."

"Mom! Brian! Susan Sophia had three kittens!"

It crossed Rachel's mind that she should certainly make some effort to save the kittens from the earthquake. Kittens. She opened her eyes and found Davey's face half an inch from hers. "One's all white," he reported excitedly, "and two are tuxedo cats. Are you going to come look?"

Jessica was pulling on Rachel's toes. "Please, Mom!"

"Davey," Brian complained groggily, "your elbow's in my throat."

"The kittens are here, Brian!" Davey shook him.

"I heard," he said, burrowing his head into the pillow. "Rachel's going to check them out and bring me a full report."

Rachel sat up, pushed her hair out of her face, and shooed the children from the room. "We'll be right there," she promised with a yawn. "Give us one minute."

As the children ran from the room, Jessica checked her watch and Rachel knew there could be no dawdling. She pushed on Brian's shoulder. "Come on, Brian."

"Why?"

"It's after ten."

"It's Sunday."

"We have to see the kittens. And the kids just found us in bed together." She frowned at him as he rolled toward her. "Aren't you embarrassed?"

Slowly, he propped himself up on an elbow. He was sleep-flushed and disheveled, his stubbly chin accentuating his sexy appeal. "Disappointed. I was going to sleep another half hour, then give you a shower."

Rachel turned down his offer. "I can take my own shower."

"What I had in mind requires two."

"No time for that now," Rachel said briskly, throwing the blankets back. Then she looked into his spellbinding eyes and leaned down to kiss him quickly. "But hold the thought."

Both children were bent over the box when Rachel and Brian made their way into the kitchen. The kittens were a tiny huddled mass of black and white, laying in the protective curve of Susan's body. The cat's eyes were half closed in weariness or pride, it was difficult to tell which.

"You did good," Jessica told Susan, gently stroking her head. "Your babies are beautiful."

Susan Sophia lifted her head into the movement of the girl's hand, beginning to purr. Jessica looked up at Rachel, her eyes bright with excitement and delight.

"Davey says I can name the white one. But how do I know if it's a girl or a boy?"

Rachel looked at Brian with a grin. "You're the wild-life expert."

"You're the one who was raised on a farm," he said, handing her a cup of coffee.

"Wheat is neither male nor female."

Brian squatted down beside Jessica. "Actually, it is a little hard to tell without getting very personal, and Susan Sophia wouldn't like it if we handled them too much yet. What about a name that doesn't have to be male or female. Like . . . snowflake or sugar."

"Crystal!" Jessica said, suddenly inspired.

"That sounds like a girl," Davey protested.

"If it turns out to be a boy, you can call it Chris," Brian suggested. There was a conference of looks from Davey to Jessica to Brian, then a communal nod.

"You're Crystal," Jessica said, rubbing the tiny head with her small index finger.

"What about the other two?" Rachel asked.

Davey grinned broadly. "I've already decided. Vanderweghe and Drexler."

"What kinds of names are those for kittens?" Jessica demanded, indignant.

Davey gave Brian a look that clearly mourned Jessica's lack of knowledge. "They play for the Trailblazers."

"What if the kittens are girls?"

While Davey pondered that problem, Rachel knelt between them and gave the cat's head a stroke. "Then you could give them first names. Like Cathy . . . or Theodora." She suggested the last with a teasing laugh. "And they can still have their last names."

Davey looked up at Rachel as though she had just redeemed herself for many past transgressions. "That's a great idea. Thanks."

"Sure."

ANY KIND OF OUTDOOR ACTIVITY that day was out of the question, as the children refused to leave the kittens. Jessica and Davey sat at the kitchen table compiling a list of first names on the chance that the tuxedo kittens did turn out to be females. Rachel caught up on laundry and tried to restore Brian's house to some semblance of order. His once-a-week housekeeper insisted that she could manage, but Rachel felt obliged to do her share.

With the children in residence there were always jackets and schoolbooks and games and other indicators of their presence strewn around, and no amount of reminders seemed to cure the problem entirely. But Jess and Davey were working together and, by all indications, even having a good time. Rachel would gladly tidy up herself to avoid disturbing that tenuous peace.

Brian was lying under the sink on a towel with plumbing tools spread around him as he worked on a sluggish drain. Unable to resist taking advantage of his vulnerability, Rachel reached down to tickle his ribs as she stepped over him on her way to the refrigerator.

When she found herself staring up at an elbow pipe and the underside of the cabinet a moment later, she decided that had not been a wise move.

"Unless you want to try my idea for the shower in the kitchen sink," Brian warned with a hard kiss on her mouth, "don't harass the plumber."

Rachel scrambled up onto her knees. "You'd think for what you guys get an hour, you could throw in a little sense of humor."

A sturdy swat landed on her backside as she crawled out from under the sink.

Midafternoon, Rachel was returning to the kitchen with a stack of freshly laundered tablecloths and place mats when she overheard a conversation the children were having with Brian.

"Everybody knows how it happens," Davey was saying. "I seen two cats breed once."

"Saw," Brian corrected from under the sink.

Rachel marveled that he thought to correct grammar rather than prepare himself for what was obviously coming.

"Yeah, saw." Davey was sitting cross-legged on the floor by Brian's knees. "They kind of stick together until it's all over."

"Cause they're kissing," Jessica said from the table where she was still working on the list.

Davey cast her a long-suffering look. "It wasn't their lips, dummy."

"Oh." Apparently grasping the significance of Davey's correction but not necessarily horrified by it, Jessica moved to the other side of Brian's knees. "Well, why is that?"

"Do people stick together when they breed?" Davey asked.

Rachel drew a deep breath and decided to maintain her hidden position in the hallway. Brian, at least, had the advantage of his face being under the sink.

Rachel heard a wrench applied to a pipe. "Well, first of all..." There was a grunt as Brian applied pressure to the wrench. "Animals breed. People have sex or they make love."

"What's the difference?" Jessica wanted to know.

"Sex can simply be a way for a man and a woman to . . . to enjoy each other's company," he replied. Something heavy dropped to the floor. "Hand me that washer, Davey. Thanks. And some people look at it that way. But many men and women save it for those with whom they feel something special."

"Love?" from Davey.

"Right. And what passes between you when you make love is something very important."

"A baby," Jessica said.

"Not always—but sometimes."

"Eggs and sperm make babies." Rachel shrank a little closer to the wall as Jessica contributed her knowledge of the specifics to the conversation.

There was a smile in Brian's voice and the sound of him scooting out from under the sink. "Right. And when those magic ingredients are put together, a man and a woman hold each other close because it's such a wonderful thing to share."

"Well, which is it that you and Mom are doing?" Jessica asked candidly. "Having sex or making love."

Rachel screwed her eyes closed through the seemingly interminable silence that followed.

"Making love," Brian finally replied. His voice was firm and convincing.

Doing an abrupt about-face with her stack of clean table linens, Rachel went back to the laundry to find another way to occupy her time until the echoes of that conversation had faded.

Chapter Nine

"What kind of a sweater are you looking for?" Rachel asked, offering a small white sack to Brian. Warmly dressed against a sunny but blustery day, they wandered slowly down Cannon Beach's main street.

He reached into the bag for a chocolate and popped it into his mouth. "Something to make me look worldly and sophisticated in the photo for the dust jacket of my book."

She glanced up at him, grinning. "Something with a mask?"

Brian stopped in the middle of the sidewalk, hands on the hips of his jeans. The wind caught the tail of his green-and-white scarf and fluttered the dark hair on his forehead. "You do not consider me worldly and sophisticated?" he demanded.

"No," Rachel replied without pause. When he looked amusedly disappointed, she held out the sack of candy as a peace offering. "Another starfish?"

Ignoring the proffered bag, he walked past her with an injured air and a lift of that eloquent eyebrow. "No, thank you."

She ran after him. "Actually, it's a compliment," she said as she skipped to keep pace with his long strides.

He stopped again and looked down at her, and for a moment, she really wasn't sure that he was teasing.

"Well, you enjoy everything too much to be worldly," she explained, "and I always think of someone or something that is sophisticated as not being genuine. And you're the most natural—real—person I know."

A small smile softened his expression and grew increasingly indulgent as his eyes went over her face, feature by feature.

"Unless," she added softly, "by sophisticated you mean complex. You are that."

Brian took her chin in his hand, and ignoring the few midweek, midafternoon passersby, stared into her dark eyes. "Well, here's an uncomplicated, unsophisticated, unworldly thought for you," he said, leaning down so that their mouths were a mere inch apart. "I love you." Then he closed the distance and kissed her.

Rachel emerged from his embrace feeling the glow that had warmed her from within for the past two weeks—since the night they had first made love. Brian was so perfect for her—life itself seemed so perfect when she was with him—that whatever problems had once stood between them ceased to exist. She'd been handed a wonderful gift, and she refused to question it.

Brian put his arm around her shoulder and led her forward. "Now, quit distracting me, so we can find a sweater. Penny agreed to try to do without you this afternoon in the interest of this project, so let's get serious about it so we can retire to less public surroundings and more private endeavors."

She pinched the flat waist under her fingers. "Lech."

"Hey, we all have our talents."

When they had gone a block, Rachel stopped, pointing to a shop across the street. "Let's try El Mundo for Men, Brian. My friend Susie works there."

"All right." Taking her hand, he waited for a station wagon to pass then sprinted across the street.

The shop smelled comfortably of natural fabrics and some spicy, exotic fragrance. Rachel spotted Susie across the shop with a customer and waved, indicating that they were in no hurry.

She pulled Brian toward a rack of hats against one wall. "Here's what you need to give you that bon-vivant sportsman image. A hat."

"No." Brian pulled in the other direction, but Rachel dug her toes into the carpeting.

"Come on. This could accentuate your personality." Knowing he disliked the idea, she felt a perverse urge to tease. "Women turn on to hats, Brian."

"Women don't read my books."

"You wouldn't have a bestseller if women weren't reading you, too. What about this?" She pulled down a brown tweed Tyrolean and strained up to put it on his head. As she studied him thoughtfully, he looked into the mirror behind the rack. He turned back to her with a frown.

"I'd have to include a chapter on yodeling."

"It is too alpine looking." She pulled it off his head and replaced it with a Crocodile Dundee hat, complete with fierce, three-inch teeth sewn into the band.

He studied himself and asked quietly, "How could I wear this knowing some poor crocodile is gumming his dinner?"

"I wish I had known you were this hard to please when I got involved with you." Rachel laughed, fitting a white pith helmet on him. "Now, this has a certain elegance."

"I look like Prince Charles headed for the polo field. Rachel..."

"Okay, just one more," she wheedled, reaching up for a western hat with a rolled side brim and braided leather sweatband with a blue and black feather tucked in it.

Brian obligingly bent his knees as she reached up to put it on his head. She tilted it low on his brow and stepped back to check the effect. In the shadow of the brim, his teal-blue eyes took her breath away. He looked gorgeous. As she continued to stare at him without comment, he hooked his thumbs in the belt of his jeans and planted his feet apart.

"Well, pilgrim?" he asked in a fair John Wayne imitation. "What do you think?"

"Hi, Rachel. What can I help you with?" Their playful hat shopping was interrupted by a pretty dark-haired woman with a mischievous smile.

Rachel quickly swept the western hat from Brian's head and put it back, smiling sheepishly at her friend. "Sorry. We were playing with the hats. Susie, this is my friend, Brian Tate. Brian, Susie Burns."

Brian smiled at Susie while indicating Rachel with a tilt of his head. "It's such an embarrassment to take her places."

"How well I know." Ignoring Rachel's gasp of indignation, Susie shook her head sadly at her friend's lack of social graces. "I'm almost grateful that I'm too busy these days to keep company with her. So you're not shopping for a hat?"

"No. A sweater. Something simple."

Susie nodded and started across the shop, Rachel and Brian trailing after her. "Pullover? Cardigan? V-neck? Henley?"

Rachel and Brian frowned at each other, realizing that this was going to require more effort than they had thought. But with Susie's expert help they emerged twenty minutes later with a gray heather London Fog V-neck.

"Let's go home and put it on with that—" Rachel began, sure she knew just the right shirt to be worn under it.

"No," Brian said firmly as he checked the traffic before crossing the street. "We're going home and take it off," he said, his voice filled with seductive promise as he looked down into her upturned face. "Take it all off."

"Oh." Rachel wrapped both arms around his as they hurried in the direction of home. "What a great idea."

ALMOST TWO WEEKS OLD, the kittens were beginning to look less like little mice and more like the offspring Susan Sophia was so proud of. Crystal, already beginning to show signs of Persian in her ancestry, was a fat and fluffy butterball. One of the tuxedos, Drexler, now had the given name of Cathy, but the other, the first to stand and the first to try to escape the box, maintained his masculine identity, growing a little faster than the other two, strutting when he walked.

Susan Sophia and her brood were Rachel's only companions one rainy night in the middle of the week. A note on the refrigerator from the children reminded her that they were at a special baby shower at school for one of the teachers.

But where was Brian? She checked all the places where he might have left a note but found nothing. It began to occur to her that the need to get away might have come upon him. Perhaps he was gone on one of his unscheduled trips.

She'd be the first to understand that things might be closing in on him. Particularly for a man who'd lived most of his life alone, the constant presence of two children was demanding and depleting. Even she found the needs of a second child a challenge to her energy and her patience.

Jessica and Davey had settled down to coexist fairly amicably, but conflicts arose a dozen times a day that were simply the normal process of a child dealing with another child.

Brian's ability to cope with the children had amazed and amused her. Listening to him scold with daunting firmness or comfort with care and kindness, she was reminded of his claim that children made him nervous and he'd prefer not to have them around. He was so especially suited to the role of father that she wondered if he now saw things differently himself. They hadn't discussed it lately. In fact, they had totally avoided all subjects of a serious nature during the past few weeks, almost since the day he'd had that discussion with the children about sex.

And she had been laboring with insecurities since that day. She was now head over heels in love with him, and she knew he loved her. But he hadn't suggested any kind of permanence in their relationship, and she was beginning to suspect that he wouldn't.

In fact, she thought, pacing across the dark kitchen, this might be his way of showing her that despite all that had passed between them in the past month, nothing had changed. And if he felt the need to go off on a camping trip, to take to the woods to seek the comfort he found in nature, then he was free to do it because he was bound to no one. She hadn't the right to worry, and she hadn't the right to complain. Hadn't she suggested the no-strings relationship in the first place?

She laughed mirthlessly when she thought about how little she had known then—about life and love and men.

She had been so sure that a man and a woman could enjoy things together, share children together, even make love, if it came to that, and still maintain a certain distance, a separateness that protected each party's independence.

Then it had come to that and she had seen how wrong she was. It was impossible to enjoy the same things and not be bound by the memories, to share a month of a child's life and not see yourselves in the growth that took place and be proud together. And more, it was impossible to lie in each other's arms at night and not be changed the following day. One couldn't learn the secrets of love, of one's own deepest self, from a man and not want to be bound to him forever.

Rachel sat down at the table with a cup of coffee and realized that Brian must have sensed that need building in her. As well as he knew her now, it must have been as detectable as a change of hair color. The woman with whom he'd embarked on this free and open relationship now wanted to close the exits and make him hers. It came home to her with a sense of despair that he was probably still running.

The children came home at ten, and Rachel hurried them through their baths and preparations for bed, relieved that they were so excited about the party at school that neither stopped to wonder where Brian was. She tucked Jessica in and then Davey and noted that he hugged her a little more tightly than he usually did. She hugged him back and tucked the blankets up under his chin.

"You know," the child said after she turned off the light, "I used to think you were in the way with me and Brian. But you're not. He still likes me even though he loves you. And you do a lot of nice things for me. Things nobody ever did for me before. Like putting my favorite sandwiches in my lunch, and patching my jeans. It's like having a mom, you know?'' Rachel heard him swallow and wanted to offer him some reassurance. But her throat was too tight to allow speech, and Children's Services would be finding his uncle one day soon. ''I know I'm gonna have to go pretty soon, but I never had all this before and . . . it was nice.''

Rachel lay awake in the middle of the bed when Brian came home half an hour later. Having convinced herself that he would be gone for days, or longer, Rachel was stunned and disoriented when the bright bedroom light went on. She sat up, her hair in a wild tangle, her eyes wide and distressed, her nightgown falling off her shoulder from thirty minutes of tossing and turning.

Surprised and angry, she sat up, clutching the blankets to her chest, and demanded, ''What are you doing here?''

Still wearing his leather jacket, his dark hair beaded with rain, Brian stopped just inside the room, confused by her question, concerned by the look in her eyes.

''What's the matter?'' he asked.

''You're missing for hours without a word,'' she accused, ''and you ask me what's the matter?''

He raised an eyebrow at her tone and took several steps into the room. ''I left—'' He began to explain when Davey burst into the room, his eyes wide, his smile uncertain. Rachel now recognized the look as one that said he knew he was in trouble.

''Rachel, I . . . I was supposed to tell you that . . .'' He pointed to Brian, to whom things were suddenly becoming clear. ''Brian got called to this special meeting at the college and said he'd be back—'' He looked at the Star Wars watch that he wore everywhere, even to bed. He looked from Brian to Rachel and smiled sheepishly. ''Before eleven. But I forgot that we were going to that thing at school and I wouldn't be here to tell you. Then I was gonna leave you a note, but I forgot.''

He studied the two brooding adults and sighed deeply. "I blew it again, didn't I? I'm sorry." When his confession was greeted by silence he offered nobly, "I won't watch television for a week."

Brian snaked a hand out and pulled him close, ruffling his hair. "It's okay. But messages are usually important or people wouldn't bother leaving them. Try to remember that."

Davey nodded. He glanced at Rachel. "I didn't remember till I heard Brian's car just now. Then I thought it'd be okay 'cause you never asked us where he was or anythin' when we came home. Then I heard you yelling at him. It was my fault."

Rachel put her head in her hand. It was beginning to ache. "It's okay, Davey. Go on to bed."

She heard Brian walk the boy back to his room, then his footsteps sounded along the hall as he approached their bedroom. He walked in and removed his jacket and pushed up the sleeves of his sweater. He looked tired but composed. She felt exhausted and drained of energy.

She looked at him with weariness in her eyes. He sat in the chair by the bed and rested the ankle of one leg on the knee of the other, waiting for her to explain.

Rachel relaxed against the pillows. "It's been a rough evening."

"What time did the kids get home from the party?" he asked calmly.

"Ten."

He frowned, his manner strangely objective. "And you wondered where I was all that time? Why didn't you ask them when they came home?"

Rachel stretched back and braced her hand on her pillow, looking at him evenly. "Because I thought I knew."

When his continued stare told her that that statement didn't compute for him, she sighed and explained. "I thought you'd left us. That you'd taken one of those trips you told me about where you have to get away and get yourself together."

Anger slipped into the calm set of his features. "Without telling you?"

"My understanding was that you wouldn't have to tell me," Rachel said, a trifle casually because she felt pressured and embarrassed and because the problem remained even though they had stumbled into discussing it by accident. She tossed her rumpled hair and met his gaze. "That you would consider yourself simply free to go when you felt the need. That wife and children would just have to understand. Of course, we aren't—wife or children, I mean. We're all just passing through..."

He was off the chair and on the bed like a shot, his steely fingers capturing the hand with which she made a careless gesture. For a moment they sat staring at each other. His teal-blue eyes were hurt, her dark ones weary. It took a moment of glaring before she could realize that she'd accused him falsely and before he could see her anguish.

With a gentle tug on the hand he held, he pulled her to him, then closed both arms around her as she leaned into him and began to cry.

"I was worried," she said into his shoulder, wrapping her arms around his middle. "I know it breaks all the rules we established, but I can't keep a clinical distance, reminding myself that we haven't promised each other anything. Damn it!" She pushed away to look up at him with tear-filled eyes. "Brian, I think we've turned a corner all right, only you've found nothing there."

Pain formed in Brian's throat then slid down to the pit of his stomach and settled there. He dropped his hands from her and closed his eyes a moment, gathering strength. It had to come to this. He had been a fool to have thought it wouldn't.

Two months ago, when he'd agreed to this relationship, he hadn't really known himself, and he certainly hadn't known her. He hadn't seen the brilliant, warming depths of her, or the needs within himself that found such comfort there. He hadn't expected that she would let him in that far, and he hadn't expected to want to go. It was a revelation to him how vulnerable love made one.

But as much as they could draw from each other, each had needs that couldn't be compromised. She had once put it so simply.

"I love you, Rachel," he said. "I turned the corner and found everything. But I can't give it back to you. You once told me that you need boundaries and I need space. That's our downfall in a nutshell."

She'd had a long evening to agonize over this and she had vowed that she would not cry. She took a Kleenex from the box on the bedside table and dabbed at her nose. She tossed her hair back and asked calmly, "So we let everything die without a struggle?"

He shook his head, his expression weary. "I don't know what we do, Rachel. I swear to God I don't."

"And why worry about it?" She made an impatient gesture with the hand holding the balled-up tissue. "This way you can just declare the situation hopeless and walk away."

Brian looked at her a long moment, his expression hardening. Then he got to his feet. "I'll talk to you when you're calmer."

Rachel grabbed his brawny wrist and used it to pull herself to her feet. The pressure of her full weight didn't even budge him. She squared her shoulders and pointed to her breastbone. "I am not going to *get* calmer. I am frustrated and angry, and I'm tired as hell of tiptoeing around your fear of family."

Had she been any other woman, he would have walked away. But she was Rachel, and though she'd shoved a fist into a raw nerve, something of her took hold of something in him and held it. He waited in silence for her to go on.

For an instant her eyes were filled with regret then she seemed to steel herself and they took on a look that reminded him of the way she dealt with the children when they were challenging her. General Patton couldn't have driven her from her position.

"Remember when we first started seeing each other and you had this thing about not wanting any children?" He didn't nod or reply, he just continued to watch her. "Well, look at the father you've turned out to be. Jessica's own father never cared for or about her as you have. Davey's father might have loved him, I don't know. But he's dead and Davey's had no one until you, Brian." Her voice rose in frustration. "I'd put you up against any man out of *Parents Magazine*."

He folded his arms and looked her in the eye. "Except that I need space."

"Oh, bull, Brian!" Rachel shouted. He shushed her, pointing a finger toward the door to indicate the children asleep across the hall. She went on more quietly, but losing none of her vehemence. "Forget your father! Forget the need to hide because you feel unlovable! You are lovable. The kids adore you and I'd go to hell with you if you asked me, even if we couldn't come back. Remember how much Ben loved you. He was a good man and you valued your relationship with him.''

''Rachel, I am not biologically half Ben Tate. I am half Kenneth Donovan. I am not going to have a kid and turn on him. I'm not going to have a wife and make every day of her life a choice between us.''

''Bull, again! You're one hundred percent Brian Tate. Stop rationalizing the plain old ordinary fear we all have of taking on a family by remembering what your father did to you and making of his feelings more than they were. Put the blame where it belongs. You weren't a bad kid and you weren't in the way—he was selfish. Believe in yourself, Brian. You'll never go on from here if you don't. You are not like him.''

Feeling as though he'd been beaten, Brian ran a hand over his face and tried to collect his thoughts into some semblance of order. Had he really become that psyched out over his father? Was this fear he had of being inadequate just ordinary?

Seeing the dissipation of his resistance to her, Rachel looped her arms around his neck and asked reasonably, ''Where do you think I'd be today if I hadn't believed in myself? If I'd listened to a husband who told me I was not very bright and sexually inadequate?''

Brian couldn't quite believe the smile forming on his lips.

''Sexually inadequate?'' he repeated slowly with a grin of disbelief.

She nodded, her eyes softening. ''Can you believe it? Me, the temptress of the shower and the kitchen sink.''

He chuckled despite himself and pulled her close. For a long time they held each other, each taking what was needed from the embrace while somehow knowing that a small rift had formed that couldn't be simply sealed by a heartfelt hug.

They finally pulled apart and Brian fixed Rachel with a level gaze. His eyes were filled with regret, she thought, and suddenly Rachel was the one who was afraid.

"This is not a great time to be making long-lasting decisions. Davey's in a state of flux, and frankly, so am I." He swallowed, his voice lowering to a grave note. "You know, it's going to be hard to let him go."

Rachel felt emotion well up in her throat and in her eyes. "Do you have to?" she asked.

He nodded with a fractional smile. "I've thought about that. But if he does have family somewhere, he should be with them. He doesn't remember his dad, but he loves the idea of him—it's easy to see that. He should be with someone who can perpetuate that for him. It's important to a boy."

Of course it was; Rachel could acknowledge that. And Brian, to whom a loving father had been nothing but a futile hope during all those early, formative years of his life, would understand that better than anyone. Yet the parting seemed to her such a miscarriage of loving justice. Brian and Davey belonged together. As far as she was concerned, they should be a foursome including Jessica and herself, but she wouldn't dwell on that at the moment. Her dreams had been jostled too severely tonight as it was.

"Look." Brian threaded his fingers into the hair at her temples and his blue-gray eyes looked into her face. She remained quiet under his hands, but he saw that need in her eyes reaching out for him. He deliberately held down his response and saw her eyes register the hurt. He ran his thumbs soothingly over her still damp cheekbones.

"I know you like things tidier than this, Rachel, but I just can't offer you perfect order at this moment. All I can promise is that I love you and that no power, no event, not even rejection of it on your part could ever change that or diminish it in any way." He sighed and pulled her closer to kiss her lightly on the mouth. "If you can hold to that for a little while longer, I promise to try to sort this all out right after we know what's happening with Davey."

She nodded, leaning her forehead against his chin. "I know. I'm sorry. I would never have brought it up now, but I was all upset when you weren't home and I thought...well..." She drew away to look into his eyes, her own soft and apologetic. "I'm sorry. I love you, Brian."

Brian kissed her again then pulled on the covers she had pushed to the foot of the bed. "You'd better get in," he ordered gently. "You're shivering. Go to sleep. I have some paperwork related to that college board meeting and I'd just as soon get it out of the way tonight. I'll be in in a little while."

She didn't want to go to sleep. She wanted to make love to him, to convince him that her love could carry him beyond all his doubts and fears, and banish his memories of his father's indifference forever. But he had asked her to wait and she had promised.

THE TELEPHONE CALL came the following Saturday afternoon. Brian and Rachel had taken the children to Seaside, several miles north of Cannon Beach, where a festive midway stretched from the highway to the beach. In the summer, every shop, arcade and fast-food booth was open and both sides of the street were filled with tourists and what locals chose to brave the summer invasion.

But in the winter, when the wind blew and the ocean stretched out like a rumpled sheet of pewter silk, traffic was thin. Many of the shops were closed, but several arcades remained open, catering to the fun-seeking natives.

"Want to see how good I can shoot?" Davey asked Rachel as he delved into his jacket pocket for quarters. They stood in front of a whimsical mural of a duck pond, where wooden representations of waterfowl swam past in robotic formation. Lined up on a sort of counter that surrounded the scene were a dozen rifles, bolted in place, with a slot for inserting coins to arm the weapons.

Davey stood on a box provided for children, took what looked to Rachel like very professional preparations, aimed and fired. There was a mechanical honk and a mallard fell. Jessica applauded.

Several more ducks fell in rapid succession, then Davey missed one.

"You jerked," Brian said, standing at his shoulder. "Remember to squeeze the trigger."

"Can I try?" Jessica had climbed on the box beside Davey and, using the counter for leverage, was boosting herself up for a closer look at what Davey was doing.

Brian pulled her off the counter and stood her on the box.

"I don't think so, Jess," Rachel said, bracing herself for an argument. When Brian looked down at her in surprise, she said defensively, "Well, I'm not sure it's a good idea for her to learn to handle something so dangerous."

"That's your decision, of course," he replied, resting a hand on the butt of the rifle where Jessica stood. "But do you think it's wiser for her to be ignorant of something potentially dangerous, or to know how to deal with it safely?"

Rachel stood her ground. "I don't want her to know how to hurt things."

Brian looked back at her evenly. "Do you also want her to stand helpless, if something wants to hurt her?"

"That's why she has me."

"Oh." He raised an eyebrow. "Can you use a gun?"

She drew a breath. "No."

"So you would protect her by being a shield. Who would take care of her once you were disposed of?" He looked into her steady glare and grinned. "Although there is a distinct possibility that you could argue anything to death."

Capitulating, Rachel reached into her purse for quarters and handed them over.

"You're sure?"

"Yes." She stepped back, prepared to watch. "But if she grows up to be a big-game hunter, I'm coming after you."

As Jessica giggled at the thought, Brian stood behind her placing her hands appropriately. "Three basic rules," he said, couching the butt of the rifle in her shoulder. "When you're shooting with other people, you always stay behind whoever is shooting. You don't try to get a closer look like you did with Davey."

"Okay."

"And you always treat the gun as though it's loaded. You never point it at anybody or anything."

"Right."

"The third rule's the most important." He turned to the boy firing away beside them. "What is it, Davey?"

Without moving his eye from his target, Davey replied, "You never shoot anything you're not going to eat."

Brian reached over to slap his shoulder. "Good. Okay, Jess. Pick a target that isn't moving."

Jessica indicated a duck perched on a little hill in the mural. "That one."

"Okay." Brian tilted her head until her cheek rested beside the rifle butt. "Close your left eye and try to find your target in the sight." He tapped the notched protrusion of metal down the barrel of the gun. "This thing."

She took a moment. "Okay."

He put his hand over hers on the trigger. "Take a breath."

Jessica drew in a deep, dramatic gulp of air, and she giggled as they all laughed.

"You don't have to inhale the gun, Jess," Brian teased. "Just take an easy breath."

Trying again, Jessica inhaled delicately.

"Okay," he said quietly. "Let just half the breath out, then squeeze the trigger."

She did and missed. As she groaned, Davey laughed. Brian sent him a look and he turned his attention back to his own target.

"It's okay," Brian reassured Jessica. "You have to work at it. Nobody gets it the first time. Just remember the steps and keep trying. Sight the target, take a breath, let half of it out then squeeze."

Brian stepped back to stand beside Rachel. Another round of quarters was required before Jessica finally hit her target. Then she screamed in delight while her supportive audience applauded. Even Davey congratulated her.

As the children played through yet another round of quarters, Brian put his arm around Rachel. "So you're not coming on safari with me?"

Rachel kept her eyes on Jessica, trying not to betray surprise or apprehension. "Are you going?"

"Probably. Some day. Not to kill, just to see. And you wouldn't have to worry about warm socks. The African bush is about one hundred twenty in the shade."

"Thanks," she said lightly. "But I'd rather look in the daisie's eye in that Jewell meadow."

He patted her shoulder and she knew he read her mind. "We'll have lots of time for that, too. No, no. That's enough. It's almost time for dinner." Brian fended off Davey and Jessica, whose ammunition was depleted once again.

"Just one more," Davey pleaded.

Brian stood firm. "That's what you said the last time."

Jessica tugged at his sleeve. "But I was just getting good."

"You'll get better," he said, "if you learn in easy stages. Let's go. Back to the car."

The telephone was ringing when they reached the house and they all scrambled over one another, laughing to get to it. Davey snatched the phone from the hook on the kitchen wall as Jessica stuck her tongue out at him.

The smile on his face died instantly and he lowered the receiver, covering the mouthpiece with his hand. He held it out to Brian.

"It's Mr. McCloskey," he said.

McCloskey, Rachel thought. McCloskey. Why was that name familiar? Finally repetition and the look on Davey's face jogged her memory. It was Brian's friend at Children's Services, the man who was looking for Davey's uncle.

After a brief conversation, Brian hung up the telephone and looked down at Davey, who waited beside him with that remarkable but eerie control firmly in place.

"They found him?" Davey guessed.

Brian put a hand to the back of Davey's head and rubbed gently. "Yeah. He'll be here on Wednesday. We're supposed to meet him at Mr. McCloskey's office."

Davey nodded and swallowed. "Will I have to go with him Wednesday?"

Brian shook his head. "I don't think so. I think they'll give you a couple of days."

Davey looked wordlessly at Brian, his dark eyes full of pain and uncertainty. Brian put his other arm around him and drew him closer, offering the shelter in which the boy could finally let down his emotional defenses if he wanted. But long conditioning had given Davey a fatalistic sense of acceptance that was more adult than child.

"Then I guess I'd better check my stuff and start getting it together," the boy said, firmly pushing Brian's arms aside.

Davey walked quietly to his room. The moment he disappeared, Jessica burst into tears and also ran for her bedroom.

"Jesus," Brian groaned and turned away to the sliding glass doors, leaning a forearm on the metal frame and staring out at the bleak day. It had begun to rain. Rachel put her arms around his waist, leaning her cheek against his back. She felt its rigidity and held him harder.

"Did I do him any favor by letting him stay here?" he asked. His voice was constricted and hoarse. "Now that he has to go?"

"Of course you did," Rachel replied. "The alternative would have been a foster home where he didn't know anyone, and they'd still have found his uncle and he'd still have to move. He was happy here, Brian."

"For a month," he said bitterly. "A pitiful, lousy month. Happiness dangled in front of him and then taken away."

"His uncle might be a wonderful man who'll be delighted to have him and who'll make him happy."

"Davey doesn't let you make him happy," he said. His voice caught, and he paused a moment before going on. "He looks for it himself, and you've got to understand him enough to let him find it. And I think you have to have been looking for it yourself to know where it is."

"And where is it?" she asked gently.

She felt him sigh in her embrace. "In some unconscious memory of his father, I think. He likes physical contact, but only when he's ready. He likes to talk about things, to analyze them beyond what most kids see. He's got a crazy, reckless streak." He uttered a little laugh. "He's a pilot's son. But he's not a brat. At some point that recklessness was brought up short and he can deal with being disciplined without pouting."

"Then your job is to explain all that to his uncle. And trust that he'll be the kind of man who'll understand."

Brian turned away from the doors and leaned against the wall, gathering Rachel to him. He looked sad. "He loves the outdoors," he said, closing his eyes. "And he's going to Boston. That's where my friend found his uncle. God."

Not knowing how else to offer comfort, and feeling in considerable need of it herself, Rachel simply stood in Brian's arms and held him.

Chapter Ten

Harry Wallis turned out to be the kind of man who would understand. Rachel acknowledged that fact with a combination of relief and regret. Had he appeared uninterested in Davey or the least unwilling to assume the fatherly duties Brian had taken on, she felt sure Brian would have resisted. But an hour of talking to Harry Wallis, Davey's only surviving family, proved that he was a nice guy.

Rachel and Brian and Davey were seated on a vinyl sofa in McCloskey's office, and Harry Wallis occupied the chair near the caseworker's desk. Rachel judged Wallis's age at middle to late forties. He was Davey's mother's brother.

"We weren't very close," he admitted to the room at large. "She was more than ten years younger than I was and very spoiled." Realizing that he was disparaging Davey's mother in front of the boy, he changed his tack. "She was pretty, though. Dark like Davey." He smiled at the child and Davey, ever controlled, gave him a fractional smile back. "I knew she had married, though I was in Vietnam at the time. But we never wrote or called or anything. I didn't know about the boy." He looked at McCloskey. "Until you called. Of course, my wife and I would be delighted to have him."

Rachel glanced at Brian, something cold and pointed sinking inside her. So that was that. Harry Wallis was the perfect adoptive parent. And he wanted Davey.

Brian turned to look at her, his eyes surprising her with their uncharacteristic turmoil. Absently, she listened to Wallis talking about his home in a middle-class Boston suburb, its proximity to a fine grade school, his membership in the YMCA, his children's music lessons, all the time her eyes trapped in Brian's.

Silence rose and then hung, heavy and loud. Brian got to his feet, and Davey, sitting beside him, started, and grabbed for his pant leg. Tears burned in Rachel's throat. That was the first overt sign she'd seen from Davey that hinted at how much he needed Brian.

Brian reached down to pull him to his feet.

"Greg," Brian said, his manner suddenly brusque. "Could your secretary take Davey for a Coke, or something?"

Surprised by the request, McCloskey just stared at him for a moment. Then he reached for his intercom button. "Sure."

While the caseworker spoke to his secretary, Davey looked at Brian with suspicion. "Are you gonna sneak out while I'm gone?"

"No, I'm not going to leave," he replied. "But I'd like a little private time with your uncle, okay?"

Davey eyed him evenly. "You're gonna warn him about the bad stuff."

Brian shook his head. "There is no bad stuff, Davey. Just give us a few minutes. I'll be here when you get back."

Rachel's heartbeat threatened to choke her as she sat forward on the sofa. A pretty young redhead came into the office and tried to take Davey by the hand. The boy resisted, choosing instead to follow her. He gave Brian a long look over his shoulder before the door closed behind him.

Brian sat on the edge of McCloskey's desk closest to Wallis. The other man watched him curiously. McCloskey and Rachel shared a questioning look.

"How many children do you have, Mr. Wallis?" Brian asked.

"Four girls," the man replied. "And you can call me Harry." His eyes narrowed on the younger man, not in suspicion, but in consideration. "Do you doubt my willingness to take Davey, Mr. Tate? Or wonder if I'll treat him as well as you have? Mr. McCloskey had all kinds of glowing things to say about you when we talked on the phone."

Brian shook his head, folding his arms. "No. I have fairly good instincts about people, and I've had several days to imagine what kind of person you might be. Had I been able to personally select someone to hand Davey over to, I couldn't be more satisfied." Brian grinned. "Except that you live in Boston and have four daughters."

Wallis nodded. "Four sisters would be hard for any boy to cope with. But what have you got against Boston?"

"Nothing. Except that Davey loves the outdoors."

With a shrug, Wallis shifted in his chair. "We have fairly easy access to hunting and fishing. I'd be willing to see that he was able to enjoy those."

"I'm sure you would." Brian drew a deep breath and got restlessly to his feet. He paced across the room, then back again, stopping in front of McCloskey's desk. He picked a pencil out of a cup and spun it back and forth between his thumb and index finger before perching once more on the mahogany corner.

"Harry," he said finally, "I'd really like to keep Davey. Could you be agreeable to that?"

Rachel and McCloskey stared at each other in surprise. Wallis simply looked back at Brian without replying.

"You're family and I'm not," Brian went on quietly. "And you don't know me from Adam. But in one way and another, Davey and I have been together a lot longer than the month we've waited for Greg to find you. We've established a rapport and he likes being with me. He's been through so much, I think it'd be much less traumatic for him to stay. I care about him a lot, Harry. I'd like to file for custody of him."

McCloskey leaned back in his chair and ran a hand down his face. Wallis turned to him.

"You never said anything about—"

McCloskey shot Brian a look Rachel found hard to interpret. "I didn't know, Mr. Wallis. When I gave you that glowing report on Tate, here, I neglected to mention that he's sometimes impulsive."

Wallis frowned at Brian as though trying to understand this sudden shift in the meeting's purpose. "You can't raise a boy on impulse."

Brian nodded, studying the pencil then dropping it back in the cup. "You're absolutely right. This isn't really impulse, Harry, it's . . . finally understanding, I guess. I had convinced myself that how I felt really didn't matter—that Davey belonged with his family. But he's come to mean a lot to me. I think we mean a lot to each other. I didn't realize how much until we came to this point."

"But you're single, aren't you?" Wallis asked Brian.

Brian considered that a moment then laughed softly. "Sort of," was his artful reply.

Wallis looked from Brian to Rachel, who held his gaze with a smile. Finally, he laughed, too. "Yeah. Okay." He turned to McCloskey. "How does your office feel about that?"

McCloskey riffled some papers on his desk, looking a little harassed. "Well . . . Brian would be the adoptive parent. As far as I'm concerned, he's qualified, probably even ideal." He slid his friend a look that told him he owed him one. "I'd vouch for him."

Wallis continued to look uncertain. "Well, I don't want to tear you and the boy apart, but he is my family . . ."

"Mr. Wallis, you haven't had any time with Davey alone," McCloskey said. "Maybe talking to the boy could help you make a decision." He looked at Brian. "Why don't you take Rachel outside for a few minutes and ask Davey to come in."

Brian paced the polished parquet floor in the outer office while Rachel sat in a chair facing the redheaded secretary's desk and waited.

He'd been a little shocked when he'd heard the words come out of his mouth. "I'd like to file for custody . . ." But then he was getting used to surprising himself—finding that he could love children, two particularly, that he could love and need a woman the way he loved and needed Rachel—that he could voluntarily bind himself with the demands of raising a child. His time would no longer be his own. Strangely, at this moment, that held no terror for him.

Rachel wasn't sure how to think of this morning's turn of events. If Wallis agreed, she'd be delighted because she firmly believed Brian and Davey belonged together. But, then, this was a decision Brian had reached without her, apart from her, and though she was bursting with pride in him, she felt removed from him.

The secretary's phone buzzed. McCloskey's disembodied voice said, "Send Mr. Tate and Mrs. Bennett back in, please."

Rachel smiled encouragingly at Brian as he offered her a hand up. He put his other hand to his stomach, murmuring as the door opened, "I'm going to be sick."

"That won't make a good impression," she warned dryly as they stepped back into the brightly lit office.

Once they were all settled again, McCloskey leaned across his desk toward the boy.

"Davey," he said, "if we can arrange it, would you like to stay with Brian?"

The boy was completely still for a moment, then he looked from the caseworker to Brian in surprise. Hectic thought was visible in his wide, dark eyes. He swallowed.

"Is he kidding?" Davey asked Brian.

Brian looked at Wallis, who shrugged and smiled.

"No." Brian shook his head. "Your uncle would like to have you stay with him. He's got a neat place in Boston with lots of good ideas about things you could do. If you'd like to go, we'd all be happy for you. But if you'd rather stay, I'd like you to live with me. That would be okay with your uncle, and Mr. McCloskey can arrange it. The choice is yours."

Watching the boy's eyes clinging to Brian's, his mouth working unsteadily, Rachel thought it would come now—the release. The collection of grief and anxiety Davey had been carrying so long was within a breath of being expelled on a sob or a scream. She waited. She felt Brian waiting.

But Davey merely firmed his lips and swallowed. "Yeah," he said, turning to McCloskey. "I'd like to stay." Facing his uncle, he explained his decision by offering apologetically, "Me and Brian are friends."

Wallis nodded and smiled. "I understand. Well..." He stood, reaching across the desk to shake McCloskey's hand. Then he moved across the room and Brian stood offering his. Wallis studied Brian for a moment, then took the hand he offered. "When Mr. McCloskey suggested I talk to Davey, I expected to be outweighed in his estimation by all your accomplishments as an outdoorsman. I expected to hear about how you took him fly-fishing and hunting for elk. When I finally got the young man to talk—" Wallis and Brian exchanged a grin and both men looked down at Davey, who didn't understand the joke "—it was 'Brian fixed my bike,' 'Brian yelled at me 'cause I rode down a hill with Jennifer—' "

"Jessica," Davey corrected.

" 'Jessica on the handlebars,' 'Brian makes the best chili.' " Wallis slapped Brian's shoulder. "You two are family. I'd be the intruder. Listen, if you ever venture east I want your promise that you'll stop in Boston."

"You've got it. And if you get a chance to venture west, come and see us."

"I will." Wallis took Davey in a bear hug. "I'm awfully glad to know you're here, Davey. We've got to keep in touch, okay? I'm not a very good letter-writer, but I can pick up the telephone. Send me a picture once in a while to let me see how you're growing."

Davey nodded, his face full of color, his eyes bright. When he put his small hand out to have it swallowed by his uncle's, Rachel noticed that it was shaking. It's coming, she thought again.

But Davey held strong emotion at bay, behaving almost normally when they stopped for lunch after leaving McCloskey's office. He seemed no more than moderately pleased that his life was finally taking a direction he had chosen.

"Do I have to go back to school after lunch?" he asked. He was wolfing down a hamburger, dabbing the tip of a French fry in catsup.

Brian looked at Davey, trying to judge, Rachel was sure, whether or not he was emotionally ready to return to the routine of the classroom. There was nothing about him to indicate that he wasn't.

"Think you should?"

"I s'pose. We're having this English test."

Rachel, having finished a small salad, took a French fry off his plate. "You *want* to go back to take a test?"

"Well, I don't want to," Davey explained. "But if I'm gonna be a writer like Brian, I need to know all that stuff. Besides, if I don't go back to school, Jessica'll be jealous, and you know what that means."

Brian grinned at Rachel over half a roast-beef sandwich. "What does it mean?"

"Trouble!" she and Davey replied simultaneously.

After lunch Brian dropped Davey off at school then took Rachel to work. As he pulled up in front of her shop, she turned in her seat to look at him, her eyes expressing a thousand things she suddenly found hard to say. She had no idea how to tell him how proud she was of him or what a fine thing he had done. She didn't dare consider what it meant to their relationship.

"I love you," she said softly and reached forward to kiss him.

He met her halfway. "I love you, too. Have we got stuff for dinner?"

Such a mundane question after such a momentous morning, Rachel thought. But that was life, she supposed, from stunning to ordinary in a matter of moments. "I think so. Just keep working, and I'll take care of it when I get home. See you at six."

Penny watched Rachel's face for some sign of how the morning had gone. "How's the uncle?" she asked.

Rachel picked up the mail from the desk behind the counter and flipped through it. "Mr. Wallis seems like a wonderful man. Everybody liked him."

Penny sounded disappointed. "Oh. So when's Davey... going?"

Rachel tossed the mail back on the desk. "He's not. Brian and Davey's uncle talked it over, and Brian's filing for custody."

Penny's mouth fell open. "You're kidding."

"Nope."

"Well..." Penny smiled broadly, waiting for Rachel to tell her more. When she didn't, she asked carefully, "So are you guys... I mean, did he ask you... will you be getting—?"

"Don't ask me!" Rachel finally said loudly. She stormed into the stockroom, suddenly frustrated beyond endurance. Penny followed. "How would I know? I'm only the second party in a casual relationship."

Penny leaned against the doorframe. "It isn't casual, and you know it."

Rachel fell into her chair. "I know it, but does Brian know it?"

"He knows it." At the sound of a voice that wasn't Penny's, Rachel spun around in her chair to see Alicia standing beside her assistant. "Forgive me for intruding, but I stopped by to see how this morning went. Does your understandable frustration with my son mean it went badly?"

Penny excused herself, and Rachel invited Alicia in, gesturing her toward the stack of boxes that served as a seat. Rachel noted that she looked worried. Alicia was a fan of Davey's and never visited her son without bringing something for the boy and Jessica.

"Can I give that a two-part reply?" Rachel asked with a small smile.

Alicia rolled her eyes and nodded. "Brian is complex."

Rachel sat back in her chair and tried to recapture how she had felt when Brian asked Harry Wallis if he would relinquish his right to custody of Davey. "Actually, Alicia, you'd have been so proud of Brian today. He's filing for custody of Davey."

Alicia stared for a long moment. "The uncle didn't want Davey?"

"Harry Wallis was a great guy. He really wanted Davey. But once he was convinced that the boy was happy with Brian, he agreed to let Brian have him."

Alicia unbuttoned her cloak and pulled it off her shoulders. "Well, my stars. There might be hope for the old boy yet." She narrowed her eyes on Rachel. "Or do you want to give me part two of your reply?"

"Part two is that he loves me..." Rachel paused and opened her hands in a gesture of helplessness. "But I'm not convinced that he wants to spend his life with me."

"Horse puckey!"

That epithet coming from the elegantly clad and genteel artist brought a smile to Rachel's lips. "Puckey?"

"I'm trying to consider your sensitivities. On the other hand, sometimes plain talk is required. You're crazy. He loves you; it's obvious to the whole world, if not to you."

Rachel nodded. "I know he loves me. I just don't think he trusts me to be what he needs... or something like that." She lowered her head to her hands in confusion. "Oh, I don't know. The four of us have such a good time together. Brian and I manage the kids and the house and our lives together with such compatibility that it's as if some precision-die maker created us for it. But he doesn't seem to see that. We start to get close, he draws back and I confront him, then we argue." Rachel stood and leaned against the taller stack of boxes next to which Alicia sat. She bent an elbow on the top box and leaned her head against her open hand. "If the day comes that I have to walk away from him, I'll survive, but I'll never be me again. And Jessica will be devastated. But I refuse to spend the rest of my life raising two children with a man who's just my lover."

"I don't blame you, of course. But maybe now that the issue of Davey is settled, he'll begin thinking in more permanent terms."

Rachel smiled grimly. "I hope so. But I seriously doubt it."

"Well . . ." Alicia pulled her cape on again. "If there's anything I can do, for you or *to* him, don't hesitate to call." She stood, buttoning her cloak. "You know, feeling love and trusting love are two very different things. When Brian was little, part of the love he trusted failed him." With a sad smile Alicia leaned down to hug Rachel. "I was sure he wouldn't have anything to do with a family in any form, yet here he is on the brink of adopting a son, and keeping you around like a wife." She patted Rachel's cheek and turned away toward the door. She paused a moment to add over her shoulder, "One day it will occur to him that whether you two have a license or not, he's committed to the relationship. Bye, dear."

"Bye, Alicia."

And when he comes to that conclusion, Rachel thought, falling exasperatedly into her chair, he'll figure, why marry her anyway.

Chapter Eleven

By the time Rachel pulled into the driveway of Brian's home, she was determined to be patient. Brian had made an enormous decision today, and at the moment, he needed nothing more on his mind. His book deadline was now three weeks away and she would do all she could to see that home life ran smoothly, that Davey really settled in, that Jessica was happy and that Brian had his writing time.

Davey talked continually through dinner, his color a little high. But he helped Jessica clear the table and fill the dishwasher then went to his room to do homework. That task finished, he argued with Jessica over television, as was customary, had a snack and went to bed. He never brought up the subject of staying with Brian, or asked any questions about the future.

Poor kid's as confused as I am, Rachel thought as she tucked him in.

Answering a knock at the door an hour later, Rachel found Alicia on the porch, a round cake-carrier in hand. In jeans, a puffy white jacket and a red angora scarf, she managed to look glamorous.

"I felt like baking something," she explained, "and wanted someone to share it with. Got any ice cream?"

Brian, stoking the fire, turned to shake his head as Rachel helped Alicia off with her jacket. "The kids finished it off when they got home from school." He got to his feet, brushed off the knees of his jeans and went to hug his mother. "Nice thought, Mom. Hold on and I'll run to the market."

"Take Rachel with you," she called over her shoulder as she took the cake into the kitchen. "I'll put on the coffee."

Pulling up in front of the small, twenty-four-hour convenience store on the outskirts of Cannon Beach, Brian turned off the Porsche's motor and looked at Rachel. "I hope you appreciate the extent to which I have spoiled you."

She raised an eyebrow. "By allowing me to accompany you to the market?"

"Well." He jumped out of the car and walked around to open her door. "That may not seem like much in itself, but last Wednesday you took the truck to be lubed, Friday you shopped for plumbing parts and just this morning you had several fun-filled hours at the state building in Astoria."

"True." With a dry glance at Brian, Rachel passed before him into the brightly lit store. "If this pace continues, I'll be completely corrupted by spring." She walked down the freezer aisle and stopped in front of the ice cream. "Vanilla?"

When Brian didn't answer, she looked up in time to lose herself in his very indulgent smile. "Do you have any idea how I feel about you?" he asked lazily.

Rachel's heart lurched. Was she going to hear it at last? Tell me, please, she thought. Make it clear.

But a brown-coated arm reached between them with a quick "Excuse me" from its owner, who secured a small container of Häagen-Dazs. The shopper, a stout woman in her sixties, lingered nearby to study sauces.

Brian cleared his throat, the sudden intimacy gone. "Vanilla is so pedestrian. Any other ideas?"

Requiring a moment to recover from her long-sought-after brush with the truth, Rachel studied the selection. "Chocolate?" she proposed.

Brian shook his head.

"Sherbet?"

"No."

Rachel shifted her weight. "Well, what kind of a cake is it?"

Shrugging, Brian picked up a carton and studied the ingredients. "I don't know. Didn't you check?"

Rachel rolled her eyes. "Do I have to do everything? I bought the plumbing parts, remember?"

Brian put the carton down decisively. "Mom always makes chocolate cakes."

Rachel handed him a half-gallon with a picture of a sandwich cookie on it. "Cookies and cream, then. That's perfect."

The decision made, they drove home with the insulated bag between them, Brian whistling, Rachel wondering what he would have said his feelings were if he hadn't been interrupted.

The scream was audible the moment Brian turned the motor off and opened the driver's side door. The sound was high and filled with anguish, and coming from the house. It was repeated again while Brian and Rachel stared at each other in surprised silence. Interspersed with it was the anxious sound of Alicia's voice.

Brian bolted for the house with Rachel at his heels. The door was yanked open by a very pale Jessica. Brian caught her shoulders. "Are you all right?"

She pointed in the direction of the kitchen. "It's Davey!"

The sound of a struggle came from the kitchen, with more screaming. But this time the sound had form; Davey was calling for Brian.

As Brian sprinted for the kitchen, Davey came running out, a disheveled Alicia in pursuit. Davey's eyes were not quite focused and his chest was heaving.

Blindly, Davey ran past Brian, who caught him by the back of his pajama top. The boy struggled against him as he turned him around and held him still, giving him a little shake as he said his name. "Davey!"

Davey looked into Brian's face and reality finally penetrated hysteria. "Brian?" The boy's voice was uneven and hoarse. His finally focused eyes went over Brian once more then his face puckered and he said accusingly, "You were gone."

"Only to the store." Brian pulled the boy up into his arms. Davey's legs wrapped around his waist and his hands clung to the shoulders of Brian's jacket. "I wouldn't leave you," he scolded gently. "You know that."

The anguish and the tension seemed to leave the child suddenly and he slumped against Brian. "I guess I just dreamed that you left." His voice broke and he began to cry, a normal, even weeping that allowed Brian to draw the first even breath since he'd opened his car door and heard the scream. He wrapped his arms around him and rocked him gently from side to side.

"He woke up and came into the kitchen looking for you," Alicia said, putting a comforting hand to Davey's back as she approached Brian. "When you weren't there, he just...got desperate. I couldn't convince him that you'd be right back."

"He told me that he thought you'd change your mind about keeping him," Jessica explained, dark-eyed and pale in her sprigged flannel nightgown. "When he woke up and you were gone, I guess he thought you really had."

"Can I do anything?" Rachel asked.

"I think he'll be okay with something warm to drink and a few minutes in a hot bath." Brian tried to sound brusque, though he felt shaken. "Would you mind running a tub for him? Mom, get yourself a cup of coffee and sit down with Jess."

He carried Davey into the kitchen and rested the child's weight on the counter. When Davey clutched the back of his shirt, resisting his efforts to move away long enough to get the coffeepot, Brian worked one-handed. He made a small portion of a coffee nudge, and added a teaspoon of sugar after the brandy. He pulled Davey far enough away to hand him the cup.

Finally composed, the boy looked suspiciously into the cup then into Brian's eyes. "What is it?"

"Ah…" Brian searched his mind for a reply that would make him drink it. "We call it camper's brew."

Davey frowned. "Yeah?"

"Yeah. We drink it around the fire after a rough day. Only you're going to drink it in the bathtub."

"Brian?" Davey put a hand on Brian's shoulder when he would have pulled him off the counter.

"Yeah?"

"It was a good day," he said. Davey looked into the cup, and Brian saw that he was almost himself again, though embarrassed and confused. "I mean, this morning was good." He looked up, his eyes and his smile tentative but bright. "I couldn't believe it when they said I could stay with you. Then…" He sobered and a pleat formed between his eyebrows. Brian saw the hands holding the cup begin to shake and the boy's mouth worked unsteadily.

"Say what you're thinking," Brian told him quietly, rubbing small circles on his back. "You don't have to hide anything or be afraid of it."

Davey drew a deep sigh and the last bout of anguish took hold of him. He wept softly. "Then...then I remembered all the other times...good things were supposed to happen. My mom said we were gonna buy a white house and have a puppy and not have to move so much 'cause my dad was gonna quit, only he died instead. Then I thought her and me would have the house and...the puppy, only she left." He lifted a shoulder, partly an expression of confusion, partly a withdrawal from pain. "Then me and Grandma were gonna do all kinds of things and she got sick and...died." He gulped on a sob and looked at Brian with a despair that cut his heart out. "I just knew you were gonna change your mind. I thought about it all afternoon. Great things are always gonna happen—but they don't. Not to me. Then I went to bed and I dreamed about it, and when I woke up...you were gone."

Davey fell against him and Brian put the cup aside, holding him close and rocking him until the sobbing stopped.

"I haven't changed my mind," he said. "You are staying with me. We are staying together. You have to trust me. Shall we toast to it?"

Brian poured himself a cup of coffee, dropped a dram of brandy in it and clinked the cup against Davey's. The boy drank it down.

"Okay." He lifted him off the counter and led him away. "Into the tub to warm you up, and then we'd better get you back to bed."

Rachel, Jessica and Alicia sat around the kitchen table, waiting for Brian and a report on Davey.

"That was scary," Jessica admitted gravely, both hands holding tight to a cup of cocoa. She looked at Rachel, obviously affected by what she had witnessed. "Sometimes I felt sorry for myself 'cause I didn't have a dad, then I felt sorry for Davey 'cause he didn't have a mom *or* a dad. That was even worse." Jessica shook her head and blew delicately into her cup. "But I didn't really understand what that would be like, until I saw his face when he was screaming for Brian. I've never been that scared, Mom. Even that time when I lost you in that big store in Portland. I was a little scared, but I knew you'd find me. Imagine what it would be like to think that you didn't have anyone."

Brian walked into the kitchen feeling as though he'd just wrestled a grizzly to the ground with his bare hands and finally emerged the victor. His neck and shoulders were stiff from the tension of the past half hour and his arms ached from holding and carrying Davey. Yet he felt oddly at peace. After years of refusing to share any serious, caring emotions with anyone except his mother and Ben, he understood why. He had given. Forced to repeat the promises to Davey over and over—I will never leave you, we will always be together—he'd had to commit himself without qualification. That was something he could not have done before he had loved and been loved by Rachel.

Rachel and Jessica looked up at him as he went to the coffeepot. Alicia was slipping into her coat.

"He's asleep," Brian said, without being asked. He refilled the cup he was carrying and put it on the table next to Jessica and across from Rachel.

Alicia put her arms around his neck. "I guess the cake and ice cream can wait till tomorrow. If I can do anything you'll call me?"

"Promise."

She gave him a tremulous smile and another hug. "I love you, Brian. I'll see myself out."

As Alicia disappeared, Brian sat at the table, frowning at Rachel. "Is she okay?"

"I think it's just maternal pride," she replied, sipping at her coffee, dealing with strong feelings of her own. "It makes a mother emotional to know she's raised a giving, caring human being."

Jessica stood and made a production of trying to be casual. "I'd better get to bed. You guys probably want to...I mean—"

"Wait a minute." Brian caught Jessica's wrist as she moved past him and pulled her onto his knee. Rachel saw that she was delighted and surprised by the action, probably having presumed that there'd be little attention left for her tonight. Rachel acknowledged silently that there were moments when his intuition amazed her.

"So how are you?" he asked, putting his cup aside to hold Jessica loosely.

"Lucky," she replied. He waited for her to explain, and when she did so, she spoke as though the reason should be obvious. "I have Mom, and Mom and I have you."

He glanced at Rachel, who caught the look and held it.

"You're gonna adopt Davey," Jessica said.

Brian looked down at her and nodded.

"That's neat." Her voice went very soft and she lowered her eyes. Rachel saw a trace of jealousy in them. Then the child yawned mightily and gave Brian a hug. "Night." Then she got to her feet and went around the table to hug Rachel. "Good night, Mom."

Rachel held her a moment longer than was necessary, then felt obliged to remind her, "Don't forget to brush your teeth again after the cocoa."

With a roll of her eyes, Jessica disappeared down the hallway. When Rachel turned back to Brian, he was coming around the table to pull her to her feet.

"Let's move to the fireplace," he suggested.

As had become a habit, he lay on his side before the blazing warmth, a bent elbow bracing his head, and Rachel lay curled up beside him. She reached to the sofa for a cushion and the afghan that lay across the arm.

Brian raised his elbow to let her stuff the pillow under it. She spread the afghan over him, then, discovering that left none of it for herself, gave him an apologetic smile, snatched it off him and covered herself with it.

"Then you have the nerve to snuggle against me for warmth," he said, mockingly indignant even as he pulled her closer and tucked the afghan in at her neck.

For several moments the only sounds in the room were the crackle of the fire and the quiet ticking of the clock. Then Brian asked, "Will you marry me?"

Rachel didn't recall receiving a blow to the head, yet she distinctly heard the proposal. With a hand to his chest, she pushed him aside so that she could look into his face. He wasn't laughing or even smiling. She put an elbow on the pillow and stared down at him. He looked quite serious. "Huh?" she asked.

He repeated, enunciating carefully, "Will you marry me?"

Rachel continued to stare at him. That had been pretty clear; she hadn't misunderstood. Wondering what was motivating him, why he had chosen the aftermath of such a traumatic scene to ask her, it occurred to her to worry about that later and reply while she had the chance. "Yes," she said.

"Good. Right after the deadline? The middle of April?"

He had thought about it. He was making definite plans. "Yes."

Rachel rested her cheek on his chest in disbelief. Then she looked into his face again as though to reassure herself that she wasn't hallucinating. Brian had proposed marriage. Excitement began to pulse in her.

He reached up with both hands to push her hair back and hold it there. "One thing," he said. She felt his body tense under her. "I'd like to reserve the right to take off occasionally when I need to. Not for long, but for a few days at a time—maybe a week."

Silence fell between them, and with it distance. Rachel pushed herself to a sitting position, her momentary euphoria doused. She was sure now that she wasn't hallucinating. That careful withholding of himself was the real Brian, all right.

Brian didn't move. He felt their closeness dissolve and leave a yawning hole where it had been. He didn't know how to make her understand how important that particular freedom was to him. And he felt hurt that she wouldn't accept it without understanding it. He stared at the moving shadows on the ceiling.

"That's always been a part of me, Rachel. I have to be able to do that."

Rachel pulled her knees up and wrapped her arms around them, staring into the fire. "I would be a part of you, Brian. I'd resent it that you'd renew yourself by separating yourself from me."

"It isn't the being away that does it," he explained patiently. "It's the being with myself."

Brian saw Rachel's back stiffen. "The best way to be with yourself, Brian, is to stay single."

He sat up and studied the rigid line of her shoulders as she dropped her knees to sit Indian-style, still turned away from him. "I used to think that," he said softly. "Until you."

He heard her sigh then she leaned her head sideways and her hair fell to one shoulder, the rich brown dancing with highlights from the fire. "Then why doesn't it make a difference?"

"It makes a difference to everything else but that."

She swung her legs to one side to turn and face him. Her cheeks were red from the fire or temper, he wasn't sure which. There was disappointment in her eyes. "Then you don't love me."

He shook his head in exasperation. "I do. But how can you deny me what I need to keep my life and myself in order and say that *you* love *me*?"

"Because you're keeping an option open for getting out. That doesn't sound committed to me."

"It's an option for renewal, not for escape."

Rachel sighed again and got to her feet. "You were right in the beginning, Brian. Your habits wouldn't fit well in a family."

He, too, rose, and he looked down at her, hands on his hips. He was angry now. "And you were right, as well. You've become too independent to fit into a relationship."

"Because..." She began to shout, then quieted when he shushed her. "Because I want to be sure you'll be there."

"Because you can't give me any slack. You want it your way or not at all."

"And what would I tell Jess and Davey when their father disappears?"

His eyes darkened. "I have never cut them short and you know I wouldn't. And I imagine it'll be some time before I can go anywhere without taking Davey with me."

"I see. You'd take the child with you. But you'd have to get away from me."

"Not get away from you," he said carefully, "but—"

"I know. Be with yourself." She folded her arms and shifted her weight to one foot. "And having Davey with you won't interfere with that?"

He assumed the same stance in imitation of her deliberate refusal to be reasonable. "No, it wouldn't. Because he isn't always trying to shake a commitment out of me as though it were loose change to which he was entitled. He invades my 'space'..." He gave the word that continued to come up between them an emphatic accent. "But he doesn't put walls up around it."

"You just said," she pointed out, "that it'll be some time before you'll be going anywhere without taking Davey with you. That isn't walls?"

"The difference is," he replied, "that I put them up. I'll stay where he needs me."

She nodded grimly. "But not where I need you."

"You need me always in front of your feet." He sighed and she heard the pain in it. And the finality. "No. I won't."

Rachel dropped her arms. "I have never demanded that of you, and it isn't fair to accuse me of it."

"Not demanded but expected." He shrugged as though the difference were negligible. "Same thing."

Her temper flared but she reminded calmly, "All I expected was friendship, remember. You're the one who wanted to turn a corner."

"It was inevitable and you know it. Friendship turned to love almost instantly, and that's when you began to grasp. Maybe you're afraid that because Jarrod couldn't give it to you, you'll never have it." He had paced across the room as he spoke, emptying random thoughts at her in frustration. When he saw her eyes come up at that, he stopped. He took several steps toward her, his mind working. "Or maybe you're afraid that part of the problem was you." He stopped directly in front of her. She seemed rooted to the spot. Anger had left her and she was stunned by what he'd said, as though seeing that possibility for the first time herself. "Maybe," he went on quietly, "you sometimes feel as unlovable as I used to. Only instead of withdrawing, as I did, you reach out and clutch, afraid love will get away."

He should have known, Brian thought, as her eyes focused on his, filled with fury once again. Telling her what he suspected to be the truth wouldn't make her see, it would just make her hurt. And seeing him as the object of her pain, she would have to remove him.

She turned to spin away from him, to run, and he caught her arm. She was coiled and tense. "Let yourself think about it." He shook her lightly. "Is it true? Are you afraid that your love for me isn't strong enough to make me come back? If you are, it's a rootless fear. I love you, Rachel. I swear it."

She pulled against him. "As long as I don't try to hold you."

He held fast. "I proposed marriage, remember. You can hold me, just don't . . . don't stand on me to keep me there."

"Brian, I don't think you want to be married." Rachel forced herself to speak calmly. "I think you asked me because you have a son now, and with that comes some feeling that you should conform. That would be wrong.''

"You're saying you don't want to get married?" he demanded with strained patience.

Rachel sighed, feeling the real demands of day-to-day living closing in to destroy the little parody of life they had created. "I'm saying that I think it's time for me to go."

"No," he said, stiffening.

"All we do is go around and around the problem," she said frustratedly. "There's no way through it for us."

"Because you won't give a little," he accused.

Rachel felt suddenly drained of anger and all other emotion. The argument seemed to demand more energy, more spirit than she possessed.

"We agreed on this a long time ago," she said wearily. "We promised not to make demands on each other that couldn't be met. Well, you can't be what I want, and I don't seem to be right for you any longer." She finished on a high note, her voice close to breaking. "It's time to let each other go."

Brian had the sensation of having been set afire, the pain was so great. With eyes dark and anguished, he studied her face and saw with dawning dread that she meant it. It was over. Gently, he dropped his hand from her arm.

"If that's what you want."

"Oh, Brian," she said on a gulp of emotion. "How could that be what I want?"

"And the kids?"

Rachel folded her arms and resolutely kept her composure. "If we tell them together, maybe they'll understand—or at least accept."

"I don't understand." He paced away from her, stopping at the fireplace to turn and glare at her. "And I sure as hell don't accept. I won't do that to Davey after what he's just been through."

Of course the children had to be their first consideration. "I'll stay with you until you meet your deadline. We ought to be able to be civil to each other for two weeks. Then we'll find a way to tell them."

"It's the coward's way out," Brian insisted.

Rachel drew a ragged breath. "Yes. Well, I never claimed to be a heroine. Good night, Brian."

Chapter Twelve

"Butter?"

"Please. And salt and pepper. Thank you."

"You're welcome. Shall I pour for you?"

"Please."

Rachel and Brian had refined civility to an art form—and neither had ever been more miserable. Rachel reflected that good manners held nothing in common with loving kindness, and no amount of Brian's careful deference would ever compensate her for the loss of his teasing and his smile.

Brian worked resolutely on his revisions, driven by the pressure of time and by the pain of being near Rachel and seeing the light gone out of her. The sunny, vital woman eager to argue with him or to make love with him was gone. In her place was a woman he didn't know, and worse, one who seemed not to know him. Days passed in a blur of work and strained politeness.

The children were standing at the kitchen table, giggling, when Rachel came home from work on a Saturday afternoon. Brian stood behind them with a smile. It was a weak one, Rachel noted, but it was a smile. She took a moment to simply stare at it after two long weeks of that cold civility between them.

"What's going on?" she asked, finally advancing into the room.

At the sound of her voice Brian looked up, the smile remaining in place as he invited her to share the moment. His eyes stayed on her, caressing her as she smiled back. Then he tore his gaze away from her and indicated the open box on the table, filled with one revised manuscript—and one sleeping kitten. Cathy Drexler curled a paw over her nose as she sought privacy from her noisy audience.

"Brian left it for a minute because he forgot his cover letter," Jessica explained. "And Drex thought it looked roomier than Susan's box."

Reaching out to stroke the kitten, Rachel laughed with the children, until she realized that the manuscript in its mailing box meant it was finished—and she had no more reason to stay.

Brian saw the fact hit her, then braced himself when she raised her eyes to him. There was a moment's pleading in her stricken gaze, then accusation, then a grim acceptance, followed by the overpowering loneliness he'd known so well himself the past few weeks.

Rachel moved away from the table to pull her coat off and go to the closet.

"Brian's taking us for hamburgers and banana splits!" Davey announced, following her. "To sort of celebrate. We're gonna leave the car so we can walk back along the beach."

An odd plan for a chilly, overcast March afternoon, Rachel thought. Until she looked over Jessica's head at Brian and saw the grimness in his face. It was time to tell the children.

"SO WHEN IS RACHEL LEAVING?" Davey asked.

Brian and Rachel, walking several feet apart along the water's edge, stopped in unison, looking at each other in surprise. During their lunch at the Lemon Tree there had been nothing about his behavior to indicate he suspected the impending separation.

Rachel turned to Jessica, who was trailing along behind them, and saw that she, too, awaited an answer. This was apparently something the children had discussed.

Davey shrugged under his blue down jacket. "Well, isn't that why we're taking this walk?" He kicked at a broken sand dollar and continued walking. "We're not dumb, you know."

Davey's frontal attack shook the calm, reasonable explanation she'd been formulating since lunch. Fortunately, Brian seemed to have recovered.

"I know." Brian put an arm around him. He searched his mind desperately for a logical explanation of something that made no sense. Finally deciding that honesty, even in confusion, was preferable to evasion, he tried to make the situation clear. "You're right. That's why we're taking this walk. But it's hard for us to explain to you something we don't entirely understand ourselves."

"Aren't you in love any more?"

Rachel knew there had to be a reassuring answer to his question, but she'd been searching for some comfort in all this for herself and had found precious little. Jessica fell into step beside her but with enough distance between them to express disapproval and outright hostility.

"We heard you fighting," Jessica explained.

Rachel nodded, finally finding her voice. "We've done a lot of that lately. I'm sorry. I know it hasn't been very pleasant for you."

"Leaving would be worse," Jessica said.

Brian and Davey stopped, waiting for Rachel and Jessica to catch up. "It would seem worse at the beginning." As the wind whipped around them, Brian pulled up Jessica's hood in a possessive, paternal way he wasn't even aware of. Rachel saw the gesture and turned away, unable to bear it. "But in the end, you'll see that it was the right thing to do after all. When you're fighting all the time, it makes it hard for good things to happen, for people to be happy."

"Why do you fight?"

"Because Brian needs different things out of life than I need," Rachel replied quietly. "And it's hard to live together when you don't want the same thing."

"But you always tell us to try to share," Davey pointed out reasonably, "and to try to see the other guy's side of things."

"That works for getting along with strangers." Brian nodded. "And even friends, but for a man and a woman to live together as husband and wife, they have to be in tune about the important things. They have to be looking in the same direction or it doesn't work."

"But how come," Jessica demanded, her voice distressed, "we all had so much fun for so long, then all of a sudden it isn't fun anymore?"

They had reached an uprooted tree trunk, flung out of the ocean in some angry storm, and Brian pointed to it. "Let's stop and sit for a few minutes."

He sat on the trunk, a child on each side of him and Rachel on the other side of Jessica. The air was full of the smell of rain and of the ocean, and sea gulls circled them, calling mournfully.

"We had a lot of fun because we were friends then. And because we enjoyed each other so much, we wanted to be more than friends. And that's where we had trouble."

"Then can't you just stay friends?"

"We will stay friends," Brian said firmly, "but we can't stay together. You can't go backward in a relationship, only forward."

"And for us, forward doesn't work." Rachel put an arm around Jessica. "So we just have to stop."

"Well, I think it's crummy!" Jessica blurted, her face contorting, tears falling freely.

"You're right." Brian patted her knee, his stormy gaze bouncing off Rachel's woeful expression as he sought to comfort the child. "We all think so. It will hurt all of us, but that doesn't mean that we can't go on—separately— and eventually be just fine."

The hell it didn't, he thought, but kept that to himself. He turned to Davey and pulled him close. "Do you understand?"

"No," the boy replied candidly. "I've moved around a lot, you know, and I never understand. I guess I don't have to. So... when?"

Brian, as well as the children, waited for Rachel's answer.

"Day after tomorrow," she said as gently but as firmly as she could. A day to pack was all she needed, and there was no point in prolonging the inevitable. She would call Penny and arrange to come in late on Monday.

For several moments no one moved or spoke. Then Jessica, tears still flowing, stood. "If you guys are going to sit here for a while, can I go back myself?"

Rachel nodded. Brian reached into his pocket to hand her the house key. She turned away and began to run.

"Guess I'll go, too," Davey said, and followed after her.

Rachel stared out at the horizon, wondering if there was any pain more unbearable than knowing you'd caused pain in someone else, particularly someone you loved. "Well, we've made one hell of a mess."

"Yeah," Brian agreed. "Hard to believe that something that feels so right can end this way."

Rachel laughed mirthlessly. "It takes great skill. We'd better go. I don't want them to be alone too long the way they feel."

"Right." Brian got to his feet, and they walked back to the house as black clouds thickened overhead.

THE DUPLEX SEEMED small and lifeless, everything about it only faintly familiar, as though she had dreamed living there or seen it in photographs. But she had truly lived in the beach house.

She pushed away images of Brian and Davey helping her and Jess load the van, and of the two of them standing arm in arm, waving as she drove away. She and Jessica changed the linens on the beds and did laundry. Together they checked the kitchen cupboards and made a grocery list.

When Rachel tucked Jessica in that night, the child looked so small and lost against her pillow that she searched her mind for a cheerful piece of news. "The landlady says you can have Crystal," she said, tucking her blankets in once more then sitting beside her. "You can call Brian about her at the end of the week, okay? That'll give us time to buy cat dishes and food and a litter box."

Jessica offered a faint smile. "And one of those little balls with a bell in it. Susan Sophia..." Her brow pleated and Rachel read her thought. She would have Crystal, but she wouldn't have Susan Sophia. She sniffed and went on, "Susan really likes hers."

"Then we'll definitely get one. Did you brush your teeth? Get your drink of water? Get on the scale?"

Jessica playfully punched her arm. "You're the only one who does that. And you always scream or say bad words."

Rachel gasped. "I didn't know you heard that. You'll be quiet about it, won't you?"

Jessica looked at the ceiling. "Well. Maybe a Peanut Buster Parfait at Dairy Queen would keep my mouth busy."

"Okay, you're on." Rachel leaned down to hug her fiercely. "Good night, sweetie."

"Night, Mom."

Rachel turned out the light and closed the door, then sank against it in emotional exhaustion.

The following day, Jessica asked if she could call Davey, and Rachel agreed. But Jessica came back to the living room, disappointed. There had been no answer. After several more tries, she abandoned the project until the following day, when she got the same result.

"Where did they go?" Jessica demanded, her eyes wide with concern. "They didn't answer all day Sunday, and not this morning. Davey wasn't at school and they're not home tonight. If nobody's been home all that time, the kittens could be starving!"

Rachel finally called Alicia to ease Jessica's mind—or that was the reason she gave herself.

"Why, he and Davey have gone camping," Alicia said with some surprise. "Where are you, Rachel? How come you didn't know?"

"I'm at home," she replied in a thin voice. Camping. A getaway trip the moment she was gone.

"Home?"

"My place."

There was a heavy silence. "He didn't tell me that," Alicia said finally. "He just told me they'd be gone for a couple of weeks or so and that he'd cleared it with the school. I guess considering what Davey's been through, they're willing to be open-minded.''

"Of course.''

"Rachel, I'm sorry." Alicia made a sound of helplessness. "Can I do anything?"

"No, thank you." Rachel forced a calm tone of voice. "Jessica was just concerned about the kittens."

"I've got them. Come on over and see them."

I should, Rachel thought. But she didn't want to see Alicia right now, and she didn't want to see the kittens. Leaving Brian's house had hurt abominably, but knowing that the moment she was out of it he had left it in search of the solace he could only find on his own hurt even more.

"Thanks, Alicia. We will be over later in the week. And please call us if you need anything."

"I will, Rachel. You're sure you're all right?"

"Sure."

Rachel repeated her conversation with Alicia to Jessica and ended with the promise, "And she says we can go and see the kittens at the end of the week."

Jessica nodded. "Crystal's okay?"

"Fat and sassy. So's Susan Sophia."

"I wonder how Davey is. And Brian."

Rachel tried to sound casual. "Well, we've had a beautiful few days. If they're camping nearby, they're probably having a wonderful time. If not—it's hard telling. I imagine camping in the rain isn't much fun."

Jessica smiled thoughtfully. "Everything with Brian and Davey is fun."

"I'm going to fold the laundry." Rachel suddenly needed movement, a project. "You'd better think about getting ready for bed."

Trying to concentrate on the roar of the washer instead of her vivid memories, Rachel pulled Jessica's jeans out of the dryer. She held the child's narrow pants up and thought jealously that those were hips that would never have to worry about getting on the scale and swearing.

Then, suddenly, her mind's eye was filled with the picture of herself, holding a towel against her chest, and getting on the scale in the bathroom of Brian's bedroom. She remembered clearly saying something unprintable.

Then Brian had appeared in the doorway, wearing pajama bottoms and a grin. "Shh," he'd said. "The kids are right across the hall."

"Oh, they're asleep." She had looked at him in horror. "Two pounds. I'm up two pounds. It's your chili! And your snacks at ten o'clock at night!"

He had wrapped his arms around her and held her tight. "Mmm." She could hear that purring quality in his voice. And then he'd made her forget that two pounds could do anything but make her even more desirable than he already found her.

"Mom?" Jessica was standing in the doorway to the kitchen, her eyes big and round.

"Sweetie, it's getting late," Rachel began to scold.

Jessica pointed behind herself, toward the living room. "But . . . Grandma's here."

"Grandma? You mean Alicia?"

Jessica shook her head. "No. She says she's Grandma Caroline. And Grandpa Frank is with her. They look kinda like the pictures on your dresser."

Rachel dropped the jeans and ran through the kitchen to the living-room doorway. And they *were* standing there, like a photo out of her past, the small, slim woman with the English-rose complexion and the big man look-ing uncomfortable in a three-piece suit.

"Mom," Rachel said in shock, her voice a thin thread of sound as the tears she had been swallowing for days rose up to choke her. "Daddy!"

Chapter Thirteen

It was after midnight, and the four of them were still talking, Jessica ensconced between her grandparents, listening to every detail as they spun out memories of Rachel's childhood.

"You jumped a hole on the handlebars of your brother's bicycle!" the child exclaimed. Then she looked up at Caroline. "She yelled at me for that. Actually... Brian did the yelling. But she stood by him."

"The difference was," Rachel offered with a thin attempt at righteous indignation, "that that was out in the country where there was no traffic."

"Right," her father said dryly, "just over a well hole you might have fallen into and disappeared forever."

"Dad..."

"The fact is," Frank Crawford said to Jessica, "that in the country or the city, in traffic or over a well hole, two on a bike isn't safe."

Rachel nodded. "Thank you." Then she gave her father a teasing side glance. The long separation and all that had happened seemed not to have affected her relationship with her mother one iota, but she still carried that guilt about her father, and he seemed a little removed from her, as though displeased. She found teasing him difficult. "And you never did anything like that?" she challenged.

He shrugged. "Never had a bicycle."

"Just a horse," Caroline said with a ladylike sniff, "according to Grandfather Crawford, that had to be retired to stud service after racing a locomotive. Now why would a sensible horse race a locomotive, I wonder, unless prodded by an unsensible rider?"

Jessica giggled. "They got ya, Grandpa."

Frank squeezed Jessica to him with a brawny arm. "You're supposed to be on my side."

Rachel looked at her watch, horrified by the time. "Jess, you've got to go to bed."

"But—"

"They'll be here for two weeks and next week is spring break. We'll have lots of time together. But tomorrow you have to go to school. Now, say good-night."

Jessica hugged Frank and then Caroline. "It's nice that Mom's brothers and sisters sent you here on your anniversary, but it's too bad they couldn't come, too."

Rachel shook her head in wonder, the shock of their appearance in her living room fresh again as she studied the faces she'd seen only in photographs since her husband's funeral. "I can't believe the family sent you to see *me* as a present."

Caroline shrugged, pulling Jessica down onto her knee. "When we all get together we always talk about the two of you and wonder how you're doing. Our last trip was so short and the circumstances so grim. We've wanted to visit but it's always so hard to find the extra money for a trip. Especially in farming. But the kids finally decided we needed a change of scene and you needed to be checked on. Came as a complete surprise to us, too. And we wanted you to be surprised. But don't worry. We've got motel reservations.''

Overwhelmed at being the subject of such a generous gift, Rachel felt all her old fears of exclusion from the family totter and then steady for reexamination. She rose briskly to her feet.

''Well, Jess and I will be crushed if you stay anywhere but here.''

''Yeah,'' Jessica said emphatically.

''But, honey—'' Caroline began to protest.

Jessica reached out to put a hand on her grandfather's shoulder. ''Grandpa doesn't want to stay in some old motel. Do ya?''

He melted visibly and looked at his wife. ''Let's try a night here. If Rachel fusses too much, we'll move to the motel.''

Caroline hugged Jessica to her. ''Your aunts and uncles told us to make sure your mom brings you back to Kansas this summer for a vacation so they can finally meet you.''

''That'd be neat.'' Jessica looked at her mother. ''I bet Davey would like to come. And Brian said he hunted stuff there.''

Rachel pulled her daughter toward the stairs. ''Mom, pour you and Dad some more coffee and I'll tuck Jess in, fix your bed and be right down.''

When Rachel walked into the kitchen, her mother was loading the dishwasher and her father was studying a sticking cabinet door.

''You got a plane?'' Frank asked her.

''You should have brought the one you flew in on,'' she said.

He shot her a quietly amused look. ''They allow corny Kansas jokes in Oregon?''

"Sorry. No plane. I don't do much carpentry."

He opened and closed the door experimentally, running his finger along the edge. "What about this Brian? Or is it Davey?"

Caroline looked up at her husband's question and shook her head at Rachel. "Once a father, always a father. Even when your child is twenty-eight. It's none of your business, Frank."

"Davey is a child Jessica's age," Rachel said, leaning against the counter. "And . . . we lived with Brian for six weeks."

Frank turned away from the cupboard, an eyebrow raised.

"Davey is Brian's?" Caroline asked.

Rachel nodded. "It's kind of a long story."

"Brian anything like Jarrod?" Her father turned away from the cupboard.

Caroline closed her eyes and pleaded, "Frank . . ."

"No." Rachel shook her head. "Nothing at all."

"Good."

"Daddy, I'm sorry!" The words burst from Rachel in tearless grief. Suddenly seeing her parents tonight after all those years of separation brought home to her more clearly than all her memories what a grim time that had been. She and her father had screamed at each other. Her mother had pleaded and cried. And she, Rachel, had stepped over all of them and done what she wanted to do. And paid.

She turned to her mother, words and anguish spilling out. "I know how much I hurt you and how disappointed you were in me." She turned back to her father, who was studying her in confused silence. "Every time I telephoned you, I could hear the coolness and the disappointment in your voice, and I wanted to explain to you that I...that I *really* loved Jarrod and that he loved me. That I wouldn't have hurt you deliberately for the whole world and that I—"

"Wait. Wait. Whoa!" Frank advanced on her, finally stopping the flow of words with one big, calloused hand. Then both hands closed on her shoulders, and she looked into his weathered face, into brown eyes that were loving and kind. "Is that what you thought?" he asked in amazement. "That we held any of that against you because you hurt us?"

"Oh, Rachel." Rachel felt her mother's arm come around her as she moved to stand beside her. But she couldn't look away from her father's eyes. There was no coolness there, no distance, no grudge. Just love.

"I was mad as hell at you at the time because I knew he'd hurt you, that *you* would hurt you, and you wouldn't listen to me. But you're a part of us, girl. Our daughter. Every family celebration when we've got all the other six kids around us and all their kids, we still miss you. We always miss you." The brown eyes filled and the strong mouth gave a dangerous quirk. "We love you, Rachel."

His arms closed around her as though she were five years old and she felt as though she could have died with the sudden unburdening. "Haven't you yelled at Jessica and even swatted her because you wanted to prevent her from hurting herself?"

"Of course." Rachel pulled away to look at him. "And I understood that. But I just thought...maybe I just didn't belong anymore."

He sounded angry now. "How could you think that?"

"Frank, don't yell," Caroline said firmly. "She was very young and you were always very loud. She just got her signals crossed, that's all. The question is, do you understand now, Rachel? We have never, would never, stop loving you. If we were ever angry at you, it was because you had hurt yourself and not us.''

Rachel nodded, anxious, relieved to believe it. ''Yes.''

''Good.'' Caroline grinned. ''Now tell us about Brian.''

They talked until four. Rachel alternately laughed, cried, praised Brian and complained about his inability to share himself completely with her.

The three of them were sitting on the sofa again, sipping more coffee, and Rachel absently thought it was no wonder no one was sleepy. ''Well, how many times has he gone on these trips since you've known him?''

''He's on one right now,'' she replied in an injured tone.

''But you've left him,'' her father pointed out. ''How often did he do this when you were together?''

She thought about that. ''He didn't. But when he asked me to marry him, he wanted to have that option. To be able to go at a moment's notice.''

''Without telling you?'' Caroline asked.

''No.''

''Then why is that so horrible? It's no different than a man who travels for his company, or a—''

''But he says he renews himself that way,'' she explained, frustrated that they didn't see. ''Why would he have to be away from me to do that?''

''The land has a calming effect on a man.'' Frank spoke quietly, leaning into a corner of the sofa. ''It's very basic. The same dust we're made of. It calls to us—to some of us louder than others. Why can't you let him have that? It doesn't diminish what you mean to him.''

''Remember, Rachel—'' Caroline put a hand out to pat her daughter's knee ''—when things were going bad with Jarrod? We were talking on the phone one Christmastime and you said, 'Jarrod and I may as well be miles apart for all the talking we do.' Remember that?''

She nodded, sensing what was coming.

"Well, then you had a man at your side day and night, but you never really had him. He was there, but he wasn't. Now here's a man who took in a child, would love your child, and you, if you wouldn't hold him so hard. Who would be with you, even if he had to renew himself by getting away once in a while."

Rachel shook her head and let it fall back against the sofa. "I am so confused."

"You've always been one to wrestle down whatever you wanted, and that's good," Frank said, a smile in his voice. Then it became sober. "But that kind of guts can get you in trouble on two occasions. You can wrestle down something that isn't worth it and you're stuck with it, like Jarrod. Or you can find yourself face-to-face with something that's tough as you are and isn't gonna let you win. If wrestling's your only way to handle it, you're gonna lose."

Caroline stood. "Well, while you've got wrestling on your mind, Frank, let's get to bed. Does this sofa fold out?"

"You're going to sleep in my bed." Rachel accepted her father's hand up. Then she smiled at him. "And if you two plan to wrestle, remember that Jessica's next door to you and misses nothing."

A minor argument ensued on who would sleep on the sofa and who would sleep on the bed, but Rachel stood firm. "I have to be up in a couple of hours to get Jess off to school and myself off to work. You'll probably need to sleep in." She frowned as a thought occurred to her. "I hope you won't be bored. I'd leave my van here for you to drive, but I need it for deliveries."

"Don't be silly," Caroline assured her. "We're going to walk around and see the town. Then, when you come home, we'll take you and Jess out to dinner. We can think about some serious touring next week, when Jess is home from school. Maybe Penny will let you have a day or two off."

Rachel had written them about Penny and how valuable she was as an employee and a friend. "Right."

When she was sure her parents had everything they needed, Rachel gathered up her nightgown, slippers and a change of clothes for tomorrow, or, rather, today and hugged them good-night.

She shook her head as she prepared to leave the room. "I still can't believe you're here."

Caroline inclined her head toward Frank. "Wait till the snoring starts; you'll believe it."

Frank turned to Caroline, pulling himself up to his full height. "Woman..." he began to threaten. Rachel closed the door on them, thinking jealously that her parents might get some wrestling in after all.

For a sleepless hour on the sagging sofa, Rachel thought a lot about wrestling. "You can wrestle something that's tough as you are and isn't gonna let you win," her father had said, her father who loved her after all, "and if wrestling's your only way to handle it, you're gonna lose."

Her mother thought she was holding Brian too hard. He had accused her of not giving him any slack. She remembered the miserable, lonely years with Jarrod and her determination, when he was gone, that she would never put herself through anything like that again.

In her attempt to secure a stable future for herself and for Jessica, she had tried to shape her relationship with Brian the way she wanted it—all details tied up, boundaries drawn, promises made and kept.

But Brian had a freer spirit, one that needed room in which to move. To him, details were unimportant, boundaries chafed and promises didn't have to be made because he would do what was right when the time came without having to be held to a pledge.

For the first time, Rachel saw Brian's need to get away in terms of what it meant to him rather than what it meant to her. And for the first time, she realized that that particular perspective was what love was all about. It didn't really matter if she understood, or if she functioned in a different way, as long as she could let him do whatever he needed to be a partner in their relationship.

Rachel sat up with the sudden impact of new insight. Why had she never seen that before, she wondered. She'd never thought of herself as small or selfish; why had that concession to Brian's need for freedom been so hard to make?

She remembered her conversation with Brian that night in front of the fireplace. "Could it be that you sometimes feel as unlovable as I have felt, but instead of withdrawing as I did, you grasp, afraid that love will escape?"

Rachel lay back, pulling the blankets up to her chin. She had felt unlovable all those years, and not because of Jarrod. She'd been burdened by the guilt of having hurt her family when she left with him, and later by the fear that in leaving she'd lost her place in its tight circle. She had felt stranded and alone. Instinct had made her close her hand on Brian's love and make a fist around it.

She heaved a deep sigh and pushed the blankets back, holding her hands up in the dark. She held them high with the fingers spread. Her fear was gone now, her burden lifted. Walls could have windows, boundaries could have gates.

Rachel drew her hands in and leaned into the back of the sofa. She longed for Brian with a pain that was tangible. It rolled over her like a studded tire. She would call him in the morning, but she doubted that he would be there. And if he was—and he let her explain—would it change anything? Would he be afraid to try again?

She tried to think about him and Davey, snug in their sleeping bags in some cleverly secured tent. They were both probably feeling free of female influence in their lives and all the confinement it had put on their relationship. When they finally did come home, could she convince them that she and Jess could be assets in their lives once again?

They'd be gone for two weeks, Alicia had said. That would be at least ten more days. An eternity. Rachel turned into her pillow, doubling her knees up against the excruciating longing.

BRIAN LAY ON HIS BACK on the warm, down-filled sleeping bag and let himself drown in thoughts of Rachel. During the day he fought to keep her image at bay by concentrating on his knowledge of beautiful Mann Lake and sharing it with Davey, by doing all he had to do to keep their camp comfortable, the inside of their tent warm and secure against the persistent, sage-scented eastern Oregon wind.

But with Davey snug and asleep in the bag beside him, he allowed himself the luxury of remembering how Rachel's silky limbs felt entwined with his, how capable her small hands were, how her hair felt and smelled as it swept across his chest in the wake of her kisses.

"You okay, Brian?"

Davey's question made him realize that he had groaned aloud.

"Fine," he replied, drawing a steadying breath. "You?"

"Yeah." Davey paused. "But I miss Rachel." He uttered a small laugh. "I even miss Jess."

Brian smiled in the dark. Thoughts of Jessica always made him smile; she was Rachel uncomplicated.

"Me, too."

"Then why don't we go get 'em?"

"Cause . . . Rachel and I . . ."

Brian paused too long and Davey filled in. "Need different things. You guys told us. But how different?"

"Very different." As different as boundaries and uncluttered space. Then his brow furrowed as he realized that for three days it had been just him and Davey in a wild, unfettered world, and he'd been completely confined in thoughts of Rachel.

"Rachel felt like my mom," Davey said. "Better than my mom, even. My mom used to yell. Rachel can scare you without yelling."

Brian chuckled and turned his head toward Davey. "You going to be okay?"

He heard the boy shrug. "I guess. I've still got you. Are you gonna be okay?"

He thought about that a minute. "Probably never quite the same, but okay."

There was silence for a time and Brian began to think Davey had fallen asleep. Then his voice came out of the dark.

"Should I be calling you, Dad?"

Surprised, Brian considered his reply. "Only if you're comfortable with it."

"Would you be?"

"Sure."

"Well, maybe I should. It's neat, you know, but scary, too. You'll be my dad, but I'll have to be your son. There'll be things I'll have to do for you, too. It won't be just you doing for me. I'm scared of that sometimes—like, maybe I won't always do things right."

"Nobody *always* does things right. Love makes the times you do things wrong unimportant."

"Yeah?"

"Yeah."

"Then maybe I need to not be afraid and just do it."

"Maybe."

Silence fell again and Brian heard Davey shift onto his side, away from him. He relaxed into the downy bag and closed his eyes.

He heard a small breath drawn. "Dad?"

His heart beat loudly. "Yeah?"

"Good night."

"Good night, son."

Brian opened his eyes and stared into the dark. "Maybe I need to not be afraid," Davey had said, "and just do it." He lay awake for a long time.

"NOW, YOU'RE SURE you're going to be okay?" Rachel was standing at the kitchen table where Caroline and Frank still sat in their nightclothes, enjoying a second cup of coffee.

"We'll be fine." Frank popped a last bite of toast in his mouth and shooed her toward the door. "Go on. Think about where you want to eat tonight."

"I'll call you at lunchtime to see if you need anything." She waved from the front door then ran out into a crisp, sunny day. She tried to take the beauty of the morning as a positive sign. Ten days stretched ahead of her as an interminable string of hours.

Rachel called her parents just before noon.

"No, don't come home for lunch," Caroline said firmly. "You're going to be seeing enough of us for the next two weeks. Go out on your own and relax."

Rachel caught what sounded like male conversation in the background. "Who's Daddy talking to?"

Caroline laughed. "The contestants on *Jeopardy*. They never know the answers unless he tells them, you know. Who am I to burst his bubble?"

"All right, Mom. See you about six."

"Bye, dear."

Rachel closed the shop and took Penny to lunch, but regretted her generosity when they returned and she learned the details of her next delivery.

"A boat?" Rachel checked the order sheet and looked up at Penny, who was on a ladder, replacing a demo balloon that was out of stock with a new design. "I have to deliver a balloon bouquet to a boat?"

"Xumpfh." Penny had push pins in her mouth.

"Where is it moored?"

Penny took time to force a pin into the top of the balloon then removed the second pin from her mouth. "It isn't," she said without turning around. "Our subject is fishing on the river. You have to take it out to the boat."

"What!" The word was more an exclamation of anguish than a question.

"A small boat will pick you up at Englund Marine's dock in Astoria and take you out to the boat."

"We don't deliver beyond Astoria," Rachel reminded, her spurt of good humor evaporating. She felt tired and overwhelmed.

"They paid extra." Penny climbed down the ladder, folded it and carried it to the back room. "It's an anniversary, for heaven's sake. Where's your enthusiasm for love and romance?''

At Rachel's stricken look, Penny offered a quick hug. "I'm sorry. That was thoughtless. Come on, it's such a pretty day. An hour on the river will do you good."

Rachel froze in place. "An hour?"

"You can go home when you're finished," Penny promised, "and I'll close up. They'll probably sing your praises to all their friends and you'll end up with more balloon deliveries than you'll know what to do with, and eventually more money."

As Penny put Rachel's hat on her head, Rachel gave her a saccharine smile. "With more money I'll hire someone competent."

Penny shrugged. "It'll *take* more money to get someone competent. Here." She reached into the back room for the bouquet and handed her the dozen silver ribbons. "The boat'll be at Englund's dock in half an hour. Don't waste any time."

As Rachel drove to Astoria, she fought the urge to have a bona fide tantrum. Even when everything else went wrong she could usually count on Penny for cooperation and support. But to break all the rules she had established for deliveries and waste her entire afternoon when her parents were visiting and she was stressed out about Brian . . . She couldn't imagine what had gotten into her.

Rachel parked on the highway in front of Englund's, pulled her dozen balloons out of the van and squared her shoulders. Ballooney-Tunes's name was at stake here. She had to do something about her attitude. Holding the balloons against the wind from the river, she walked to the end of the marine supplier's dock and waited. Within minutes she heard the roar of an outboard and a small boat appeared from the other side of the structure.

A man about Brian's age sat in the boat, holding the tiller. He wore jeans and a blue down vest over a gray sweatshirt. A blue knit cap was pulled down over his ears.

Bright blue eyes squinted up at Rachel. "Are you from Ballooney-Tunes?" he asked in a mild drawl.

Her attitude slipping, Rachel looked at him, then at the dozen balloons she held, then at him again. "No," she said. "I'm testing a new theory in aerodynamics."

He chuckled and beckoned her to the boat. She went down the steps to the platform, held the balloons aloft and accepted his hand into the boat. It rocked gently and she sat carefully, grateful she had chosen to wear pants today. But Brian would have never approved of her stockings and small-heeled pumps for this excursion. She hoped her blazer would keep her warm enough.

"I'm Dave Hughes," the man shouted over the roar of the motor as they moved away from the dock.

"Rachel Bennett," she shouted back, pulling down on the balloons as the wind created by the movement of the boat threatened to take them.

He gave her an oddly speculative smile.

"I'm sorry I was snide," she said.

He shrugged it off. "A sense of humor never offends."

That was homespun and profound, she thought, wondering who he was and how he had drawn the job of transporting her out to a boat. Maybe he was related to the couple celebrating their anniversary.

He turned in his seat then, to face the direction in which they moved, and conversation was suspended. Rachel looked around at the clear blue sky, gulls and ducks at play in it, at the smooth river reflecting the brightness of the sky, and felt the longing for Brian rise up in her with a force that made her want to cry out.

It had been gray and raining that morning she and Brian had spent on the river, but it had been beautiful then, too. They had made that seemingly innocent agreement in the duck shack that had resulted in the best and worst moments of her life. No, she thought resolutely, she wouldn't think that way. Just ten more days and they could fix it. If Brian wanted to fix it.

They'd been underway more than half an hour when Rachel spotted several boats ahead. They appeared to be anchored, bobbing on the calm surface of the river. On the first boat they passed, a white-haired man sat in a folding chair, his rod secured in a holder on the side.

Hughes smiled at her over his shoulder. "Waiting for sturgeon!" he said.

She nodded understanding. They passed the second boat and Rachel strained to see in the distance, looking for another. She saw nothing but little reed-covered islands, flocks of ducks and the lush banks of the river.

She sighed and transferred the balloons to her other hand. Holding them against the wind required a clenched fist and her hand now ached from the effort.

Fifteen minutes later, frozen and about to run out of patience, Rachel prepared to demand that the boatman disclose their destination. But he chose that very moment to turn to her and shout, "Almost there!"

Her hands numb, her feet frozen, Rachel nodded and squared her shoulders to wait. I have to dredge up a smile, she thought. I have to wish them a happy anniversary without sounding jealous or irritated or sarcastic. I have to be cheerful and warm. That was hard without Brian, she thought. Everything was hard without Brian.

Suddenly the trees that bordered the banks closed in on them and the sound of the motor quieted as Hughes slowed the boat. They were in a sheltered area lined with...duck shacks. Rachel made a startled movement, looking around at the awkward structures, some of them broken down, some of them with window boxes, some of them simply rough but cared for...like Brian's. They were in the slough.

Hughes turned the boat and drove it through the open doors of a boat shack, into a small bay. Hiking boots and jeans stood on the dock and caught the line Hughes tossed, making it fast around a piling. Rachel flung her head back to run her eyes up the boots and jeans, topped by a fisherman's knit sweater. At sight of the man's face, her breath caught in her throat, her heartbeat suffocating her. Brian.

He smiled down at her and she felt her heart stall.

"Hand the balloons to Dave," he said. Momentarily unable to think or speak, she turned to do as he asked, some still-functioning part of her mind detecting collusion at work here.

Hughes shrugged. "He makes harsh demands on his friends," he said, laughing softly. "What can I say?" Then to Brian he added seriously, "You're right, Brian. She's something else."

With the toe of his boot, Brian indicated a spot on the dock in front of him. "Put your foot here."

Coming to her senses now, Rachel looked at the substantial height of the dock in relation to the level of the water. The last time they did this, she speculated, it must have been high tide.

"Brian," she protested, "I'd have to be a giraffe!"

He and Dave exchanged a look over her head. "It's that or go back with Dave."

There was more than teasing in that look. There was the suggestion of a promise she'd be a fool to turn away from.

Unbuttoning her blazer, she pulled up on the leg of her wool pants, planted her foot as close as she could to Brian's boot then raised her arms. He took her hands, yanked, and she landed beside him on the dock.

"Hold those a minute," Brian told Hughes as the other man tried to hand him the balloons. Hughes rolled his eyes and settled back to wait.

Brian turned to Rachel, hands on his hips, and looked down into her still astonished eyes. For a moment he simply drank in the sight of her, then he swallowed as though something hurt.

"I've learned a lot in the last four days," he said quietly. "If you'd like to hear about it, we'll send Dave home and you can spend the night with me in the duck shack."

"The kids . . ." she began.

"Will stay with my mother." As though he couldn't help himself, he reached out to smooth her windblown hair. "Davey's already there. Your parents will take Jess there after school and stay for dinner. I left them the Porsche. I told them we'd be back by dinner tomorrow."

"You met my parents?" She had a vague memory of male conversation in the background when she'd called at lunchtime.

He smiled. "I stopped at your place on the chance that you'd be there when you weren't at the shop. They're great." With a chuckle he added modestly, "They think I am, too."

Rachel gave him a long look and squared her shoulders. "Well," she said, lifting her chin. "That makes them and you." But instead of getting back into the boat she walked around the dock and out of the boat shack.

Hughes laughed and Brian watched her walk away, a small smile forming.

"God," his friend said feelingly. "Better you than me. Take these things. I'm getting out of here before she uses you for duck food. I hate to see a good man go that way."

Laughing, Brian took the balloons from him and cast his line. "Thanks, Dave. Say hi to Katey and Abby. I owe you one."

The duck shack was toasty warm and Rachel sat in the chair she had used the last time she was there, taking her pumps off and holding her frozen feet to the fire. The intimacy of the room wrapped around her, memories assailed her, hope taunted her, yet terrified her. Her heartbeat threatened to break her ribs as she tried desperately to remember all the things she'd wanted to tell Brian. She suddenly found herself wishing she had the ten days in which to collect herself.

Brian studied the back of Rachel's head as he closed the door behind him, and knew he had a chance. Her head held straight meant she was resolute. Inclined to the side, her shoulder tucked up, meant she was vulnerable. She had missed him. Now all he had to do was convince her of the hell he'd been through since she had driven away from him four days ago.

He fastened the ribbons of the bouquet of balloons to the footrail of the upper bunk then walked around in front of her. He got down on his haunches and took a stocking-clad foot in his hand. It felt like an ice cube. He snatched the socks he had ready from under the claw feet of the stove.

He grinned up at Rachel. "Panty hose or those short things?"

It took her a minute to comprehend. "The short things," she finally replied. Then, as he rolled the hem of her pants up to pull down the knee-highs and replace them with the deliciously warm, red-toed woolen socks, she asked, "And what would you have done had I been wearing panty hose?"

The second sock in place, he got up on his knees and joined his hands lightly behind her neck. He looked into her wide, watchful eyes and lost himself in the longing he saw there. "Put them on over the stockings," he said.

Despite his serious demeanor, there was merriment in his eyes and she pursed her lips at him. "You've gone gentleman on me all of a sudden?"

He felt a reinforcement of hope when she sounded disappointed. "Just long enough for us to talk. Then, depending on what you decide, all's fair."

Her jaw took on a stubborn set and she looked just a little injured. "How dare you disappear—" she gestured with her hand like a magician "—then pop back up, plot against me with my family and Penny, and haul me all this way up a cold river?" Make me think I have to live without you ten more days, then suddenly appear, leaving me tongue-tied and terrified that I won't think of the right things to say. "Who is Dave Hughes, anyway?"

"Only the best outdoor writer in the country," he replied, then added with a grin, "next to me, of course. And a good friend. He lives in Astoria."

Rachel resisted the grin. "Why couldn't you come to me?"

He leaned forward to kiss the tip of her nose. "With my mother, your parents and our collective children around? I thought we should meet here, where the duck shack agreement got us in trouble in the first place. We need a new set of rules," he said. "Something more realistic than the let's-play-together-and-not-get-involved idiocy we thought would work the first time."

She nodded, relaxing. "That makes sense to me. And I have things to tell you, too." She wanted to fly into his arms, to hold him, to feel him against her and be sure that he felt her. But he wanted to establish new rules. She folded her arms and waited.

"The day after you left, Davey and I took off for two weeks on Mann Lake in eastern Oregon. We were going to camp and fish, talk about things." He paused, and with a sound of helplessness totally unlike him, he shook his head. "And I was going to get over you. I was going to find the serenity that always came to me on a riverbank or on a lake. Well—the weather was beautiful, the fish were biting, Davey was a brick. He didn't pester me; he stayed within sight; he did his share of the setting up, cooking and dishes without complaint; and when I wanted to talk, he talked. I guess that was one good thing that came out of this. Davey and I met on a new level." He seemed pleased and a little amazed. "We are..." He paused a minute, perhaps composing himself. "Father and son. Anyway..." He looked into her eyes, his deep and dark but holding no mysteries. "You know what I discovered?"

"What?" she breathed.

"That being in touch with you is a hell of a lot more critical to my sanity than being in touch with myself. I missed you, Rachel. I can't separate myself from you for whatever reason without feeling like my world has come to an end. Please." He moved his hands to her face, gently tracing a thumb over her quivering bottom lip. "Come home, Rachel." He put his mouth gently to the tremor on hers then looked into her eyes, his filled with a naked yearning. "Marry me. I can't face a lifetime without you. Let's get this family on its feet once and for all."

That was all the impetus Rachel needed to throw herself forward into his arms. "Oh, Brian. I want to! But I've been thinking while you were gone that I've no right to demand that you be anything other than what you are, or need anything different than you've always needed simply because I want to share your life. I'm sorry that I've held you too tight. I wouldn't do that again."

As she finished speaking Rachel realized she had a death grip on his neck and loosened it, sitting back on her heels, looking sheepish. "Well, the adjustment might take a while."

Laughing, he pulled her to her feet and moved with her to the bottom bunk. He pushed her gently onto it then joined her, pulling her close, holding her hard.

"Do you have any idea how much I've missed that?" he demanded, his voice a little unsteady. "You holding me as though you couldn't bear to let me go." He kissed her cheek then rested his face against it. "And that was never the kind of holding that was at issue."

"I know. I understand the difference now. You're sure you want to get married?"

"Positive. You?"

"Yes." She pulled away enough to look at him. "You wanted to establish some new rules."

"Right. I get one and then you get one. Okay?"

She nodded. "Okay." Then she asked, "But why not me first?"

"Because it's my shack."

"True. Okay. Rule number one."

"Rule number one." Brian stared at the bottom of the bunk above them, one hand behind his head, the other around Rachel, his hand gently strumming up and down her arm. "I will always... always love you. No matter what. When it comes to matters of you and me, I won't try to keep a clinical distance, or think things through, or even make sense. I will just feel and use my feeling as a standard for action, because what I feel is love. That's it," he said, sounding satisfied. The sound of his words hung above their heads, trapped between the bunks as warm, alder-scented air from the fire filled the room. "Okay, your turn."

Rachel thought, feeling the comforting warmth of being wrapped in Brian's embrace, wrapped in his love, and came up with it. "Duck shack rule number two. Whether you need space or whether you need to be held, I'll be there to do it. Because I will always, always love you. There," she said, satisfied.

He put a hand under the hem of her sweater, his eyes dark and indulgent. "That was rule number one."

She pulled at his top button, her smile warm and promising. "Some things can't be improved upon."

Epilogue

Where'll we go?''

It was a Sunday afternoon in June and sunshine poured
into the kitchen from the sliding glass doors. Davey knelt
in a chair, leaning over a map of the United States that
was spread out on the dining-room table. He jabbed a
finger somewhere slightly left of middle. "Wyoming!" He
answered his own question. "They have mammoth skel-
etons there."

As he spoke, Vanderweghe leaped onto the table and sat
directly on his finger, purring as though it were a silk
cushion. Davey picked up the cat, held it against him,
stroking it absently. "Imagine, Jess. Bones twenty feet
long!"

Jessica, leaning over the table from the other side,
pointed to California. "Let's go to Hollywood, where the
movie stars are."

Davey looked disgusted. "You see them on TV all the
time. Nobody's seen a mammoth in millions of years!"

"Who'd want to?" Jessica demanded. "If all that's left
bones?"

Davey rolled his eyes as Rachel closed the oven door on a pan of brownies. She went to the table to look over his shoulder, drying her hands on a towel.

"I don't want to go to Hollywood," he groaned.

Rachel had to agree. "Me, either. I had in mind someplace a little more quiet."

"Well, I don't want to spend our vacation looking at bones." Jessica folded her arms, vehement.

"That leaves forty-seven other states," Rachel said. When Davey frowned, prepared to correct her, she pointed to the Pacific ocean. "Hawaii doesn't count. We can't drive there."

"Oh, yeah."

The idea of spending a month in the motor home Brian had bought had made so much sense at the time. The four of them could travel in comfort. Food, a bathroom and beds available around the clock would be a definite plus on their first adventure as a family. But every time the children began to argue, all Rachel could think of was that they would be spending twenty-eight days confined together in a couple of hundred square feet of space. She prayed for steady nerves.

The two months since her marriage to Brian had not really changed the pattern of their daily lives. They had strived so hard for normalcy when Davey's grandmother died that the transition from friends to family had been without incident. The children's arguments had become a little more intense, but then so had their friendship. Jessica still bore a bruise on her chin from an altercation in which she had become involved because she considered Davey outnumbered. Rachel judged the trade-off as fair.

From his kneeling position on the chair, Davey put an arm around Rachel's waist. "Well, where do you want to go?"

Rachel gave his shoulders a squeeze, still surprised and delighted by his gestures of affection. She'd been a little concerned at first that Jessica would resent having to share her with Davey. But Brian showered Jessica with attention and affection, and she seemed satisfied that sharing her mother entitled her to share Brian with Davey. There'd been less jealousy between the children than Rachel had expected.

Rachel looked over the map and her eyes stopped right in the middle. Kansas. She'd love to go to Kansas and visit with her family, show off her husband and her children, sit on the front porch and swing, sing with her father as the sun went down. She wanted to get reacquainted with her brothers and sisters as adults, meet their families, see if the neighbors still lived there and take Brian to the drive-in movie, where all serious relationships were explored.

But, she thought with a sigh, she had just seen her parents several months ago, and the choice of where to vacation should be Brian's. He'd just finished a three-week session of working day and night to complete revisions on his book so that it would be ready for the Christmas market. And yet he'd carried out his share of duties with the children and helped her scout out a larger shop for Balloney-Tunes. Business was good and growing.

Brian was everything he had promised to be and more. She often wondered how she had managed to live so long without him.

The powerful sound of the Porsche pulling into the driveway had the children running for the front door. Rachel would have been willing to fight them for the first hug, but she had developed a healthy respect for their ruthlessness. She chose to check on her brownies instead. Vanderweghe, cast aside, followed her.

The children met Brian as he closed the car door. He put an arm out to each, and Davey and Jessica closed in, each circling his waist. Their eagerness to greet him when he came home was a pleasure that would never grow old for him. It was foremost among a host of honors that often had him wondering lately how he'd gotten so lucky.

"Davey wants to visit bones!" Jessica complained as they went from the sunny outdoors to the darker stillness of the living room.

"Mammoth bones," Davey specified. "*She* wants to visit Hollywood." Then he snickered. "Prob'ly thinks she's gonna end up in the movies or something." He peered around Brian at Jessica and made a monstrous face. "Maybe if they make a new Mrs. Frankenstein."

Jessica lunged at Davey, who took shelter behind Brian.

"Disneyland!" the boy said, stopping Jessica in her tracks. She looked up at Brian with a broad smile. "Yeah!"

"No," he said calmly, pulling both children toward the table and the map.

As they grumbled and complained, he put a finger to the middle of the map. Vanderweghe leaped up onto the table and sat on it. "Kansas," Brian said as he picked up the cat.

Rachel turned away from the stove and said simultaneously with the children, "Kansas?"

Brian nodded. "Kansas."

She went toward him, her eyes wide and startled. "Why?"

"To see your family," he said, dodging Vander-weghe's batting paw. "I'm sure you'd like to show us off, wouldn't you?"

"Well, yes, but I thought you..."

"What do you guys think?" Brian looked down at the children, finally catching the cat's paw and holding it.

"Dodge City," Davey said in delight.

Jessica beamed. "Grandma Caroline and Grandpa Frank."

Rachel shook her head, still stunned. "But...are you sure you want to spend your vacation with my family?"

Brian looked from Rachel to the children, then back into her eyes again. "I'll be spending the vacation with *my* family."

"We could bring Grandma Alicia," Jessica suggested.

"No, she's going to Mexico with Tom Benedict." Alicia's relationship with the city councilman was now serious. "She's being very coy, but I have a feeling she'll be coming back with another name."

"Do you want to go to Kansas, Mom?" Jessica asked.

Rachel moved to Brian, took the cat and handed it to Davey, then put her arms around her husband's neck. She held him close, silently thanking him for reading her mind, silently promising him that she would reward him. She pulled back and smiled into his eyes. "I would love to go to Kansas. Thank you."

That look of love in Rachel's eyes was another pleasure that made Brian feel every day as though he'd done something to please the gods. Marriage to her had given every moment a richness he had never known was possible. While he and Rachel had simply lived together, every moment with her had been precious, but now that they had promised to be there for each other forever, every look exchanged, every thought shared, every touch possessed a quality of eternity. Forever. They would love each other forever. The knowledge made him feel weak.

"Brian?" Jessica was tugging on his belt.

"Yes." He moved Rachel to his side and put a hand to Jessica's hair. She looked concerned and intense.

"We need to talk about something."

"Privately?" he asked.

"No." Jessica glanced at Davey, who gave her an awkward pat on the shoulder then sat down. "It's kinda about all of us. But me, mostly."

"Okay." Brian sat, pulling her onto his knee. "What is it?"

"Well..." Jessica fidgeted, a gesture unlike her usual calm directness. Brian waited quietly. "You married Mom, right?"

Brian nodded, smiling. "You were maid of honor."

"Yeah." She glanced across the table at Davey, who gave her an encouraging nod. "And you adopted Davey."

"Right."

"Well..." Jessica twined her fingers together and gave Brian a small, uncertain smile. Then she sobered and said with dark-eyed steadiness, "I'm the only one whose name isn't Tate. I...but I...don't think I'm Jessica Bennett anymore. I feel like I'm Jessica Tate."

Brian felt Rachel's hands settle on his shoulders. He concentrated on that gesture, borrowed strength from it until he could compose himself enough to speak.

"Your mother and I realized that," he said gently, rubbing a hand between her thin shoulder blades. "But you've been Jess Bennett for a long time, and a name is kind of important to a person. We didn't think we had the right to just take it away from you unless that was what you wanted."

"What would we have to do?"

"I would adopt you, just like I did Davey."

Jessica smiled. "Yeah?"

Brian swallowed. "Yeah."

"Can we do it before we go to Kansas, so that when we visit Mom's family, *we'll* all be the same family?"

"We can start the paperwork tomorrow. But the fact that we've decided on it makes it official. You are now Jessica Tate."

Applause from Rachel and Davey greeted the declaration. Jessica blushed and smiled. "Great. One more thing."

"What?"

Jessica glanced again at Davey, who put his elbows on the table and appeared to be trying to hide his face behind his folded hands. "Davey and I made a deal. I can call you Dad if he can call Mom, Mom."

For a moment Brian thought Rachel's grip on his shoulder would cut off the flow of blood in his carotid artery and render him unconscious. Then she walked around the table to Davey and pulled his hands from in front of his face. It was crimson.

"I'd like to hear you say it," she ordered softly.

Davey swallowed, cleared his throat, licked his lips. "Mom," he said.

Rachel smiled, gathering him in her arms, wondering how one woman could be lucky enough to have acquired the world's finest man and its two dearest children in one lifetime.

Brian looked at Jessica and didn't have to ask. "Dad," he said, then collapsed in giggles against him. He hugged her, laughing, and she pulled back to say with a soft sincerity that nearly destroyed his composure, "Daddy."

IT WAS ONE in the morning. The house was still, the children, Davey and Jessica Tate, long since asleep. Brian and Rachel lay together in front of the fire, loath to let go of what had been a momentous day.

"And you know the very best part?" Rachel asked, pushing herself up against Brian's chest to look into his eyes.

He reached up to brush her hair back, the unusual combination of contentment and excitement on her face making him wonder what was on her mind. "What?"

"That thousands more days like today are waiting for us." At his quick smile, she added, "Oh, I know they won't all be as special in the way that today was, but they'll be special because we'll have them together." Her eyes misted as she considered that knowledge. "Blows your mind, doesn't it? And all because of an agreement made between two innocents in a duck shack."

He laughed softly. "We were pretty dumb, weren't we?"

"Yeah." She leaned forward to kiss him. "But we got smart."

Give in to Temptation! Harlequin Temptation

The story of a woman who knows her own mind, her own heart . . . and of the man who touches her, body and soul.

Intimate, sexy stories of today's woman—her troubles, her triumphs, her tears, her laughter.

And her ultimate commitment to love.

Four new titles each month—get 'em while they're hot. Available wherever paperbacks are sold.

Temp

**In the spellbinding tradition
of Barbara Taylor Bradford, a novel of
passion, destiny and endless love.**

Season of Loving

Shirley Larson

He possessed everything: wealth, power, privilege—everything except the woman he desired and the son he loved more than life itself.

PAMELA BROWNING

...is fireworks on the green at the Fourth of July and prayers said around the Thanksgiving table. It is the dream of freedom realized in thousands of small towns across this great nation.

But mostly, the Heartland is its people. People who care about and help one another. People who cherish traditional values and give to their children the greatest gift, the gift of love.

American Romance presents HEARTLAND, an emotional trilogy about people whose memories, hopes and dreams are bound up in the acres they farm.

HEARTLAND...the story of America.

Don't miss these heartfelt stories: American Romance #237 SIMPLE GIFTS (March), #241 FLY AWAY (April), and #245 HARVEST HOME (May).